praise for

"Sadie and David's journey to salvage love and a family legacy will steal your breath and reaffirm your belief in second chances. A must-read for anyone who cherishes a heart-pounding romance as much as a heartwarming happy-ever-after."

—USA TODAY BESTSELLING AUTHOR
SUSAN MAY WARREN

"*Here With Me* might sound like a Hallmark movie on paper but Sadie and David's story goes so far beyond, reaching deep into readers' hearts. Their story went beyond a novel I was reading to truly speak to my heart and challenge me in ways I never expected. All while making me smile at the beauty and romance and how utterly adorable certain characters were."

— HANNAH CURRIE, AUTHOR OF DAUGHTERS
OF PEVERELL AND CROWN OF PROMISE SERIES

"I loved the characters and their interactions, and there are swoony kisses. Then there were the plot twists that had me saying, "No, no, don't do that!" All in all I loved the book and am eager for the next one."

—MARGARET, GOODREADS

"To anyone out there looking for a high-stakes story of love and redemption, ripe with life lessons: you'll love this one! Don't miss this incredible second book in the Home to Heritage series - drive, fly, or swim to the little town of Heritage, and sit yourself down right next to Otis - you'll surely find home in the pages of *Here with Me*."

—SARA, GOODREADS

here with me

HOME TO HERITAGE

here with me

MANDY BOERMA

sunrise PUBLISHING

Here With Me
Home to Heritage, Book 2
Published by Sunrise Media Group LLC
Copyright © 2024 by Sunrise Media Group LLC

ISBN: 978-1-963372-04-5

For more information about Susan May Warren, Tari Faris, or Mandy Boerma, please access the author's website at the following address: www.susanmaywarren.com, https://www.tarifaris.com/, or www.mandyboerma.com.

Published in the United States of America.
Cover Design: Tari Faris and Sarah Erredge
Editing: Barbara Curtis

A Note from Tari Faris

Dear Readers,

I met Mandy at a writer's retreat in Florida. We became fast friends, and I had no idea of the great adventures God had in store for our friendship. Shortly after meeting her, she became my first reader for *Until I Met You* and continued with each consecutive book. In some ways, she knows Heritage even better than I do. So when the opportunity arose for her to write in Heritage, I jumped at it, and I am so glad I did. Not only is Mandy a fantastic writer and storyteller, but she also helped expand my view of this little fictional town and Heritage is better for it.

Here with Me is an amazing story of redemption, second chances, and love. It fits so well into the world of Heritage that it will always feel like a story of my heart—just written by someone else.

From the moment we heard about David in my novella, *P.S. Goodbye,* I knew he needed a great story. I had planned his story to be in *Since You've Been Gone*, but I just couldn't get a strong idea. When Mandy approached me with an idea for David's story, I knew it would be the perfect fit. Only I had no idea just how perfect it would be.

Working with Mandy on this book has truly been one of the highlights of my career. Thank you, Mandy, for always bringing your best to the table, never giving up, and making Heritage richer with your story.

Mandy is definitely an author to watch. Don't forget to check out her other book, *You'll Be Mine*. It isn't a Heritage book but you will love it!

Tari Faris

As for God, his way is perfect;
the word of the Lord is tried:
he is a buckler to all them that trust in him.

2 Samuel 22:31 (KJV)

To Julie. For celebrating the good
and bringing the coffee when it's not-so-good.

one

IT WAS TIME, BEYOND TIME, TO LEAVE HERITAGE, Michigan, and return to Costa Rica—if only David Williams could convince his directors at Christ in the World Mission that he was ready.

To be needed.

To help people.

To go.

Instead, David was stuck in a tiny town, practically trapped in his late grandparents' old farmhouse. His only use? Fulfilling his sisters' designs to turn this place into an Airbnb.

The cool August breeze whispered over his skin as David worked at a makeshift table, a couple of sawhorses for his miter saw, in the driveway of the old farmhouse.

Gravel crunched under tire wheels, but he didn't need a distraction now.

"Still working I see." Nate Williams, his cousin, walked across the gravel driveway.

David set the board aside. "These are the last shelves I need to cut to finish up the built-in."

Picking up one of the freshly cut boards, Nate nodded to the front door. David grabbed the remaining two pieces on the saw, checked to make sure the power was off, and followed Nate toward the front door.

"Heard anything from Lance?" Nate pushed through the door of the old, two-story farmhouse and tossed his keys on the table.

David set the boards against the new built-in he'd constructed in his grandparents' living room. "Do you know what they decided?"

"I sent off my recommendation yesterday via email, but I'm not part of the meeting today."

David tried to hold back a wince. He had hoped Nate was part of it. After all, it could only help to have his cousin and pastor of the local church on his side. But maybe the letter from Nate would be enough to convince the board he was well enough to return to his job as a teacher for the children of missionaries in Costa Rica.

Nate ran his hand along the last set of shelves David had installed. "This looks good."

David grunted a thanks. The shelves did look good. Especially as a backdrop to the two couches and coffee table that his sisters had ordered. They called it "farmhouse chic"—whatever that was. All he knew was that it was the last project his sisters wanted before they listed the place as an Airbnb. Of course, they couldn't do that until after he returned to Costa Rica. Who knew how many people would want to come vacation in Heritage?

The clock chimed the bottom of the hour. The day was ticking past him at a snail's pace. With the offices closed for Labor Day, surely the director wouldn't make him wait until Tuesday for an answer, or would he?

David picked up his cordless drill on the coffee table then pulled a couple of wood screws out of his carpenter's belt—he was almost out of them. Hopefully he had enough to finish installing the shelves.

David measured and marked where the shelf would go, and Nate stepped closer, taking the shelf and pressing it against the wall. Then he picked up the level and set it on top. "Are you sure you're ready to leave all this behind and return to Costa Rica? Your sisters have enjoyed having you here these past six months."

David adjusted the shelf and checked the level. "School is starting next week. I really wanted to be back before this new year began. Besides, I haven't seen them much. They're busy with their own lives." Leah with her new baby, and Caroline had her hands full with two girls and another baby on the way.

David lined up the screw in the predrilled hole then lifted the drill. When his hand started to shake, he lowered it as his gaze shot to Nate. The guy's stare fixed on the wall—at least he hadn't seen. He drew a slow breath and stretched his fingers then tried again. This time he connected with the screw. David slipped his hand into his belt for more screws and pulled out the last three. Just his luck. Short three screws for the final shelf. "I'm gonna need to run and pick up more screws to finish these last few shelves."

"You should have messaged. I could have stopped at Hoover's on my way over."

Hoover's. The local hardware store—the one he'd turned his back on all those years ago. No way could he shop there now. It would be easier to drive to Ludington.

"I'll run to Lowe's." David looked at the time. Three forty-five. "But I'd like to be here when that call from Lance comes in. I hate talking and driving."

"You don't have to continue to hide out here." Nate walked into the kitchen and filled a glass of water at the sink.

Hiding hadn't crossed his mind. But he liked to keep the past in the past.

David followed, pulling out a root beer from the fridge. He

opened the top, and the pop fizzed before he took a long drink, taking his time to respond to Nate. They'd had this conversation a few times now. "I get out. Talk to people when I do."

"You've been home six months, and you've hardly left the house."

"I've counted every day I've been here. That's why I need to get back." David picked up his wallet and keys to his grandpa's Subaru Brat and walked to the front door.

Nate, close behind, grabbed his own keys off the table by the door as he followed David outside. "If you're eager to get back to work, you could do that here. You could be out in the community. There are people here that need encouragement. For example, would it be hard to run to Hoover's Hardware? It would certainly take less time. How hard could it be to say hi to Gary?"

Gary wasn't the problem. It was Sadie. But if she was in town, Caroline or Leah would have mentioned it. They'd certainly told him when Sadie had moved away. He hadn't believed them, because for as long as they'd dated, her dream had been to take over the family business. It had become their dream. Proof that dreams changed.

Still, David had managed to go all summer without going to Hoover's. Why change that today? Heading there might dig up memories best forgotten. Memories he worked hard to keep buried.

Once they were on the porch, Nate's phone pinged.

His cousin pulled it out then shook his head as he typed out a quick message. "I've gotta go. Church duty calls."

Nate hurried to his motorcycle and buckled his helmet in place before heading back toward town.

The sun beat down on David, the temperatures hinting of the changing leaves and the cooler weather sure to come. He checked his watch. Three fifty-one. Gary Hoover had always closed the hardware store at five back in the day. If that was still the case, David could be there and back in under thirty minutes. Maybe

Nate had a point. He could easily pop in and say hi, get what he needed, and be home. Bonus, it wouldn't take as much time as traveling to Ludington.

Almost ten years had passed since David had spoken to Gary in person. When David and Sadie had broken up, he assumed Gary would disappear from his life. But Gary hadn't. Just like a true father, he'd stayed in contact, even sending monthly support.

David drove into the city center of Heritage. Otis, the bronze hippo that moved around the town square, sat in front of the new ballet studio, almost like he enjoyed the fresh entertainment. Never able to figure out how Otis moved, David accepted the lovable town oddity.

David stopped at the intersection of Second and Teft. No matter how many times he pulled into town, the updated square surprised him. Long gone was the Manor and the row of condemned houses. An old schoolhouse had been renovated and turned into the library. It sat on one corner with a gazebo in the middle. A playground filled the southern part of the square. Maybe his sisters weren't too far off base with the Airbnb idea. The town did hold a certain small-town charm.

Up on his right, the diner's front window sparkled in the afternoon sun, and directly in front of him a huge banner hung over the street advertising their 150th town anniversary in October.

David continued through the intersection down Second Street until he found a parking spot along the square and cut the engine. The shop sat on the corner of Richard and Second just across the street from the southeast corner of the square. It was right next to the bank, but the entrance had been moved around the corner to Richard Street on the southern side of the building. That would have been Sadie's and his first change to the store. He shook away the memory as he got out of the truck and hurried across the street.

As soon as he turned the corner, the rusted Hoover's Hardware sign greeted him. The letters had faded even more, so that one of the o's was completely gone.

The friendly jingle of an overhead bell announced his entrance into the shop. Gary had always kept the store in immaculate condition, but today, dust laced the air and the endcaps of the aisles held anything from paint brushes to hammers—seemingly with no rhyme or reason. Charlotte's web had nothing on the huge cobweb spun along the wood paneled wall behind the register. Gary had never allowed spiders free rein of his store.

"Be right with ya!" The distant voice came from somewhere among the shelves, but there was no mistaking Gary's deep timbre.

The man's gait faltered for a second as he stepped out of the aisle, his eyes widening. He set down a five-gallon paint bucket. And there was just enough of a pause that David's heart sank. Maybe this hadn't been a great idea. But before he could think of what to do next, Gary rushed forward and grabbed David's shoulder and looked him over. "Ten years looks good on you, son. The final bits of boy have disappeared."

Son. David's throat tightened. Gary probably used the term with every male under the age of forty, but it still triggered a sense of what had been. What could have been. The guy almost looked proud of him.

Before David could consider what to say, his gaze landed on Gary's arm that was wrapped in a blue sling and seemed to be strapped down to his chest. "What happened to your arm?"

The older man offered a slight shrug, lifting his uninjured shoulder. "I fell working on the upstairs guest bath a month ago. Landed on my shoulder wrong. Emergency surgery on my rotator cuff, and my arm is useless until it heals. Just a few more weeks in the sling."

One month ago? How had he missed this tidbit of gossip? David had been working away in his grandparents' home a month ago. Maybe this was what Nate meant when he said that David should get out more and see the needs of people around him. Guilt clung to him like day-old sawdust.

Gary walked back to the bucket and bent to pick it up.

"Let me." David didn't know much about rotator cuff surgery, but lifting heavy objects probably wasn't part of the recovery.

Gary slapped David's back. "I appreciate that. I'm getting too old for this. Definitely time for the next generation to take over. But kids are busy these days. One of my daughters only pops in and out maybe once a month now."

Gary had three daughters, but he must mean Sadie, otherwise he'd just name his daughter. With their complicated past, he couldn't blame Gary for being vague. He couldn't ask. Wouldn't ask about Sadie. So, he nodded, and Gary kept talking.

"The high schoolers looking for volunteer hours just don't work for us, with all the heavy machinery and specialized merchandise."

David followed Gary to the register at the front of the store, and set the bucket where Gary directed.

Gary patted him on the back, squeezing his shoulder. "Now tell me, what brings you in today?"

Business. Good. David could handle that. "Need a box of two-and-a-half-inch wood screws."

"Ah. Screws. Those are on the back wall, just like always. It's a bit disorganized—things have just gotten away from me—but I'm pretty sure they're back there somewhere."

David's phone chimed in his pocket, and he pulled it out. Finally. He held up his phone. "I need to respond to this. I'll be right back."

"Take your time, son. I'll be here." Gary continued toward the back of the store, and David turned and stepped outside, looking for shade so he could read his phone screen. The afternoon sun slipped behind a cloud as he walked to the back of the building, away from the square.

Lance
Let's chat next week. Tuesday
morning. 10 EST.

No. No. No. No. No. This couldn't be right. If they'd approved him to go back, they'd simply say the words. The only reason Lance would want to talk was because they weren't going to send him back yet.

David
School starts next week.

I'd love to work through
things ASAP.

Chat now?

Lance
Marco can't right now. Tuesday
morning. 10.

Marco wanted to talk, too? David clenched his fist and then stretched his hand. If they wanted to bring in the executive director, it meant he'd officially miss the first day of school in Costa Rica. This couldn't be God's will. But then again, what did he know? No matter how much he prayed lately, God still seemed to be silent.

Anytime, God. I'm ready.

Still no response.

Nothing more could be done today. Tucking his phone away, David walked back to his grandfather's gold truck and opened the door and plopped down in the driver's seat. Ugh. He still needed those screws. Not that he had a pressing deadline to finish the built-ins anymore. No. He wasn't giving up that easy. He'd fight for what he wanted.

He left the truck and hurried back up the few steps toward the hardware store. The bell welcomed him a second time.

"Coming." A feminine voice rang out, and David could hardly process the familiarity before Sadie stepped out of the back aisle. She froze. Her long, light brown hair was braided, hanging over her shoulder. Her hazel eyes took him in, a touch of vulnerability in her gaze. "You." The word came out breathy and tense.

"Sadie." His voice wasn't any better. But it had been ten years. Ten years since she'd talked to him. Ten years since he'd held her. Ten years since she'd broken his heart right before their college graduation. He opened his mouth again, but nothing came out. His brain had stopped working.

The softness in her gaze vanished, and the welcoming smile disappeared as she held out a box. "I take it you're the wood screw guy."

She was mad at him? She was the one who'd stomped on his heart, not the other way around. She'd been the one to walk away and never look back. He opened his mouth but snapped it shut. He'd moved on and so had she. They didn't need to have this discussion again. His throat tightened, and he worked to swallow the moisture before it evaporated from his mouth. "Two-and-a-half-inch wood screws—that's me."

Her left ring finger was bare. He'd heard she'd gotten married, but maybe he'd heard wrong. He tried not to dwell on news of Sadie, so on the rare occasion one of his sisters brought her up, he quickly ended the call. But hearing she'd gotten married would have been hard to forget. Even so, there had been no one since Sadie, because no one had measured up.

She briefly nodded and walked to the register without a backward glance.

"It's been a while." Almost ten years. And not a day went by that he didn't think about her.

"We don't have to do this, David." She rang him up, not looking at him.

Do what? Catch up? Find out how she'd been? How long she'd

be in town? David gulped and looked at his shoes as he pulled out his wallet.

Sadie said the total, and he handed over the cash, his hands oddly still. He wanted her to look up again. To see her eyes, catch a glimpse of her smile. But it was better if he didn't. He couldn't consider those things anymore. Not since her wedding.

She handed him his change and the screws. Her fingers barely touched his skin, yet little sparks shot all the way up his arm. She looked up, holding eye contact now.

"You been here long?" He should go. He had his change and his screws. But seeing Sadie again...well, he wasn't ready to walk away just yet. Not if it was going to be another ten years.

"Just got into town." She tucked her hands in her back pockets and rocked back on her heels. "Have a good one, David." She nodded to the door.

He could take a hint. He stepped closer to the door without looking away from Sadie. "You too."

David pushed the door open, and the jingling of the overhead bell broke the moment. He hurried out of the store. And that was why he should have gone to Ludington. Because seeing Sadie Hoover? It only reminded him of everything he'd lost. Everything he'd never have.

One thing was certain, he wouldn't be back. Ten years hadn't been long enough to swallow the disappointment of today. He'd lay low and continue to do the one thing he'd done the last ten years.

Avoid Sadie Hoover at all costs.

⌐

She'd waited ten years to move back to Heritage, ten years to chase her dream of owning the family hardware store, and ten years of visits to her parents, praying she wouldn't run into the man who'd torpedoed her life.

Too bad it couldn't have been eleven or twenty. Or never.

Instead, she'd had to reset the count—four days had passed since she'd seen David Williams. Hopefully, that number would continue to go up. Sadie Hoover pulled the ham and provolone from the fridge and set them on the counter of her kitchen in her new-to-her apartment.

The alarm on her phone sounded, halting her movements. Great. Where had she left her phone? The vintage kitchen was barely big enough for two people, so how could she lose her phone?

She paused and followed the muffled notes of the alarm to one of the half dozen cupboards. She opened it. Of course, next to the bread. She grabbed both. This was David's fault. It was the wrong season for a visit from the spirit of Boyfriend Past. "Lottie! That's the fifteen-minute alarm."

"I heard it, Mom." Lottie's voice carried a thick layer of nine-year-old sass.

The front door burst open, and Romee, Sadie's youngest sister by four years, burst into the apartment. Romee's long brown hair tumbled around her face in wild curls, her glasses slipping to the end of her nose. She closed the door with a flourish and pushed her glasses up with one fluid movement.

"Look at this place. It's really coming together." Romee toed off her black flats by the door.

"Really?" Sadie scanned the area. It was definitely cleaner than a few days ago when everyone had helped her move in the furniture, but all she could see were boxes. On the vintage oak coffee table she'd found thrifting last month. On the dining room table that had once been Jeremy's grandmother's. She even piled them at the end of her queen-sized bed. At least she'd gotten Lottie's room ready. First day jitters at a new school were enough without being lost in a sea of boxes.

"So, Dad said David is back." Romee squeezed by Sadie in the kitchen and selected a mug.

Leave it to a sister to make herself at home, even before Sadie had. Turning back to the sandwiches, Sadie layered ham and cheese on two slices of bread. "He was in the store, not back. I think he still lives in Costa Rica, which means it was a one-time thing. By the look on his face when he saw me, he'll make sure of that. I just wish he'd gotten fat. Or gone bald."

"What you're saying is that he's still hot." Romee eyed her over the rim of Sadie's favorite Cedar Point mug.

Hot didn't really cover it. David always had been good looking with his coffee-colored eyes and auburn hair. Clean shaven, incredible bone structure, and full, kissable lips. And boy, had he known how to use them. So okay—yes, he was still hot. "He's older. Broader. And not in my life."

Romee wiggled her eyebrows. "But he could be." Her sister gave a questioning look at the sandwich. "When did Lottie start eating like a linebacker?"

Sadie blinked at the sandwich then started pulling off the layers. If David had her this discombobulated after one encounter, she prayed he'd be leaving the country soon, very soon. Maybe she'd offer to buy his ticket.

Sadie packed up the now normal-sized sandwich and put it in Lottie's new tie-dyed lunch box. Romee picked it up, zipped it closed, and put it in Lottie's matching backpack by the front door.

"No more talk of David." Sadie shook her head. Her chest ached, and her heart squeezed. Hadn't she gotten over the pain of his departure years ago? "He chose to leave me behind. He didn't want me then, and he definitely doesn't want me now. Besides, I have Lottie."

Swallowing another big gulp, Romee looked over the top of the cup. "Jeremy would want you to move on. And he liked David.

Well, except for the whole dumping you and taking off thing, but it's been ten years. Maybe—"

"No. I have a new life." Sadie turned from Romee and walked out of the kitchen into the main room, past the dining room table. She squeezed between the sectional sofa and a row of boxes to the small hallway that led to two bedrooms. "Almost ready, Lottie?"

Lottie's heavy footsteps came running out of her room, her purple hairbrush in her hand. She now had a huge bump on top of her head that hadn't been there when Sadie braided her hair after breakfast. Her freckled nose wrinkled as she waved the brush around. "Mom, I hate my hair. Fix it."

Sadie took the offered brush. "Fix it, please."

Lottie acquiesced to the proper request, and Sadie quickly brushed out the braid and re-did her daughter's thick red hair. She might hate her hair now, but give it a few more years, and the girl would love it. Thick, wavy. The color would cost women hundreds in a salon. She had her father's hair and her mother's beauty. "Five minutes, kiddo. Have you made your bed and brushed your teeth?"

"Going now. Hi, Aunt Romee!" Lottie gave a quick wave and rushed back to her room, straightening her lilac T-shirt as she left.

"Mom. It's still surreal to hear her call you that." Romee leaned against the wall outside the kitchen and sipped her coffee.

"We still talk about Bonnie and Jeremy often. But when she asked if she could call me Mom..." Sadie's throat tightened.

Romee pushed her glasses up. "When is the adoption finalized?"

"October twenty-second. And it should be pretty easy. I do wish Jeremy could be here to see it, even if his sister, Doris, is unhappy with me for moving away from Grand Rapids."

"Let Doris be unhappy. Jeremy was clear in his will that he wanted you to take custody of Lottie, not his sister. Lottie is going to love it here. We both know Heritage was an amazing place to grow up. Even if it moved you farther from me."

"We're going to miss your daily drop-ins, but you could always move home."

"Because Heritage is full of promising violinists looking for an instructor. Grand Rapids is my home now. My music school is there. Besides, you are going to keep plenty busy with the store." Romee picked up the store key on the counter and placed the ring around her finger, spinning it.

"It's a little crazy to think I'm taking over." Sadie had always pictured taking over the store as a child. When David had started talking marriage, she pictured taking it over with him. Then he'd left, and she'd let the dream die because she couldn't fathom taking over the store without him. "Do you think it's a mistake? I mean, I thought I had two years to get ready for this."

"Dad needs you now, and you need a job. It makes sense for everyone."

"I just feel like I should know more about the state of the store before I take over. Did you know Dad's accounting isn't even on the computer?"

"So, you'll learn on the job. And you'll get to set it up the way you like. Which is perfect for your control-freak personality."

"I'm not a control freak." She crossed her arms across her chest. "You're just a slob."

One eyebrow shot up, and Romee stepped to the closest box. Without breaking eye contact, she opened the flaps and pulled out what must have been the first thing she touched. Then without even looking at the purple cut glass vase, walked over and set it on one of the empty shelves in the corner. That was Sadie's favorite vase, and she always kept it on a wood trivet in the center of the dining table.

For one heartbeat Sadie stared at it then turned away. She'd fix it later. After she unpacked the trivet. It would be in the box with the vase.

Maybe she did like to have a certain order to life. But with David leaving her, then Bonnie, and eventually Jeremy, she'd learned that everything went smoother when she only depended on herself. She even stopped asking God for His input. Let someone else take the wheel? No thanks.

Just to prove to Romee that this hadn't bothered her, Sadie walked back into the kitchen and opened the cupboard above the coffeepot and pulled out a mint green tumbler. The final alarm sounded as she poured the coffee. "Lottie! Time to go."

Lottie dashed back into the living room and slung her new backpack on her shoulder. "I'm ready. Bye, Mom."

"Not so fast there. Don't I get to take you today? It's the first day of school." Sadie picked up her computer bag off the small dining table, pulled the strap onto her shoulder, and held out her hand for the store keys Romee still held.

"Please, Mom. I'm almost ten. I can walk to the bus stop. Alone. Oma said Lucy will be there. We're going to be best friends." Of course they would. Because Lottie made friends wherever she went, just like Bonnie had.

Sadie bit back the chuckle wanting to escape. Lottie—little Miss Independent. "Very well. Find out if Lucy is in ballet. Maybe you could take lessons too?"

Lottie bounced her backpack on her shoulder. "Sure thing."

"Let me snap your picture real quick." Sadie pulled out her phone, and Lottie posed in front of the door. "Can I at least walk downstairs with you since I'm heading to the store?"

Lottie threw open the door. "Okay. But no farther. And don't stand at the door and cry when I walk away."

Together, the trio walked out of the apartment and down the wooden stairs to the alley that ran behind the hardware store. The cool morning air hinted at the start of fall.

"The leaves will change soon." Lottie pointed at the fall tree full of green leaves behind the shop. "Dad would've loved that tree."

Sadie slid her arm over the little girl's shoulder and hugged her to her side. Grief, the unwanted companion that it was, showed up at unusual times. "He sure would've."

Lottie shrugged off Sadie's arm and twirled when they made it to the bottom of the stairs—the moment of grief passed. "Okay, Mom. I'll see you after school. Bye, Aunt Romee."

Lottie skipped ahead of Sadie, stopping at the corner and running back. "Mom, Otis is sitting in front of the hardware store. Almost like he's trying to peek in on you."

The cool morning breeze rushed down the side of the building as Sadie walked up to the corner. Romee kept pace with her. The sun peeked over a grove of pine trees behind them, casting their long shadows down the sidewalk toward the square. Sure enough, Otis sat on the sidewalk at the corner of Richard and Second, right under the window that faced the square, as if trying to draw attention to the big, dirty window of Hoover's Hardware.

"Otis always knows what's happening around town. He's in on all the big events." Sadie pulled in a breath. Maybe Otis's watchful eye meant her new endeavor would be a success. Otherwise, Otis would have a front seat to her making a mess of things.

Lottie jumped up to kiss Sadie on the cheek and then dashed off again.

Sadie waited while Lottie made her way all the way to the bus stop at the corner of Richard and Henderson and gave her a final wave then fell into step with another little girl. Maybe it was Lucy.

Romee stood beside her, sipping her coffee. "I'd hoped I could walk a little farther with her."

"Nope. Lottie's determined to meet Lucy. And don't go stealing my mug. I love that one."

Romee inspected the old mug. The words Cedar Point could barely be seen on the side. "You're attached to this mug? Looks ancient."

If thirteen years was old for a coffee mug. She got it just after her freshman year of college. Maybe it was ancient. She and David had met at college, both involved in the same outreach program on campus. One weekend, the group had gone to Cedar Point in Sandusky, Ohio, where she'd found the mug in the amusement park's gift shop, and David bought it for her. Maybe it was time to let the memories rest, a final release to prove seeing David again after ten years hadn't wrecked her mental state. "No attachment. Maybe you should keep it. Or better yet, trash it."

Romee waited for more, but she'd be waiting a long time, because Sadie had talked about David about as much as she was willing.

Her sister finally shrugged and turned toward their parents' place. "Well, I'll run home before anyone notices I'm missing. And I'll be back to bug you at the store in a bit. Maybe I can bring you lunch before I head for home?"

Sadie waved as Romee walked off before climbing up the few steps to the front door of Hoover's. She pushed her store key into the lock, but there was no resistance when she turned it.

The store was unlocked? She ran through her memories from yesterday. Maybe she had been a little distracted after seeing David, but there was no doubt that she had closed and locked the door last night.

Wrapping her fingers around her keys like they were brass knuckles, Sadie wondered if the crime rate in her small hometown had skyrocketed. Unlikely, but still, maybe she should invest in something other than her keys for protection.

Five aisles stretched inside the store with the front counter running along the side wall, but nothing looked different from last night. The register was still closed. And everything smelled the same—a mix of sawdust, paint, and sweat.

"Hello?" Sadie's voice wobbled through the empty store only to hear a familiar and gruff response from the office.

Shoulders relaxed, Sadie shoved her keys into her jeans pockets. Dad.

Sadie walked down the third aisle. A paintbrush had fallen on the floor, and she picked it up to hang it back up, except the paint brush sat between a hammer and a flathead screwdriver. Why wasn't it with the paint supplies? Below the hammer sat a different brand of paintbrush, a garden shovel, and a Phillips head screwdriver. Looked like she'd be reorganizing soon.

She hung the brush up and headed to the back of the store. "Dad, I thought you were taking some time off. Not coming in to open the store on my first official morning." Sadie bent over and brushed a kiss on her dad's cheek as he flipped through the ledger on his desk. Goal one: get the books online. "That's an awful deep V between your brows."

"It's all good, kiddo. Just making sure the books are in order for you. It might be a little harder to let go of the reins than I imagined."

"You thought you had more time. Me too. But it's okay. We'll figure this out."

"You're so good at organizing. But I remembered a few invoices I hadn't recorded yet. I wish I was handing it to you in better shape." Her dad stood up, stretching to his full height. His shoulders were a little rounder, his back not as straight as it had been before the fall. His dark hair held some gray, and the wrinkles in his forehead were deeper. These last few months had been hard on him. It might have changed her plans, but it was time to take over. Her dad needed the break.

"I'm sure it will be fine, Dad. I'll get everything online and fix whatever chaos is in those books."

"I don't think entering numbers into QuickBooks or whatever you're using will change the numbers." Her dad stepped behind the chair, his good hand running slowly over the back. "I guess this is yours now."

So, it was. After all these years, even without David. This was hers. Her dad pulled the chair back and gestured for Sadie to have a seat. She placed her bag on the desk and sat down.

Her dad walked to the door. "About those books..."

"It's fine, Dad. I've got this. And I'd like to hire a few people to help around the store." Sadie pulled out her computer and opened it up in front of her.

Her dad's feet shuffled on the ground. "I can help out at the store some."

"I know, Dad. But you still need to heal from your surgery and make it through rehab, too. That's part of the reason I'm here. Plus, I need time to settle in as the new proprietor. Make the store mine, you know? Oh, did you bring the keys to the back room?"

Her dad's face turned into what she could only describe as a grimace. "About the back room—it's sorta a mess."

His phone rang out and he pulled it from his back pocket, a sheepish grin on his face. "Your mother is calling. I'd better get home. I'll be back later."

"Please bring the key next time. And tell Mom I said good morning." Sadie settled behind the desk as her father exited the office and answered his phone.

When the bell jingled to signal he'd exited the store, Sadie opened her purse and pulled out a framed picture of her and Lottie for the desk. They'd been at Jeremy's favorite cabin on Lake Michigan, north of Chicago, and they were both windblown, sun-kissed, and all smiles. The reminder of her why—why she was back in town, why she wanted the store to be successful, and why she had pulled it all together after another heartbreaking turn in life. To make sure Lottie had a comfortable home, surrounded by people who loved her.

Four hours later, Sadie wished for those smiles. Her eye twitched, and she rubbed at new wrinkles on her forehead. When her dad mentioned the books weren't in great order, Sadie had wrongly assumed he meant they were disorganized. Not that the store operated in the red.

In. The. Red.

For months.

Sadie pulled open the top drawer of her dad's desk—hers now—and dug around inside. And since it was her desk now, she could raid his secret chocolate stash without guilt.

Instead of pulling out candy, her hand found a stack of envelopes. From the bank. She opened the top one and scanned the letter inside. Her stomach tightened and turned over.

There's no way this letter was right. But there was no mistake—payment due September 30th. When had her parents taken out a mortgage on the business?

Why had they taken a mortgage out on the business?

Hoover's had been in the family for years. And they'd missed a few payments, so the bank was recalling the loan. The full amount due.

Sadie closed the computer and placed the note on top. If they couldn't make the payment by September 30th, Sadie wouldn't have a store to run. She had twenty-seven days to fix this.

This was why she'd wanted two years to get ready to take over. Diving into any decision without all the details never ended well. She'd jumped blindly, making this move, changing her life, to chase a dream she'd given up on.

All for what? To discover the store was underwater. How could this happen?

Her hand trembled. But the red letters stamped across the page couldn't be ignored.

She looked down at the statement again. When she trusted people to handle the details, bad things happened. Two words stared up at her, cementing that thought.

Past Due.

two

AVID HAD SPENT EVERY MOMENT OF THE three-day weekend outlining a foolproof argument, but ten minutes into this Tuesday morning conversation with Lance and Marco, already he'd been met with his fifth no. Too bad David couldn't erase that word from their vocabulary.

There had to be a way to express his concerns that would make his field administrator, Lance Everett, understand the importance of returning to Costa Rica. The collar of his button-down shirt chafed as David was met with another no. Why had he picked a dress shirt for this video call?

He picked up his coffee cup on the corner of his grandfather's antique desk in the study David had painted a few weeks ago as Lance once again refused David's request. Too bad the coffee didn't help the discouragement go down. Or bury the distracting thoughts of Sadie. Thankfully, he wouldn't have to see her again. He'd make sure of it.

"I understand what you're saying, Lance. You want to see me

actively involved in the community. But you've also told me to take time to rest and recoup, which is what I've done."

Lance's face on the computer screen could rival a tired parent who'd been saying the same thing on repeat. "David, you went through a traumatic experience, and the mission board, me included, are concerned for you. We want to see you healed on four levels—physically, mentally, emotionally, and spiritually."

"I understand. I am in the best physical shape of my life. My medical exam showed that." Thanks in no small part to the new gym that opened up in town.

Lance leaned forward. "Agreed. But emotionally, are you ready? Your hands are still shaking."

David closed his eyes briefly and made sure his hands were off camera. Yes, they were shaking. "There's no medical reason for that, though. The doctor doesn't know why I'm shaking."

Marco Perez, Executive Director, chimed in. "Which has us concerned, David. What is the something else that's causing it?"

Who knew? He'd have to face it at some point. But David was learning how to handle it. It wasn't like his shaking prevented him from doing anything. He might have to slow down and concentrate more, but it didn't stop him.

"I've not spent this much time studying the Bible since college." Not that it had made a difference. All that time reading the Bible, and still no direction. Not one word from God. All his prayers seemed to just bounce off the ceiling. "Emotionally, I'm fine."

"Fine?" Lance looked down at the papers in front of him and back up. "Nate says you have barely interacted in any way with the people around you. That doesn't say emotionally fine."

That traitor. Nate was supposed to be on his side. David's gaze flicked to Marco's face, but he seemed to have his mind made up too. David ran a rough hand through his hair and sank back into the desk chair. "Okay. But Chris is pulling double, juggling his job and mine. Tell me what I need to do in order to go back."

Marco nodded but his stern expression didn't change. "Don't worry about Chris. We've brought in a temporary guy to fill your position."

They'd replaced him? His stomach churned, and he flexed his hand. "Is it someone I know?"

"It's a young guy. Fresh out of college. He was looking for a short-term opportunity, so it was a perfect fit. You've left the program in incredible order, and he had no problem stepping in. Don't let this discourage you, we want you back, but we want you healthy." Marco leaned forward with an encouraging lift of his eyebrows.

"What would that look like?" David worked hard to not let his resignation slip into his voice. What choice did he have in the matter? These guys were the key to getting back to Costa Rica.

"We'd like to see you connecting with people around you." Lance took a sip from his familiar Detroit Red Wings mug.

"I am connecting." Okay, so David wasn't doing a great job hiding his attitude. Instead, he sounded like a petulant child. He cleared his throat and shifted in his seat.

"You are hiding, and if you're hiding there, what makes you think you won't hide in Costa Rica?"

Properly chastised, David rubbed at his shirt collar. They had a point, and he needed to accept their stipulations and work to meet them.

If they were in person, David knew Lance would slap a hand on his shoulder and squeeze it. "We have an outline in place to help you get back. If that's really what you want to do, we'd like to help you achieve that goal. But we want the best version of you to move forward. If you decide you'd rather stay stateside, there are other options within the board that—"

"I want to go back." David needed to go back. Needed to hear God speak to him again. For God to use him again.

Lance exhaled. He looked down and back up. "Okay then. We want to see you out in the community. Nate will be there to work with you in person, but I'll be making a trip to Michigan soon, and we can meet up. I'd like to see you helping others, maybe find a temporary job. Whatever you feel you need to do to build relationships with the people around you. Why don't you work on this for the next several weeks, and the three of us can meet again mid-October to reevaluate."

David nodded. A to-do list. That was manageable. And no one would mark all the boxes and get back to Escuela Biblica de San Jose faster.

Already ideas were spinning through his head. He'd call the schools and see if he could tutor in the afternoon or volunteer at the nursing home where his uncle had lived before passing away. Maybe he could get a Sunday afternoon program up and running. If the mission board wanted to see him involved in the community, he would be the busiest person in Heritage. Maybe he could help with the planning for that fall fair...festival...town anniversary—whatever that sign had said.

"And, David." Something in Lance's voice pulled David's attention back to his field administrator and longtime friend. "As you readjust your focus, pray about your future. It's okay if God changes your plans. Often He works in ways we cannot explain, and it's only when we follow His plan that we find peace."

Good advice. Too bad all David heard was crickets. Ending the call, David closed his computer screen and reclined back in his office chair, steepling his fingers in front of his face.

Movement caught his eye, and he turned his head to see the cat someone had dumped on his property. He'd taken her in and named her Mamá Gata after he found her with five kittens under his porch steps before a storm blew through. She turned a circle and plopped down again, allowing her kittens close to nurse. The kittens were almost old enough to wean, and he'd need to find them homes before he returned to Costa Rica. Because he would go back. He'd do whatever it took.

David pulled open the top desk drawer and removed a pad of paper to make a list. If Lance wanted him to be involved in the community, then he'd get involved.

At the top of the list David wrote:

Volunteer

Then he wrote down locations he could contact.

Better to solve the problem than to dwell on the reality that Nate didn't approve his return.

A car door closed outside the office window. David pushed back from the desk, but one of the kittens pawed at his feet. He bent down to pick up the black kitten and cuddle it close. The soft body snuggled into his chest, purring.

"Hello?" Nate called out as he entered the house.

"In here."

Nate's face appeared in the doorway. "How did the meeting go?"

"You mean the one where they told me you didn't think I'm ready to return to Costa Rica?" David cringed. So much for not sounding bitter. He set the kitten down next to its mama and stood from the chair. "You seemed to have left that part out of our conversation on Friday."

Nate leaned against the doorframe and crossed his arms against his chest. "I didn't say you weren't ready. I just expressed my concern with how you've locked yourself away. I only ever see you here and at the gym."

"I've been to family dinners."

"The few your sisters have insisted you attend."

Nate didn't understand. It was hard to reconnect with them because he was leaving again. If he got too close, he'd miss them all the more when he left. Being alone in Costa Rica without family— it was hard. He missed seeing his nieces grow, missed his sisters, missed all the big life moments. If he started partaking in all the family fun, it would just make it harder later.

David grabbed his notepad and a pencil and nodded toward

the hall. Nate stepped backward. David left the office and walked down the hall to the main living area and plopped down on the couch. "So, I need to show you and the mission board I'm active and involved in the community. What time is Bible study tonight?"

"Seven."

"I'll add that to my list. Also, I need to find a job or a consistent place to volunteer."

Nate carried a bottle of water from the kitchen before he settled on the couch across from David. "With all the high school kids looking for volunteer hours, the area is pretty saturated, but you know, I think I heard that Hoover's wanted to hire someone. You've worked there before. That would be a good place to start."

"Nope. Not Hoover's." Not after he'd seen Sadie. Gary said his daughter popped in and out. He must have meant Sadie, but David wouldn't chance it. One meeting in ten years was one too many. He'd even dreamed of time gone by last night, of happy moments and scorching kisses. He'd gone years without dreaming of Sadie; he didn't want to start again. Especially since she'd married—even if she didn't have a ring on. "Definitely not Hoover's."

"I haven't heard if anyone else is hiring. You could see if Thomas needs help at the diner. They're always busy, but they also have several employees." Another of the kittens appeared, this one orange with black-and-white patches on her feet and face. It ambled into the room and headed straight for Nate's leg. He picked it up and the little fur ball snuggled into his arms.

"Practice before you take one home?" David added rehome kittens to his list.

Nate huffed while he scratched the kitten on the head. "I mean, it's a losing battle. Olivia wants one, so it looks like you win, man. One less kitten when they're ready for a home."

Good. Now he only had to find homes for four kittens and mama cat.. Because he was leaving for Costa Rica as soon as he checked off this to-do list. All while staying far away from Sadie Hoover and her all-too-familiar smile.

The kitten squirmed and Nate set it back down. "I'll ask around and see if I can find any odd jobs for you."

David nodded. After all, letting Nate dictate some of his work might get his approval sooner rather than later. "Okay. Let's do it."

Finally, David had direction. A list and a plan. He'd prove he was ready to return to Costa Rica, and he'd make certain he didn't bump into Sadie again for at least another ten years.

The bell jingled as the door to the hardware store opened and a customer walked out. It had been five days since David had walked into the store, but even so, every time the welcome bell jingled—even when Sadie knew it was someone leaving—her heart rate picked up and sweat dotted above her upper lip.

It wouldn't be David. Because there's no way he'd come back into this store on purpose. He'd been a champion at avoiding her after he sprang the news of Costa Rica on her, so he wouldn't willingly waltz back into her life now.

The bell jingled again, and like Pavlov's dog, her heart picked speed, and she started sweating.

"Good morning," Sadie called out as she stood up and squeezed past the open box in the center of the aisle to greet whoever walked in.

Bob Whittiker stood inside the store, his hands in his pockets and his posture slightly hunched. The stark wrinkles of his face were even deeper as he looked around the store.

"What can I help you find? I'm doing a bit of rearranging, but I'll have it cleaned up shortly."

Bob stopped at the top of the aisle Sadie had been working in. An opened box with smoker pellets sat next to a pushcart filled with a project Sadie had taken off the shelf. He harrumphed at the sight and pointed at the aisle like he would point at a mess a dog made in the house. "What is all that?"

"Well, typically people smoke and grill outside, so I thought it would make more sense to have the pellets next to the charcoal in the outdoor living section." Sadie brushed the dust off her jeans.

"Where are the paint brushes now?" Bob glared down the aisle.

"I moved those to the paint section. What kind would you like?"

"I'll get it myself. I don't understand why you'd try to fix what's not broke. I've found my way around this store since you were in diapers. It was fine the way it was." The man beelined to the paint section and reappeared less than a minute later with a brush in hand. He paid and grumbled about young'uns changing things.

"Have a good day, Mr. Whittiker," Sadie called out with her best cheerful voice. The door had barely closed when she let her shoulders slump.

One cranky man, but how many more regular customers would be unhappy or unable to accept the changes she wanted to make?

Might as well finish the outdoor living section before someone else came in and fussed about the mess. The bell jingled, and Sadie's dad hollered a greeting.

"Hey, Dad. Did you bring the keys for the back room?"

Her dad wrinkled his nose and grumbled something under his breath.

"No worries. I'll get it later. Let's step into the office." Sadie led the way to the back of the shop.

"I take it you opened my chocolate drawer." Her dad settled into a black plastic chair in front of his old desk.

Sadie tapped the letter she'd left on the desk yesterday with a pencil. "Why didn't you tell me?"

"I had planned on straightening everything out, but when I

fell...well, this transition happened sooner than I expected. I didn't want it to be your problem."

"Since I'm taking over the business, I think this falls under my problem."

Her dad leaned forward. "Your mother and I took out that loan when the roof needed replaced. I kept thinking the store would turn and we'd be able to pay it off, but with each month, we got further and further behind."

"What are we going to do?"

"I'll fix this. It doesn't really affect the store or you."

"How can you say that?" Sadie bit back angry words and took a deep breath. This didn't need to turn into a screaming match. "If the bank forecloses, they can take the store."

"I know. I know. But I'm going to do what I can to make sure that doesn't happen. The store has been in the family for four generations now." Her dad's shoulders rounded. He looked down at his hands and threaded his fingers together before he looked up, his eyes rimmed in red and glassy. "And I promise that it'll remain in the family for generations to come."

Sadie opened the envelope and stared at the number again. The amount due was more than Sadie could scrape together. "I have some money set aside, but this is far more."

"Honey, I don't think this is your battle to fight." Her dad stood. "I'll talk to Bo Mackers at the bank."

"Since I'm taking over, this is my battle." Sadie stood, too, keeping eye contact with her dad. She would not back down from this challenge. She might have jumped into this without all the details, but she couldn't trust anyone else to solve her problems. And this was definitely a big one.

Her dad adjusted the straps of the sling at the back of his neck. "If you're certain. But, kiddo, we'll do what we have to—"

"I'll see what I can do." It might not have been her battle before, but she'd blindly jumped into this mess. She'd have to figure it out now.

Dad rubbed his hand down his face and let out a breath. "If you insist, I'll go tell your mother. She's been worried about this. She wanted me to tell you before you moved."

"And you should have. I honestly don't know if I would have made the move, but I'm here now. The fourth generation taking over. We'll get it sorted. Together."

Dad walked around the desk, hugged her, then left. Sadie called the bank, hoping to make an appointment for tomorrow, but the bank manager was out on lunch, and his assistant asked her to call back later.

The day sped by between greeting customers and trying to organize the office and her thoughts. The bell jingled again, and Sadie stood, rolling her shoulders. Lottie would be home soon. The day had passed in a blur and she'd had entirely too much time questioning everything that had led her to sit behind her dad's desk. But she needed to let that tension go. Get ready to greet whoever walked in the doors. Customers and sales were even more important now with so much on the line. Every transaction mattered.

Inside the door, two women stood. Recognition dawned, and Sadie's stomach turned over as her footsteps briefly faltered. At least it wasn't David.

It was the next best—or worst?—thing. His twin sisters.

She knew she'd have to face them sooner or later. Unfortunately, it happened to be sooner.

Leah and Caroline were still just as beautiful as she remembered, their long red hair styled completely different. Leah wore her curls wild and free, while Caroline had straightened her hair into a smooth, tailored look.

Sadie continued walking forward, working to keep her footsteps even.

She opened her mouth to say something, but what? The only

thing that came to mind was So how have you been since your brother dumped me? Probably not the best opener.

Before she could come up with something better, the sound of the bus's brakes filled the quiet air. Was it three already? The day had passed in a blur. Lottie would be barreling in the store any moment. Lottie who had hair just like David's sisters. Who had hair just like David. This could be bad.

"Hi. Welcome to Hoover's. What can I help you with today?" The twins turned in unison and studied her. Sadie glanced down at her simple black T-shirt and jeans. She'd managed to brush off all the dust, but the twins examined her like she was a ghost.

Leah with her easy-going personality made the quickest comeback. "I could ask you the same question. I didn't know you were in town. It's been what? Eight years since we've seen you?"

"Nine years." Not since the breakup. Nine years and eight months and five—no, six—days. Not that they would really know, or that she expected them to. "What brings you in today?"

Caroline exchanged a look with Leah. "I wanted to get a new drill for—"

The front door of the store burst open, and Lottie skipped in. Throwing her backpack at Sadie's feet, Lottie launched at her. Quick reflexes were the only thing keeping Sadie standing as Lottie's full weight hit her.

"Hi, Mom! Today was awesome. You'll never guess what Lucy said on the bus!"

Sadie set Lottie down and gripped her shoulders. "Lottie, didn't we talk about running in the store? We have customers." Sadie gestured to the two women looking at them with rounded eyes.

"Oh! Look at your hair." Lottie pointed at Caroline's slick straight hair. "It's so pretty." Lottie pulled her own wild mess of curls in a low ponytail over her shoulder and ran her fingers through it. "I wonder if I could make mine look like that. Mom, will you do my hair that way tomorrow?"

Lottie turned back to Caroline. "Can I touch your hair?"

"Lottie!" Sadie stepped closer and draped her arm around the girl's shoulder. Heat climbed Sadie's neck, and her ears burned. Leave it to a nine-year-old to embarrass her in front of her ex's sisters.

Lottie shook Sadie's arms off. "Sorry." She looked anything but sorry. "Mom, can I run see Oma? She promised she'd make cookies today, and I want one before Aunt Romee eats them all." Lottie bounced on her toes.

"Go ahead. But remember when you come back to enter a little bit quieter. There may be customers." Sadie gestured toward David's sisters.

"Okay. I'll try." Lottie hugged Sadie and rushed back out the door, the bell jingling wildly. Sadie picked up the forgotten backpack and walked behind the counter to move it out of the way.

So much for being put together in front of David's family. Not that it should matter. Sadie huffed a nervous laugh. "Sorry. We're working on manners."

Another look passed between Caroline and Leah. This one she could guess. Lottie had red hair and brown eyes—just like David—and she could easily guess they were doing math in their heads. Which was stupid. She could say something to refute their troubled expressions, but she didn't owe them that. Most everyone in town knew Lottie was Bonnie and Jeremy Linden's little girl and that Sadie was adopting her. If they hadn't heard, it wasn't Sadie's fault, and she was under no obligation to clear up their assumptions. "Anyway, what brings you into Hoover's today?"

Caroline studied Sadie carefully while she spoke. "I'd like a new power drill for Grant. His is wearing out."

Sadie gestured for them to follow her and showed them all the drills she had in stock. Caroline quickly picked one up. "Oh, good. This was my top choice."

That was fast. Hopefully, they would pay and leave quickly.

While Sadie rang up the drill, the sisters asked her questions, never dipping below the surface. How had she been? When did she get back in town? How long was she staying? Fine. Last week. Forever.

In a small town, it was guaranteed she'd see them. Now she had. The initial awkward conversation over, she could move past it.

Except as the bell jingled and they were leaving, Leah looked back at Sadie. "David's in town. I'll be sure to tell him we saw you."

Sadie froze. Of course she would. Because why not? Sadie's ears burned again. Go ahead. After all, she'd already seen him. It was no big deal.

Sadie couldn't think about David and his sisters. She had bigger problems. She pulled her phone out and dialed the bank's number. They answered but put her right back on hold. She leaned on the counter. Leah still stood on the front steps. Why was she still there? Sadie rose up on her toes.

Lottie was on the sidewalk chatting with Caroline outside the shop.

In her nine-year old excitement, she gestured at Caroline's hair again.

Caroline knelt down and Lottie touched her hair. Leah copied her sister's action and pretty soon the three of them were all laughing.

A pit formed in Sadie's stomach, and she rubbed at it, but it only made things worse. Okay, so maybe Sadie should have addressed the twins' assumptions, because it suddenly felt like a big deal.

A much bigger deal.

The bell jingled again, and Lottie skipped into the store, humming a happy tune with a ziplock bag filled with a few cookies. Dealing with the twins' assumptions would have to be a problem for later, because someone finally answered at the bank.

three

C HECKING OFF HIS TO-DO LIST MIGHT BE harder than David thought because the last twenty-four hours he'd made zero successful phone calls. There were no volunteer options or jobs in sight.

Seth Warner, known as The Storm after his appearance as a Ninja Warrior, had recently opened a gym, and David had been a regular since. "Hey, man. Looks like you need some water."

"Thanks." David caught the bottle Seth tossed his way, opened it, and drank half. Then he tucked it in his bag and added another twenty-five pounds to the machine, hoping it might help clear his mind.

His muscles tightened as he gripped the handles of the chest fly machine and pressed his hands closed. Sweat dripped down his face as he finished another set of ten.

"Woah, man. Couldn't wait for me today?" Nate's voice echoed through the gym as David relaxed, letting go of the machine.

David grabbed his water bottle and drank some more as he wiped sweat from his face. Nate fell into step beside him as they crossed the room to the free weights. David gripped a weight in each hand and sat down on the bench. "I've hit every dead end I can hit today, so I came early."

"Nothing eases frustration like a good workout, and from the looks of it you've been here a while. Are you going to feel up to some basketball?" Nate selected his weights and sat down on a bench across from David.

"I'll be fine." Sweat dripped into David's eye, burning. He had to be involved, and even if he didn't feel like basketball, he couldn't turn down Nate's offer to play. Not again.

"I take it you discovered the lack of volunteer positions available right now?"

"I mean...how is that possible?" Whose bright idea was it to require high school students to volunteer?

"High school service hours. I even have more hands at the church than I know what to do with. Every surface has been scrubbed clean, and the yard looks great. This week they're deep cleaning the nursery and repainting the Sunday school classrooms." Nate curled his weights up and down in sync with David.

Once they were done, they placed their weights back on the rack. "The guys will be here waiting," Nate said. "Let's go play some ball."

David pulled out a cloth from his bag and wiped his face.

"I'm waiting for a call from the nursing home, but if they don't need help, I have no idea where to go." Cool water ran down his throat as David finished his bottle. He stopped at the refill station.

"Hey, guys." Austin walked up to them as David pulled the bottle away and drank it down. He refilled it again as Austin and Nate talked.

"I wish I could help you out." Austin picked up a basketball and they walked into the gym. Jon, Luke, and Thomas were already on the court. "We've got our hands full, though."

"You still looking for work?" Jon caught the basketball Austin passed to him. He dribbled it a few times then spun it on his finger.

"What's going on?" Luke grabbed the ball from Jon and passed it to Thomas, who dribbled it between his legs before he passed it.

Nate caught the ball. "David here is looking for a job or volunteer work."

"Sorry we didn't have a need." Thomas shook his head.

Jon divided the guys into teams—Nate and David with him against Thomas, Luke, and Austin. The guys lined up at center court, and the friendly game started.

After a while, Jon passed the ball to David, and he made a quick layup. Thomas caught the rebound and tucked the ball under his arm, then walked to the bench. "Water break. You know, I heard Hoover's Hardware was looking to hire. And the high schoolers can't volunteer there because of their equipment."

Of all the places Thomas could throw out, he had come up with Hoover's? Nate slapped David on his shoulder and water dribbled down his chin. Great.

"I don't think Hoover's would be a good fit." David wiped his chin.

Jon plopped down on the bench. "Why not? Didn't you used to work there?"

A long time ago. Memories of quick kisses and dreams long forgotten flickered in the back of his mind—he couldn't picture working in the store without Sadie by his side. It had always been her dream, which eventually morphed into theirs.

"You even dated Sadie Hoover, didn't you?" Luke. Thanks, man.

David nodded. "That's why I can't work there."

"Breakups happen. Besides, she moved out of town." Thomas drank some water and tossed his bottle back in his gym bag.

"If I remember right, you guys were serious." Jon wiped sweat from his face. "What happened?"

David stood and grabbed the ball from Thomas. "I wanted to

go to Costa Rica, and she didn't. She broke up with me when I told her about my plans. Enough talk. Let's play."

David dribbled the ball as he walked back out to the court.

"It's ours." Thomas stood and motioned to pass the ball back. David did, and the game resumed.

Ten minutes later, David's phone rang from inside his gym bag. Finally! The call he'd been waiting for. "I gotta take that, guys. Be right back." He jogged to his bag and dug out the phone, answering it as he stepped outside the gym while the guys continued the game.

"Michelle, thanks for calling me back."

"Always happy to chat with people who want to volunteer." Her gravelly voice oozed friendliness. He could picture her relaxed in an office. She probably had succulents on her desk.

Hope unfurled in David's chest. This was it. His last hope, and maybe, just maybe, she had something he could do. "That's great. I have some ideas of ways I could be of use to you."

A friendly laugh sounded. "That's great. Really. But we don't have a need right now. With the high schoolers working to get their hours in, our activities calendar is jam-packed. We don't have time or space for more activities. And I don't have any openings for employees—part-time or otherwise. I'm so sorry. Things might open up at the end of October. That's when the kids have to have their hours turned in by. I am guessing things will drop off after that. I can give you a call then."

Two months wasn't soon enough. David's shoulders rounded, and he rubbed his forehead. "Thanks, Michelle. I appreciate you calling me back."

David hung up and dragged his feet back toward the guys. He plopped down on the bench as Austin made an easy three-point shot. Jon rebounded the ball and bounced it to Nate to start their trek back to their net. Even three against two, the guys moved quickly.

David sat, watching the game continue. Wasn't this just like life? He'd been sidelined. Completely useless sitting on the bench, waiting for direction. And like a delinquent player who'd been benched, David waited, hoping God would put him back in the game.

"No luck?" Nate wiped his face as he walked toward David.

"Nope." How was he supposed to be involved in the community when no one needed help?

Thomas plopped down next to him, leaning forward, his elbows on his knees. "I said it before, but Hoover's. Give them a call."

Jon slapped David on the back. "It would get you involved in the community. Unless Nate can find some fix-it jobs for some of the older folks around town."

Nate shook his head. "There aren't that many that don't have family looking after them or who would be willing to accept help. A few widows, but not enough for the hours you need. I'll ask around though."

That left Hoover's.

"Call Gary." Luke zipped up his bag. "It's time for me to head home. Hannah had a roast in the crock pot. The house has been smelling good all day." Luke put the ball up as he walked out, Thomas with him. Austin waved as he headed to the other side of the gym, probably to run through the ninja course.

Jon stood and stretched. "You're coming for dinner tomorrow, right?"

"Leah has texted me eight times today. I'll be there."

Jon grabbed his bag and left.

Silence fell in the gym, and David stood to pack up. Nate waited, his gym bag over his shoulder.

"I'm gonna have to call Gary, huh?" David rubbed his chin. Maybe it wouldn't be so bad.

"You don't have to."

But what choice did he have? David had called or talked to just about everyone in town. No one was hiring, and thanks to the new high school community service hours, no one needed volunteers.

David pushed open the door and the cool evening air chilled his damp skin.

He said goodnight to Nate and climbed into his grandpa's old truck. He started the engine and sat there. It was only six. The store had closed an hour ago. Gary would be finishing up dinner. Years ago, David had saved Gary's number. It wouldn't be hard to call and chat with the man. He had said he could use help around the shop.

Before he could lose courage, David pulled out his phone and called him. Gary answered on the third ring.

"Hey, Gary. David Williams here."

"David. What a surprise. What can I do for ya, son?"

David swallowed at the endearment. It shouldn't surprise him. Gary had called him son when he'd seen him at the shop.

"You mentioned you could use some help around the store."

"Ah. About that." Gary hesitated a moment, and David tightened his grip on the wheel even though he hadn't moved from his parking spot.

Not the enthusiastic and overwhelming yes David had hoped for, but considering his past with Sadie, perhaps he should expect the hesitation.

Gary cleared his throat. "We, uh, could use some help. But unfortunately, we aren't in a position where we could pay someone."

It took a lot for Gary to admit that. David knew how much the man kept his personal business personal. Never in all his years working in the store had he heard Gary mention anything to do with the books. Even when he'd planned to pass the store on to David and Sadie, he said they'd discuss the money issues later. Always pushing the conversation off. Of course, they never got to the point where it had been time to discuss finances, either.

David shifted into first gear but didn't move the car. "Good news for you, Gary. I don't need to be paid. I'm looking for something short term. It would only be a few weeks, but I'd be happy to be an extra set of hands."

"Well." Laughter sounded over the phone, but then cut off. The line was quiet for a beat, and David pulled the phone down to look at the screen to see if the call had dropped. Gary hadn't hung up. Another beat, and then he cleared throat. "It would be like old times."

Not really. Sadie wouldn't be there. But that would be for the best. "Perhaps."

"I tell you what, meet me tomorrow at the store around ten. We can talk then. And it gives me time to talk with the new proprietor."

New proprietor?

But did it matter? There were no other options. He needed a job to show Lance he was willing to be out in the community. Working for free would look even better. He was helping. Giving back. Making connections.

Even if the impossible might happen, David would have to make it work. He'd do whatever he had to in order to get back to Costa Rica.

If that meant facing the new proprietor of Hoover's Hardware—whoever that might be—he could do that. He had to.

David nodded. "Okay. See you in the morning."

Why had Sadie told her dad she'd deal with the bank?

She stared down Eddie Fry who sat across the desk in his plush office. His freshly pressed suit and neatly styled hair. How could her high school classmate have grown up and become so put together? And old?

His thick-rimmed glasses perched precariously on his nose, in no way hiding his woolly eyebrows in need of a good plucking. "I understand your concerns, Ms. Hoover, but there's very little I can do. I'm sorry."

Well, she was too. Sorry for jumping into a family-run business after her husband up and died on her and after her dad had surgery. Sorry she'd let herself get carried away without looking at all the little details before uprooting her entire life.

Maybe she should have let her dad deal with the bank. He could have gotten a meeting with Bo Mackers, since they were friends, rather than her waiting two days for a meeting with Eddie.

And what was with the Ms. Hoover? Formal. Aloof. No small-town closeness here. The words sucked the hope right out of Sadie's lungs. She ran her thumbnail along a cuticle. She really needed to file her nails and put on some lotion.

"I'm sure your hands are tied, Mr. Fry." She could be formal too, even though he'd been her study buddy in advanced chemistry. "But I just took over the hardware store, so if I could have a few more months, I'm sure I could pay the amount the bank is seeking."

Eddie folded his hands on top of the desk and let out a sigh. Perhaps she was wearing him down, and he'd give her some more time.

Eddie looked up, adjusting his glasses. "I want to help you. I do. But it's not my call to make. I tell you what, though. I will talk to Bo Mackers and see what he says. I can call you later this afternoon with an answer."

"Thank you, Eddie." Sadie stood up and quickly left the bank. As soon as she made it outside, she leaned against the brick wall of the building, the rough texture scraping through her forest green sweater.

She pulled out her phone and opened up her banking app, looked at the numbers. Jeremy had left her with money. She'd set aside a huge chunk into a CD for Lottie's college fund. Untouchable now, and secure for Lottie.

But with the remainder...she'd hoped to buy a house. Have some cushion for the what-ifs in life. If she poured it all into the store, there would be no cushion left. No house. But if she didn't and it went under, where would she be? Living off the cushion, which wouldn't go far. And even if she gave everything she had for the store, she still needed several thousand more to save it.

Sadie stood up and tucked her phone into her pocket. She had to find the positives.

She took a few steps forward into the sun, the warmth heating her body. She hadn't even realized the brick had been cool, chilling her. Normally she hated being cold. Living in Michigan, she had to laugh through the winter months. At least she had a warm apartment and a comfortable place to sleep.

And her rent was free.

Wait.

Sadie's steps faltered. If the store was foreclosed, she'd lose more than her job—she'd lose her apartment over the store, too.

"Morning, dear!" Margret Bunting called as she walked past Sadie toward the diner. Sadie's stomach growled, but no food would be entering the tempest of coffee sloshing in her gut. Not until she had direction. Or money.

Maybe it would be a winning diet plan and she could drop the few pounds she'd gained since Jeremy died.

Sadie sidestepped Otis, who still sat in front of the window of the hardware store, and rounded the corner to the front door. The familiar jingle welcomed her, and her dad stood up from behind the counter, his gaze shifting to an aisle—his unspoken way of letting her know they weren't alone.

"Didn't go well?" Her dad's soft voice rolled over her.

He could say that. She nodded toward her office. "Can you meet me when you're done?"

A look crossed her dad's face, almost sheepish. "Well—"

Oh no. "What now?" She couldn't handle too much more—the loan was more than enough.

His eyebrows dipped so low a V formed between his brows. "You said you wanted to hire someone, so I did."

They couldn't afford to pay their loan. How on earth could she pay an extra employee, no matter how much she needed one? "You know I can't pay anyone."

Her dad wrinkled his nose. The last time Sadie had seen him this hesitant, he had to fess up to her mom that he'd dropped her favorite crystal bowl—which had originally been Sadie's great-grandma's. "That's not a problem, because he doesn't need paid."

"You know we can't have the high school students volunteer here."

"What if I told you he wasn't in high school..." Her dad looked over her shoulder and beckoned someone closer. Sadie looked behind her, but no one was there. Her dad pulled out a handkerchief and rubbed his face before tucking it away. "It's temporary. A few weeks. And the best news? You already know him and work well with him."

That narrowed down the choices. There were only two hims she had worked in the store with over the years. Her brother and... David. Toby wouldn't come all this way from Florida to help for a few weeks. He had his own job and a wife.

Oh no.

No. No.

No. No. No.

Her dad nodded, and his face looked anything but apologetic.

He cleared his throat behind Sadie. She closed her eyes and rubbed her head.

A loud ringing split the air, and Sadie pulled her phone from her back pocket. Saved by the bell. Literally. She held up her phone. "I need to take this."

Sadie made a beeline for her office, not looking at him. Maybe if she didn't actually see him, she could ignore his presence. She closed the door of the office and answered her phone. Eddie jumped right to business.

"I talked with Mr. Mackers, and he has agreed to extend your loan."

Air rushed out of Sadie as she let go of the breath she'd been holding since picking up the phone. She straightened her back, her shoulders popping. She'd not realized how much tension had gathered. "That's great. Thank you!"

"Well." Eddie hesitated. "There's more. Mr. Mackers says he can extend the loan until October 31, but..."

Her shoulders tensed. There was always a but.

"You'll need to pay half the amount due today."

"Today?" Sadie sat down in the chair behind the desk.

"I've told Cindy, our teller, to be on the lookout for you. We're open until five."

Sadie thanked Eddie and leaned back in the chair. It creaked under her weight as she closed her eyes.

Half the amount?

Running the numbers in her head, she pressed her hand against her forehead. She already knew how much she'd have to cough up—it didn't matter how many times she calculated everything. She'd be out almost everything in her savings account. She'd have a tiny bit left but not much. Not enough to live on if the store went under.

Jeremy had wanted to make sure she and Lottie were cared for. He hadn't seen a failing store in their future. If she parted with what remained of his life insurance, would she even be able to save the store?

Sadie leaned forward and let her head thump on the desk. An extra month would give her a total of seven weeks to scrounge up the funds. But how could she do that, run the store, focus on

Lottie, and prep for the adoption hearing? Without help, she'd never pull it off.

He flashed in her mind. Once upon a time, they'd been a good team. David had always been an incredible salesman.

Why, God? Why him?

It would be easier if she could refuse his help. Tell him she didn't need him, but the reality was...she did need him.

Oh, that burned to admit. But if she was pouring just about everything she had into this store, she couldn't afford to be prideful.

She needed help, and David was the only one offering.

Sadie sat up and unbraided her hair. Pulled the hairbrush she'd stored in the top drawer out and ran it through her hair and rebraided it. Ready to swallow her pride and face David, she added a fresh coat of lipstick. If she had chocolate, she'd eat a piece, but since she hadn't replaced her dad's stash, she dug out a breath mint.

Because there was no way around it. She had to face him. Had to accept his terms of unpaid employment.

Sadie stood, rolled her shoulders back, and took a deep breath. Here goes nothing.

As she walked back to the front of the store, her dad and David stopped speaking as she approached. David dipped his chin. A shock ran through her spine as his mocha brown eyes met hers. His deep voice rolled over her like hot chocolate. "Hi, Sadie."

Okay, when she'd wished for chocolate, she hadn't meant his alluring gaze. From now on she'd make sure she had some in her desk. "David. Why would you work here unpaid?"

He nodded, his hands sliding into his pants pockets. His arm muscles tightened, straining against his sleeves as he moved. Why didn't he have a jacket, and how did he manage to have such incredible biceps? "My mission board wants me to be working in the community while I'm here. Every other place in town is full of volunteers."

Well, at least he didn't want to work with her any more than she wanted to work with him. That probably shouldn't sting... but it did.

At least he wouldn't be here long. And the looming end date would stand as a good reminder that no matter how good looking he still was, no matter how much physical appeal he still had, he'd leave again. Just like before. At least this time she would have all her guards up, her walls in place, and her heart would stay intact.

Small mercies.

"Perfect. Do you have days and times you prefer to work?" Sadie stepped behind the register next to her dad. The pride that filled his gaze confirmed her decision.

"My schedule is pretty open. I can work as much or as little as you need." David lifted his chin, his eyes flashing.

Maybe when they were together, she could have identified those emotions in a single glance, but Sadie couldn't allow herself to think about David's feelings in this matter. In fact, she'd work to ignore his feelings altogether.

Her dad wasn't wrong—they had been a good team. And for the sake of the store, her future, and for Lottie, she'd figure out how to work with him again. But she'd take some time to mentally prepare to be in such close proximity. "Why don't you start Monday at ten."

Sadie made sure her dad could cover the store a few more minutes and stepped outside.

She needed air. And she needed to visit Cindy at the bank to pay off part of the loan and say goodbye to her savings.

She would take the weekend to collect her thoughts and prepare to work with David. She'd do anything to save her store. Empty her savings account? Check. Work with the man who broke her heart? Check.

Hopefully it would be enough.

It had to be, because she didn't have anything left to give.

four

HE'D SAID YES TO A FAMILY DINNER HOURS before he knew he'd volunteer to work with Sadie. If he could rent a TARDIS, he'd travel back a few hours and find an excuse to say no to this meal. As it was, his niece Vangie bounced next to him with all the energy of a three-year-old as she scooped another bite of green beans into her mouth.

Weren't kids supposed to be picky eaters?

David shoved the mashed potatoes around on his plate. Could he convince Vangie to eat some of them? His appetite was non-existent. Working with Sadie? Had he really agreed to work for his ex-girlfriend? The only woman he'd ever really loved.

After all these years and all the twists and turns their lives had taken, he'd be working at Hoover's Hardware with Sadie. Not as her partner like they'd always envisioned, but as a free lackey.

"Unca David?" Vangie tugged on his sleeve. "How are the kittens?"

David set his fork down. All eyes at the table were on him, and he shifted in his seat. The meal with his family had been oddly quiet. Maybe it was simply because he'd been pre-occupied with his meeting with Sadie today. "The kittens are good. Growing quickly."

"Almost time I can take one home?" Vangie brushed against David.

"I'd say in another week or two."

"I want two." Becca clapped her hands. Caroline used a napkin to wipe her daughter's hands.

"You want two kittens, or you want Dos?" Caroline glared at David. "Honestly, who names kittens by numbering them?"

Becca clapped her now clean hands. "Dos!"

Vangie tugged on David's sleeve. "I want Uno."

Perhaps Caroline would have two kittens in her future, even if she didn't want that many.

Grant pushed his plate forward. "It's clever. He doesn't have to think of fancy names."

Mamá Gata and her five kittens—Uno, Dos, Tres, Cuatro, and Cinco. Better and easier than coming up with names. And maybe he wouldn't get attached when he had to find them homes when he left.

Vangie rested her head on David's shoulder. "I'm all done. Unca David, want to come play tea party with me?"

And leave behind the now cold glob of mashed potatoes still on his plate? "Absolutely, kiddo."

David pushed his chair back, but Leah appeared behind him, her infant daughter wrapped in a blanket in her arm. Leah placed her free hand on his shoulder. "Vangie, why don't you and Becca run upstairs to play together in Isabella's playroom. This afternoon I set up an art table for you with new crayons and fresh paper. You can draw Uncle David another fairy house."

Vangie had given him a picture several weeks ago. "I attempted to build the last fairy house you gave me. One of these days you'll have to come see it."

Vangie's jaw dropped, and her hands splayed on the table. "You built me a fairy house?"

David nodded, and Vangie threw her arms around his neck. "I can't wait to see it." She gave him a sloppy kiss on the check and ran off.

Caroline shook her head at David. "Way to make sure you're the favorite uncle. She'll never stop talking about coming to see you now. You'll have to follow through on your dinner invite."

"How about next Saturday? I'll provide meat and the makings for s'mores, and you guys can bring the sides."

"We can't next weekend. Could we do it in two weeks?" Caroline looked at the calendar on her phone.

His weeks just ran together, but two weeks gave David a little extra time to clean things up and maybe add some pink paint to the trim of the fairy house. "That's fine with me. Leah?"

"Works for us. You done, David? I can take your plate." Leah brushed his shoulder as she picked up his plate before he could even respond.

He stopped her by holding the edge of the plate. "Your hands are full. Let me do this."

Leah shook her head. "You hold Isabella. I'll clear the dishes."

She carefully handed him the tiny baby wrapped in a soft pink blanket. David cuddled his tiny niece close to his chest.

He'd missed seeing both Vangie and Becca this size. He'd be heading back to Costa Rica soon, so he'd enjoy this while he could. Isabella sucked on a pink pacifier, her little cheeks working furiously, her eyes closed as she let out a sigh.

A deep longing to have a family, children of his own, awoke within him. It had to be the nieces fueling these thoughts. He shut those buried dreams down. His work, his life, required sacrifice. It was just the way it was.

"She's growing so fast." Jon spoke from the head of the table. "But I'm ready for her to sleep through the night."

Grant, who sat to the right of Jon, grunted his agreement as he grabbed Jon's shoulder, like some secret father club. "It takes a while before a baby sleeps all night."

Across from David, Caroline sat practically glaring at him. Her green eyes flashed in anger.

David racked his brain, but nothing came up. He had no idea what he'd done to make her angry. He'd finished all the renovations at his grandparents' house she and Leah had requested. She even said she liked it. Had something changed? Leah came in—she must have left the dishes in the sink because she hadn't been gone long enough for anything else—and kissed Jon on the cheek as she slipped into her seat.

"What is this? An intervention?" David couldn't handle more today. Seeing Sadie, agreeing to work with her...Wasn't that enough for one day?

Jon grunted, and Leah shot him a warning glance.

"No." Leah stood up. "I forgot dessert. Who wants coffee?"

"There's no need to make coffee." Caroline crossed her arms. "But if you have it made, I'd take a cup."

Jon stood up. "I'll get the cookies."

David pushed back from the table. "I can help."

Caroline stood up. "You have the baby. I'll help."

The baby—it had been a trap. No way could he make a quick exit with Isabella in his arms. He'd walked right into this, and he had no choice but to hear what they had to say now. If only they'd hurry up and say it.

David looked at Grant. "Do you have any idea what this is about?"

"I'm staying out of it." Grant pulled his phone out and started scrolling.

David didn't have long to wait because Jon came back in with the plate of cookies, and Leah and Caroline returned with five cups of coffee and the cream and sugar.

David took his coffee black and waited while the others fixed their own cups. He shifted the baby in his arm, pulling her closer, as he took a sip. Bitter. And not quite right—like everything else since seeing Sadie.

The night couldn't end soon enough, David just needed to hear what they had to say so could he leave. "So, ready to say your piece now?"

Leah glanced at Caroline and then Jon. "Well, you see…"

Caroline set her coffee cup on the table and leaned forward. "Sadie's back in town. Taking over the hardware store."

"I know." Boy, did he. David would be seeing a lot more of her, too. Shock filtered across his sisters' faces. Good. Nosy as all get out. "If that's all this is about, I think I'll head out now. Can I lay Isabella down?"

"Hold on." Grant looked at David over the rim of his coffee cup. "You may be done with this conversation, but I guarantee your sisters aren't, and I'd rather they have their say than listen to them rehash it if you rush out."

So much for the bro code. "And I thought you said you had no idea what this was about."

Grant shrugged and nodded toward Caroline. "I said it wasn't my problem and that I was staying out of it. But if you leave now, she'd make it my problem."

"How did you find out Sadie was in town?" Leah took a cookie and passed the plate around.

Jon and Grant took two. David passed. There was no need to try—they wouldn't taste good either.

"I'm working at the hardware store. Ironed out the details this morning."

Leah shot Caroline a look. It didn't matter if they were five, fifteen, or grown adults, their silent twin telepathy raised his hackles. "Spit it out. You don't have to use your twin powers."

Leah let out a deep breath. "Did you know she has a daughter?"

Sadie had a daughter? It would have hurt less to hammer his thumb. Not that it should matter to him. "She's married. It's not that unexpected."

"She's widowed." Caroline tossed her hair over her shoulder, but David stopped her from saying more.

"Widowed? Like her husband died?" David snuggled Isabella closer, needing to flex his hands. He patted the baby gently, thankful for a reason to move.

"Yes, genius." Grant punched his arm. A glint in his eye. "Need any other words defined?"

"I'll pull up the dictionary app." Jon picked up his phone.

Sadie was single? No. That's not how he'd think about her. Sadie was widowed. His heart ached for her pain. The heartbreak she'd endured. For her child who would grow up fatherless. "She's a single mom?"

"Yes. Her daughter is nine." Caroline's words were slow, laced with something like accusation. She leaned closer, her eyes communicating a message David didn't understand.

"Nine, David. Pretty girl. Red hair." Leah twirled a curl of her own hair around a finger.

Caroline made a V with her fingers and pointed at her own green eyes then with more force at David. "She has brown eyes."

"Red hair. Brown eyes. Make the connection, David." Grant harrumphed and sipped his coffee.

The faces around the table all stared at David like he needed to figure something out. Like he was guilty. He shook his head and shrugged.

"Come on, Bro." Leah gestured to her hair and made a V with two fingers on her right hand and pointed at her green eyes, then his. Had his sisters practiced that move?

Isabella let out a little sneeze and stretched in his arms. He looked down to see her sleepy eyes open and then slowly close.

Wait. Were they serious? A nine-year-old girl. Red hair. Brown eyes. Like his.

Of all the ridiculous things to think.

His sisters had such little faith in him? He wasn't that type of guy, and that they'd jumped to such a conclusion stung.

David stood up and paced away from the table, turning his back to his family. Isabella wiggled in his arms, and he ran a finger down her soft, pink cheek. A daughter? "No. I can tell what you're thinking, and no."

Leah bit at her bottom lip. "Are you sure she's not yours?"

He'd given up his dreams of a family when Sadie walked away from him. No one had compared to her. He hugged his niece a little closer. He'd never have the experience of holding his own daughter, and he'd be leaving his nieces behind soon enough. David spun around to face the table and walked back toward it. "I'm positive she's not mine. I can't believe you'd ask me that."

How could they think that? It wasn't possible for him to have a daughter with Sadie, but if it had been, he would never have left a baby without a father. Did they really think so little of him?

The tiny bundle in the crook of his arm started to move again, and he looked down to find Isabella's big eyes open, her mouth pinched. She grunted before a strong odor assaulted him. Saved by the...uh...stink?

He passed her to Jon. "I think that's my sign to give her back. I'm not sure uncle duties cover that."

He had to go. He shoved his hand into his pocket—yep, car keys, phone, wallet. He stepped toward the door. "Thanks for dinner, but I'm gonna head home."

He hurried out of the room before anyone could respond or stop him and opened the front door, welcoming the cool night air.

His skin burned.

Sadie had a nine-year-old daughter. She sure hadn't waited long to move on.

He'd been so devastated when they broke up. Maybe her feelings hadn't been as deep as his. Maybe that's why it had been easy for her to move on. Because news of her wedding hadn't been that long ago.

She'd moved on. And then on again. He'd been stuck in the past, wondering what could have been. No one had ever compared to her, and she replaced him. Quick.

Working with Sadie would be hard no matter the circumstances, but to know she had a daughter, and that she was widowed?

David opened the door of the small truck and sank into its seat.

In reality, this news didn't change anything. He still needed the job, and the hardware store was the only option.

Ten tips on working with your ex.

The words blurred as Sadie stared at her phone. Okay, Google, here goes. She clicked on the link because David would be here in ten minutes, and she had no idea how today was supposed to go. How was she going to work with the man who had completely shattered her heart and changed the course of her life?

A message from Romee dropped down and she clicked over.

Romee
_____
Are you ready for today?

_____ Sadie
Not even close.

What was I thinking?

Romee
_____
You were thinking about saving your store.

*gif of Superwoman.

Sadie

Assuming I can save it.

Romee

*gif of a cat jumping up and down with the words You Can Do It.

Sadie

But seriously, how do I face David?

Romee

What did Google say? Because I know you looked.

Sadie

Agree to keep the past in the past. Be professional. Don't stir up drama. Focus on your work. Always take the high road... There's more, but you texted.

Romee

That's a start. Ignore the past.

The bell jingled and Sadie sent one more message as cool air blew into the shop.

Sadie

It's go time.

David walked in wearing boot cut jeans, a navy Henley shirt, aviator sunglasses, a dark brown bomber jacket, and he was holding two to-go cups from Donny's.

Closing the space between them, he handed her a cup, his fingers brushing against her hand as she took it.

Heat crept up her neck. She pulled the cup to her face. Coffee. She closed her eyes and took a moment to savor the welcome aroma.

"It's just the way you like it. Four creams and a sugar." David's deep voice washed over her, sending a trickle of shock through her system.

He remembered how she drank her coffee? A warm pit opened up in her stomach, but her phone vibrated on the counter with a message from Romee.

David stepped back and took off his sunglasses and tucked them inside his coat pocket.

Sadie picked up her phone and unlocked it to read Romee's message.

Romee
_____

Stay strong! Be kind.

Sadie tucked her phone in her back pocket.

Be kind. She could do that.

She took a sip of coffee and savored the sweet and creamy flavor. Perfection. Except..."I drink it black now." Be kind. "But thank you."

David lifted one eyebrow, and his dimple appeared. "I guess things have changed."

Only like...everything.

Be professional. "I guess."

When Jeremy had been so sick at the end, she'd stopped taking the time to add cream and sugar. It had been more of a survival mode, and now, she hadn't added it back in. Just...because.

But she couldn't say all of that, much less to David. Leave the past in the past.

David set his cup down and shrugged out of his jacket.

"You can leave your things in the office." Sadie slid off the stool she'd been sitting on and led the way to the back of the store. Which was dumb. David knew the way to the office.

Ah, well. Be professional.

Sadie took another sip of the coffee. Absolute perfection. She'd not realized how much she missed the cream and sugar, but it made this cup of coffee the best she'd had in...well, ages.

Coffee preferences of the past, and he'd remembered. That had to mean...No.

Past in the past. It didn't mean he'd thought about her, and she couldn't assume he'd pined for her.

David took a large drink of his coffee. His Adam's apple bobbed as he swallowed. That was not supposed to be attractive. Not supposed to make her hands damp and her breath shallow.

Be professional.

She could do that.

"For starters, I'd like to move the counter, so it sits parallel with the front window. Then the register is next to the door. It's not like the line backs up, but it makes it nice to be able to pay right by the door." And now she babbled. She pointed to the coat rack inside the office. "After I clean out the back room, I'll set up a space for you, so you'll have your own personal spot to store stuff, but..."

Ugh. Put a sock in it, girl.

Sadie quickly turned on her heel and hurried back to the front of the store. A large box for an air compressor stood out in the middle of the regular tool section. It belonged with the power tools. Setting her coffee cup down, Sadie stretched her arms around the box. It was bigger than she expected, but she hoisted it up.

She took one step back, trying to regain her balance. The box weighed more than she thought.

"Let me help with that." David's hands grazed hers as he wrapped his arms around the box. Warmth shot through her, and her skin burned as his hand stayed close to hers and he lifted the box. Why did his touch still have to cause a reaction from her? "Where do you want it to go?"

Sadie directed David to the section she'd created for power tools as her phone buzzed in her pocket. She picked up her coffee and headed to the front of the store, her phone buzzing again and again. Setting her coffee down, she pulled it out. Four messages nope—five.

Romee
_____

How's it going?

Are you still alive?

*gif of Bugs Bunny chewing a carrot saying, "What's up, Doc?"

Sees-ter! I need updates. He's been there like ten minutes.

Have you guys made up? Are you hiding in the office making out?

Sadie let out a breath and shook her head. Unbelievable.

_____ Sadie

You're ridiculous.

Romee
_____

Details, please.

*gif of Puss in Boots with pleading eyes.

_____ Sadie

No details.

But...

Romee
_____

*gif of Ham talking to Scotty saying, "You're killing me, Smalls."

_____ Sadie

He brought me coffee.

Romee
_____
*gif of Thor throwing a coffee cup
on the floor yelling "Another!"

Sadie tucked her phone away as David stepped up to the glass counter. Sadie showed him where she wanted it to go. She'd already emptied it this morning, taking out the things they kept stored in there—knives, spray paint, ammo—so it would be easier to move. She'd stacked it all against the wall in her office to keep them safe.

She also had new shelves to install. She'd ordered them before she knew about the bank loan, and since they were non-refundable, she might as well use them.

David quickly set to work, moving the few remaining items that needed to be moved. "How do you want to do this?" he asked about the counter. "I can take one end and you the other?"

Sadie quickly agreed. Their polite and professional demeanors easily stayed in place.

They moved the counter over, and Sadie picked up Windex and paper towels when David offered to clean the glass.

"Do you want the items back in here?" He pointed at the empty case.

"If you remember where it all belongs, but I'm happy to put it back in." Sadie stepped out of the way as David came forward and picked up some spray paint. His arm brushed hers, and even though she wore long sleeves, goosebumps rose along her arm.

Ugh. Could she not stay out of his way?

"I remember." David's warm chocolate eyes sought hers out. "I remember a lot."

Oh no. No, he did not. Heat radiated through Sadie. Very unprofessional words sprang to her lips, but she forced them closed, pulled them between her teeth.

Leave the past in the past.

Sadie let out a deep breath and shook her head. It would be easier to walk away from that. Not take the bait. She headed toward the office. Maybe she could figure out something that would save the store.

Don't stir up drama, Sadie reminded herself as she continued to her office.

"Walking away again?" David's quiet voice might as well have been a knife thrown at her back.

That's it. Forget it. Those rules were stupid, anyway. Spinning around on her heel, she marched back to him.

"I didn't walk away. You left." She crossed her arms, hugging herself, to keep from jabbing her finger into his chest.

"I didn't leave you. You refused to talk about our future and broke up with me." David stepped closer. His manly, clean scent was the same one she remembered from all those years ago, invading her space just as much as his physical presence.

"Oh no. Don't you blame this on me." Sadie stepped closer, looking up at David, finally jamming her finger into his chest.

His very solid chest.

He didn't even have the decency to wince at her jab. But poking him had hurt her finger. She dropped her hand rather than shaking it out. "You're the one who changed our plans for the future without even talking. Then just sprang a new idea on me and told me to get on board. Or else."

David scoffed. "I didn't say it like that."

Sadie flung her arms out to her sides. "Might as well have."

"I told you I was interested in Costa Rica. That I'd been accepted as a teacher. I wanted you to go with me. You walked away."

"I needed time to think. Besides, you never invited me to go with you. You just told me you were going, and that was the end of it. I wanted to build a life together. Decide together. You just made a decision and expected me to follow. How was I supposed to know you even wanted me there? You never said as much."

"I loved you. Of course I wanted you with me."

She didn't miss the past tense. He had loved her. He had wanted her. Not now. She might still be attracted to him, but their love was a part of the past and needed to stay there.

She drew a deep, calming breath. "And I loved you and would have followed you anywhere."

His expression hardened as he took a step toward her, but she took a step back, shaking her head.

Her eyes burned and her throat tightened. She would not cry in front of him. "But I wanted a love that made decisions together. One where we could build a life together. A partnership between two people. And when you left, I realized that maybe I'd been fooling myself all along."

David stepped back. He jammed a hand into his hair, like the words pained him.

"Is that the kind of love you found with your husband? You can say you loved me, but it certainly didn't take you long to move on. You have a nine-year-old daughter. We broke up less than ten years ago."

Seriously? Was he delusional? "Oh, that's rich. You're so clueless."

"Then enlighten me."

Sadie bit the inside of her jaw to keep the words she'd regret later inside.

Part of her wanted him to think Lottie was hers, thankful that he still felt something toward her, even if it was just betrayal. But he'd learn the truth sooner or later.

And a larger part of her wanted him to know how much he'd hurt her when he'd left. He'd been gone when Lottie was born, but she figured he'd at least heard the news. "I'm adopting Lottie, Bonnie and Jeremy's daughter, you idiot. Remember their honeymoon baby, who was born three months prematurely?"

Surprise crossed his face, and he walked away from her as he rubbed his chest.

Well, good. No. Wait. That was just petty, but she couldn't deny that it did give her a little satisfaction that it bothered him.

They'd been maid of honor and best man at Bonnie and Jeremy's Easter wedding. Just weeks before their own breakup.

David had walked away from more than just Sadie when they broke up. He hadn't contacted any of their mutual friends, either.

"You're adopting Jeremy's little girl?"

"Yes." Sadie stepped back, crossing her arms and squeezing tight.

"I'm sorry. I was out of line. I heard you were a widow, but I should have known better than to trust the Heritage gossip." David stepped a little closer, his gaze boring into her. Something akin to relief flashed in his eyes, but it passed before she could be certain.

"I did marry." Her voice came out thin, and David's eyes dropped. She waited for him to look up again. "Eighteen months ago. Right after Jeremy was diagnosed with Machado-Joseph disease."

"You married Jeremy? What happened to Bonnie?" David let out a long, slow breath, like he'd been punched.

"She died in a car accident eight years ago. Which you'd know if you hadn't cut everyone off. I'd been helping with Lottie since then, and it was the next logical step."

"Did you love him?" He met her gaze, his heart in his eyes, but she wasn't doing this again.

"You don't get to ask me that."

"Sadie." A guttural sound. A plea.

Sadie shook her head. "It's in the past, David. Let's leave it there."

The front bell jingled, and Sadie jumped back. She hadn't realized how close they were standing. She whipped her head around to see her dad walking into the store flipping a key ring around his pointer finger. He'd finally brought her the key to the back room.

The perfect distraction, because this conversation was over. They'd rehashed their past. Broke every rule she'd read on Google and aired out their dirty laundry. They had a mixed up and convoluted breakup, but it didn't change anything. The past was the past.

And it had to stay there.

five

I T HAD ONLY BEEN FOUR DAYS SINCE LOTTIE HAD
met David Williams after they'd blown up their past and fought in
the middle of the store, and Sadie hadn't had a moment of peace since.

Mom, did you know Mr. Williams knew Daddy?

Mom, did you know Mr. Williams speaks Spanish?

Mom, did you know Mr. Williams takes kids on rafting trips?

Yes. David knew Jeremy. And she'd taken Spanish with him in
college, although Sadie hadn't used it much since. She had no idea
about the rafting trips.

At least things had gotten easier with David. It was like the
blowup had brought a truce. They hadn't shared anything personal
since, but at least they weren't tiptoeing around the tension now.

How he could have believed that she hadn't wanted him back
then was still a huge mystery to her.

Then again, she often held her cards a little too close. Just like
her dad and the state of this store.

Speaking of which, she forced her mind to the problem at hand.

The curser blinked unrepentantly on the laptop screen. The

numbers were still in red, and the bank note still sat in the top desk drawer, rather than a bag of chocolate. There was no need to waste money on non-essentials.

Sadie rubbed her fingers in circles at her temples. She might have to give in and take some Advil.

Even with David, who could sell water to a drowning man, and their increased sales this week, she had no idea how she'd make up the rest of the money. Maybe David could sell out the store.

Lottie's giggles filled the shop. But underneath her happy, light-hearted belly laugh, David's deep chuckle reverberated. Lottie couldn't wait to see David after school each day.

The man could make a sale to anyone who walked in the store. He chatted with the elderly, making them feel welcome, carrying their purchases to the car, and he made her little girl laugh.

It was like the man could do it all. He had to have a fault.

Maybe he snored. Or drooled.

The welcome bell jingled, and Sadie left the office to greet her newest customer, letting David know she'd take care of this one. He didn't need to do it all—even though he certainly made it look like he could.

Mrs. Allen stood inside the door of the store, looking around the shop. Her gray hair curled around her face, and her thick glasses settled on her nose.

"Hello, Mrs. Allen. What can I do for you today?"

The elderly woman shuffled forward, her sensible white sneakers peeking out from under her rose-colored, velour pantsuit. "Pastor Nate said he's found a young man who can paint my kitchen for me. For free. I'd think it was a scam, but he's a pastor. So, I'm here to look at paint colors." Mrs. Allen looped her hand around Sadie's arm.

"Do you have a color in mind?"

"My dear Roger loved yellow. So maybe a cheery daffodil color."

Mrs. Allen's husband had died almost twenty years ago, and they'd had no children. Most all of Heritage had adopted her since.

Sadie led Mrs. Allen slowly across the front of the store to the back side wall where David had set up to repaint it, a fresh off-white color called Swiss Coffee that Sadie had picked out.

The section was a bit of a mess with a tarp spread across the floor.

Lottie held a paint roller and had it pressed against the wall. David stood behind her, his hand guiding the roller in the correct W pattern. They finished, and David returned the roller to the paint tray.

"That was great. I think you're ready to try it on your own." David held out the roller to Lottie, motioning for her to step forward.

Lottie took the roller carefully and pressed it against the wall. A soft squish sounded as she pressed the roller up and then down in a wobbly W movement.

"Perfect, Lottie. Keep going." David patted the girl on the shoulder.

The child stuck her tongue out the side of her mouth as she continued to roll the paint on the wall, filling in the gaps, maintaining the W formation he showed her.

Mrs. Allen let go of Sadie's arm and pressed her hands to her heart. The paint counter had been pushed further into the aisle to make room for David and Lottie to paint. Sadie stepped around them and pulled out the paint sample ring flipped to the yellows.

"It's so good to see a father spending time with his daughter." Mrs. Allen's voice cracked, and she wiped her cheeks.

Oh no. Even though it had been almost ten months since Jeremy died, Sadie never knew how Lottie would respond to mentions of her father.

Sadie stepped closer to Lottie, trying to gauge her reaction.

The paint roller stopped moving as Lottie froze. Tears filled the little girl's eyes and spilled over, streaming down her cheeks in silent rivers as her lips trembled. The paint roller began to shake in her hand. "He's not my dad. My daddy is dead."

Lottie dropped the roller and ran toward the front door of the store.

Sadie followed her to the top of the aisle to see her exit and turn toward their apartment door at the back of the building. The jingling bell quieted, leaving the store silent.

Sadie looked from the closed door to Mrs. Allen, and then to David.

Paint splattered all over the tarp and surrounding floor, polka-dotting David's jeans and the wall. Thankfully, Mrs. Allen stood far enough back that she remained paint free.

The older lady blinked, shock written across her face. "I didn't know."

"Of course not, Mrs. Allen." Sadie couldn't blame her. David did look like he could be Sadie's father. Still, Sadie thought that most people had heard all the town gossip by now. "I'm sorry. Lottie's still processing the emotions of losing her father. Let me go check on her. David can go over the colors with you."

Sadie handed the color selection ring to David and hurried after Lottie.

After jogging up the steps to their apartment above the store, she opened the front door to find her daughter snuggled into the center corner of the sectional. Amber, Lottie's American Girl doll from her dad, sat next to her as Lottie played her Nintendo switch. "You okay, kiddo?"

Lottie barely looked up. "Sorry."

"There's no need to be. Grief is a unique journey for each of us. Do you want to talk about it?"

Lottie paused her game and looked up. "Not right now. Can I play my game for a little bit?"

"Can I sit with you?"

Lotte shrugged. "Maybe later?"

Sadie nodded. "Can you come down in about twenty minutes? Then we can close up shop early and head to Oma's. You can play your piano for me."

"Ok, Mom."

Mom. The word had brought so much joy, but today Sadie understood better the weight of responsibility that came with that title.

"Mom?"

Sadie paused at the door, looking back at Lottie.

"I left my history folder on the table." She pointed to a yellow folder a few feet away. "There's a big project this year about the history of Heritage, and I want to pick a different subject from anyone else."

Sadie nodded. She'd read the info, and they could talk it over during dinner tonight. "I heard you talking about it with Mr. Williams. Did he have any ideas?"

Lottie just shook her head and didn't look up.

"We'll come up with something amazing."

"Thanks, Mom." Sadie pushed out of the apartment and closed the door behind her. She pulled up her phone and checked the camera she'd set up inside. The connection worked just fine, and she could see Lottie. She'd just let David know she was going to close up early and be right back up.

She found David kneeling on the floor, cleaning up the paint that had flung off the roller.

He looked up as she approached. His eyes kind, worried. "Is Lottie okay?"

"We're working through it. Did Mrs. Allen pick out a paint color?" Sadie knelt down next to David. He'd scrubbed a lot of the paint, but there were still spots.

"No. She said she'll be back later." David leaned back on his heels. The understanding that seemed to emanate from his very core melted the defenses Sadie kept in place.

Warning bells rang in her head.

Why did he still affect her? Hadn't her past history with him taught her to keep her walls up? She held her hand out for the rag. "I'll finish."

David shook his head. "I am sorry, Sadie."

She let out a long sigh, closed her eyes, dropped her hand. How many years had she longed to hear those words?

"I'm sorry for how things ended ten years ago. And I'm sorry for bringing everything up this week." His warm voice oozed sincerity, and when she opened her eyes, his entire body leaned forward toward her.

It would be so easy to touch him. To cup his face and feel his smooth skin. Physical chemistry had never lacked between them, and obviously it still didn't. But there was so much more to think about now—Lottie, her future, the store.

Sadie cleared her dry throat and looked away. "David."

"Maybe it's better if I'm not here when Lottie is around."

That wouldn't change anything. Sadie shook her head. "Lottie likes you. She's talked about you non-stop since she met you."

David's lips lifted in a quirk, but Sadie looked away. She would not focus on his lips. "She's a good kid."

David sat close enough that his clean scent mixed with the paint. "Do you remember when we knocked a gallon of paint over?"

Sadie couldn't help the chuckle that escaped.

Oh, she remembered all right. She'd just finished mixing a gallon of paint for a construction company and hadn't gotten the lid on tight enough after she'd checked the color. David met her behind the counter, kissing her hello. When he finished saying hello, she stepped back, knocking the entire gallon on the floor. They'd had a huge mess to clean up. Her dad had taken the price of that gallon out of her salary, but David's kiss had been more than worth it.

"Things are a lot different now." No longer young or naive or willing to sneak kisses. "We're different. Different time in life, different futures, different dreams. My life is here, with Lottie. Your life is full of adventure, a long way from here."

David nodded, but the carefree look that had crossed his face vanished. His shoulders tightened and then relaxed, like he was forcing himself to be calm. "You're right. Things are different. But I'm here."

"For now." She had to remember this was only temporary. "As long as we both remember that you're leaving, and I'm staying." The words hurt. They shouldn't—she'd given up her dreams of a future with David years ago.

David stood up, nodding toward the door. "I'll close tonight. You need to be with Lottie."

Standing, Sadie wiped her hands on her jeans. "You don't mind?"

"Not at all." David stepped back, creating space between them. Necessary space.

Sadie's cell phone buzzed, and she pulled it out of her pocket and looked at the screen—Doris, Lottie's aunt. "Thank you. I need to take this call. See you tomorrow."

Sadie left the store and stepped onto the sidewalk before answering the call. The cool evening air wrapped around her, calming her nerves. The town square in front of the store was peaceful, and Otis sat in the midst of the playground, thankfully facing away from the hardware store.

Sadie swiped the screen of her phone to answer the call. Doris's crisp, nasally voice breathed irritation through the connection. She could almost picture her sitting at her stately desk looking like she'd just sucked on a lemon. "Lottie missed her scheduled call with me this afternoon. I've been waiting."

Sadie rubbed her forehead. She'd completely forgotten that today was supposed to be their first video call on the iPad. Doris had bought the device for Lottie for the sole purpose of video chats once a week. "I'm so sorry, Doris. Lottie had a busy day at school, and this afternoon has been tough. Can I have her call you tomorrow?"

"Tomorrow doesn't work for me. That's why we picked Fridays. I want to talk to her. Now."

Not after Mrs. Allen's comment. Doris was the last person that could help Lottie right now. "I'm sorry, but Lottie's not able to chat today. Name another day, and I promise we will connect you two."

"Today works for me. It's on you to make your schedule work on our agreed upon times. You assured me we would be able to visit when you moved my niece away from the only blood relatives she has. We'll have to wait until our next scheduled time."

Sadie made an appointment in her calendar, with three alerts, so next week she didn't forget the video chat with Lottie's aunt.

If only saving a store, supporting a grief-stricken nine-year-old, and keeping her treacherous heart from speeding up around her ex could be as easy as setting a reminder on her phone.

He should let it go.

David's hand shook as he picked up another box in his grandpa's barn Saturday morning. The sun shone through the open barn door. Dust danced in the light. Much the way the light had streamed through the now clean window at the hardware store yesterday. The way it had haloed around Sadie when he'd held her hand.

Sadie carried the grief she felt so tightly wrapped away it still had David wanting to race back to the hardware store and offer his shoulder for her to cry on. It wasn't David's fault someone thought Lottie was his daughter.

But the picture of happily ever after that came wrapped up with that—well—

Not another second could be given to that thought.

Even if things had changed with Sadie since their conversation on Monday. As foolhardy as it had been to bring up the past, hashing everything out had changed things. Gone was the lonely bitter feeling every time David thought about Sadie, replaced with gut-wrenching thoughts of what if.

What if he'd talked to her before he left for Costa Rica?

What if he'd verbally extended his offer to join him?

What if he'd reached out over the years?

Regret was a horrible companion.

Metal clinked loudly as David set the box on the workbench. Saw blades—but not lawnmower blades, which is what he was looking for.

A low rumble of a car motor sounded before it shut off and doors closed. David grabbed a rag sitting on the workbench and wiped off the dust coating his hands as he walked to the barn entrance. He wasn't expecting any company today.

Nate walked toward him as Olivia unbuckled their two-year-old daughter, Charis, from her car seat.

"You brought Olivia for backup. Something must be on your mind." David didn't have enough energy to tag team an argument with his cousins.

Nate chuckled and looked back at his wife. "We stopped to see Mr. Washburn. Do you remember him?"

"Not really."

"He's been in charge of our summer Bible camps for years. Well, until the last few. His daughter and son-in-law have been caring for him, but the end is near. Olivia wanted to make sure they had some dinner since the whole family has been called into town. On the way home, Charis said she had to use the potty, and when a potty-training toddler says it's time to go, you stop. So, here we are."

"Hi, Unca David," Charis called as Oliva hurried toward the house.

David waved back. "She does know I'm not her uncle, right?"

Nate shrugged. "Probably not. But like Caroline's kids call Austin and me uncle, I think it's okay. We're family, after all."

Family. A luxury David had given up when he moved to Costa Rica. In so many ways, he'd been a recluse long before he was forced to return to Heritage.

David walked back into the barn. "While you're here, I need some help. Bent the mower blade and Grandpa had a few extras listed on the log he kept of the items in the barn. I'm hoping they're still there. Make yourself useful."

Nate cleared his throat as he opened a box and pulled out a paintbrush. "Oh, this reminds me. Mrs. Allen wants someone—"

"To paint her kitchen. I know. She stopped by Hoover's last night for Canary or Daffodil or some kind of yellow. Thought I was Lottie's dad."

"That's why you're not working today?"

"I closed last night. Sadie said to take the weekend off. I'll go back Monday. Maybe." David set another box down. Sprinkler parts.

"Why wouldn't you go back?"

"Did you know Lottie's dad passed away? And as a toddler, her mom was killed in a car accident?"

Nate picked up a box and set it on the workbench. He wiped his hands on his jeans and then opened it. "You are in a unique position to understand that little girl's grief."

"I wasn't that young when my mom died. And I'm not sure what happened to my father. He could still be out there for all I know."

"Even so, you understand loss."

"Last night when I went to bed, all I could think about was Sadie and Lottie. I need to remain focused." On Costa Rica. Not on what-ifs and what would never be.

Nate put the brush back in the box and closed it up. "It's okay to think about something other than yourself, David."

Returning to Costa Rica wasn't being selfish. Serving God required sacrifice, and David was giving up everything. Besides, by giving up family, he couldn't hurt the people he loved. David thrust his shaking hands forward. "I don't shake at the hardware store. Explain that."

Nate moved the box and set it down, clapping his hands to remove some of the dust that had collected there. "Human interaction, David. How does it feel? A good woman—"

"No, Nate. Don't go there."

"What happened between you two?"

A complete misunderstanding. "I messed up." David leaned against the tool bench, crossing his arms against his chest. "All these years I thought when she walked away from me, that she was breaking up with me. Turns out she thought I broke up with her. She said she would have followed me anywhere. I wonder if my mistakes started before I even knew that I was making them."

Nate opened another box and pulled out a cardboard tube. He held it up and shrugged. David had no idea what was in there. Nate opened the top and dumped the papers on the worktable.

"What's that?" David looked at the papers Nate unrolled, the edges worn and yellowed, and placed them on the workbench.

"Those look like the old plans or surveys for the farm. Those should really be inside." Nate rolled the papers back up and carefully put them back inside the tube, setting them aside.

David selected another box and opened it. A huge clock packaged inside with the words Heritage, Michigan printed neatly along the top. The Victorian house that had once sat on the town square was painted a muted black behind the watch hands.

"Is there a chance you and Sadie could pick up where you left off?" Nate set the tube of plans by the barn door and packed up the box they came from.

"Sadie was quick to point out how much we've changed." David ran his fingers along the filagree of the clock inside the box. "Our futures and our dreams. Hers is here with Lottie, and I can't argue with that. I wouldn't want to hurt her. Again."

"Mistakes don't have to end a relationship, but walking away from one does. Talk to her. Apologize. Move on. People make mistakes, David. Every day. You can ask Olivia how many times I've messed up. But you know what? I apologize, she forgives me, and we move on. That's how relationships work."

David shook his head. It couldn't be that simple. Because his dad had messed up. His mom forgave him, and then his dad messed up again. Over and over. David couldn't fall into that pattern.

"Did you find the lawnmower blades? You've been looking at that box for a while." Nate peeked in the box, the large clock face still frozen in time. Nate let out a whistle. "That's a piece of Heritage history right there."

History. In part of Lottie's rambling yesterday, she had talked about her history project and how she wanted something unique and different to write about. "Know anything about this clock?"

Nate shook his head.

"Lottie says the fourth graders are all writing a paper about the history of Heritage for that town fair in October." He could take the clock into the hardware store. Show Lottie. Maybe he could even give her the clock and quit his job. "Do you think the board would be okay if I quit my job at Hoover's?"

Nate picked up another box and let it thud on the workbench. "Why would you quit?"

"Really? We've been over this. Sadie and I are in different places. Plus, I'm not sure if I'm good for Lottie."

Nate nodded. "If we're playing connect the dots, I'm not following that order. Doesn't Sadie need help at the hardware store?"

"Of course she does."

"And you can't provide that help?"

He'd helped patch up the wall, repaint. And made some pretty decent sales.

He heard the pitter-patter of tiny feet growing louder, and David turned to see Charis running toward him at her two-year-old top speed. "Unca David!"

He knelt and scooped her up. "Hey, Charis!"

"Kittens fun! Want one."

"You want Uno?"

Olivia laughed. "I think we like Cinco."

"Vangie and Becca have called dibs on Uno and Dos, so consider Cinco yours. They all need homes before I leave, so feel free to spread the word. I have two more."

"How are things at Hoover's?" Olivia stepped forward and started looking around on the workbench.

David shrugged. "I'm not sure if I should continue. Someone thought I was Lottie's dad. And things with Sadie are..."

"Tense? I get it. It would be weird. But honestly, it doesn't matter. I think you'll be good for Lottie."

David lifted an eyebrow and smirked at Nate. "You guys could certainly tag team."

"It's normal after being married. But seriously, we choose how to impact those we love. Sometimes people are only around a short time. But each relationship can have an important impact in someone's life."

The clock sat nestled in the box still sitting on the workbench. He could have a positive impact on Lottie if he gave her the clock and if she chose to look into it. She'd have that unique topic she wanted.

And even if it was only a few weeks, David was helping at the hardware store. Sadie knew the arrangement had an end date. She probably had a countdown till his departure. Too bad he didn't have a number to give her.

"You knew Lottie's dad, didn't you?" Olivia's hand found her hip and she flipped her long hair over her shoulder. "I bet you could tell her about your memories."

Nate picked up another box and settled it on the table. "Think of the impact that could have on her."

"Is this what you're looking for?" Olivia held a lawnmower blade in her hand.

Nate wrapped his arm around Olivia's waist and kissed her temple. "How did you know?"

"The lawnmower was left in the middle of the yard, only half mowed, David has grass stains on his jeans. And you guys are digging through boxes."

"Where was it?" David placed his hands on his hips. Nothing seemed to be missing.

Olivia pointed to the wall behind some old Folger cans.

Nate closed up the box and put it back where he'd taken it from. "We should be going now. Let you get back to work."

Work. David looked down at the clock.

Yes, he'd be going back to work.

six

THE IDEA OF A RELAXING EVENING AT THE PARK on Tuesday, enjoying the cool temperatures, had sounded ideal when Sadie suggested it, but as Lottie held Sadie's hand and yanked her across the playground to the monkey bars, Sadie realized she'd made a fatal mistake. Empty parks were not relaxing with an energetic child.

And energetic children wouldn't just sit and swing. Sadie glanced at the empty swing set. Her aching feet could use a break.

Even her daughter's excitement and energy couldn't help her outrun her thoughts of David. No matter what she'd done since Friday's conversation with him, she hadn't been able to escape the memory of his understanding gaze, the supportive way he stepped in to clean up without making her feel like she was helpless. The way he'd affirmed her skills as a mother when she'd wondered if she was failing.

Nothing could stop her thoughts from returning to David. Not the happy squeals of Lottie as she jumped down from the monkey bars. Or when she climbed to the top of the ladder and slid down, laughing. Or her energy as she raced toward the swings, her arms above her head.

Sadie had spent the day hauling boxes from the back room, but no matter how many trips to the dumpster, she hadn't been able to stop David's kind words from replaying in her mind.

Sadie stretched her neck, letting the cool evening air blow the hair from her face as Lottie jumped off the swing and climbed up to the top of the slide again.

At least the back room was fairly clean, thanks to David running the front of the store today. They'd been able to work without any mention of Friday night. Partly because she'd kept busy in the room that she'd found filled with mislabeled boxes.

It had almost been a relief to find a project she could take on alone, because she needed some space from her new employee. Simply being near him had made her long for things that would never be. The excess number of boxes had provided the perfect reason to stay out of his way.

"Mom! Mom! Watch me!" Lottie's voice rang out with all the happiness of a carefree child, but the volume had Sadie rubbing her temples as she watched her daughter sitting backwards on top of the slide. She pushed off and slid down, landed with a thud, and then ran to the monkey bars.

Advil. If she could make it materialize in her pocket, she'd swallow it without any water.

"Look, Mom!" Lottie grabbed the bar, pulled herself up and worked herself into a sitting position on top of the bar.

Talk about making Sadie's heart pump fast. All she'd wanted was to sit and swing for a bit, not get dragged all over the playground.

"Hi, Mr. Williams!" Lottie waved frantically, and Sadie followed her line of vision. David stood next to a gold Subaru Brat and returned Lottie's wave.

Lottie landed with a thump next to Sadie, kicking up some sand, which pelted Sadie. Thank goodness for jeans.

Lottie ran to greet David, giving him an energetic high five.

A deep laugh sounded, and the light breeze carried it over to Sadie, doing funny things to her stomach. She hated to admit that the old pull toward David hadn't died, and instead, it reignited with a stronger tug each time she saw him.

In his forest green flannel shirt that made Sadie want to run her fingers over his shoulders—just to find out if the shirt was as soft at it looked—jeans, and work boots, he did cut a fine figure. The perfect boy-next-door good looks only made him more appealing as his lips parted into a breathtaking grin. He could be on the cover of any outdoor magazine.

Sadie inhaled—she would calm her heart rate before he reached her. There was no reason it should be racing right now. No reason at all.

When deep breathing didn't work, Sadie turned and walked toward the swing that she'd wanted to sit on all night and used her foot to push herself forward and back.

"Hey." David's velvety soft voice sent a thrill through her. "This seat taken?" He held the chain of the swing next to her.

Sadie shook her head and he sat down, swinging in time with her. The perfect relaxing moment she'd pictured in her head.

"Watch this, Mr. Williams!" Lottie jumped up, grabbed the monkey bars, and then pulled her legs through to skin the cat. She let go of the bars and landed on both feet with her arms in the air like a professional gymnast.

David's eyebrows shot up, and he clapped. "Nicely done, Lottie."

Lottie bowed dramatically then pointed at the old one-room schoolhouse across the square. "Can I go to the library? It's closing soon."

Sadie barely nodded before Lottie took off at top speed toward the library.

"I'll be right behind you," Sadie called after Lottie, who raised one hand without pausing her stride. At least Lottie had given her an easy out. A few minutes' chat, and she could follow.

"I didn't expect to see you still in town." He'd gotten off a few hours ago.

"Unca David?" A young voice called across the square. A tiny little girl ran toward them with David's sisters a few feet behind.

David stood and scooped up the little girl, who squeezed him around his neck.

"I can't wait to come play in my fairy house. What kind of dessert are you making?" The little girl pressed a sloppy kiss on David's cheek. His entire body seemed to soften with the girl's embrace. The adoration between the two was clear as the child pressed both her hands on his cheeks and pushed his lips out, forcing him to make a face.

Rather than fight her, he wiggled his brows and spoke in a deep and silly—yet still somehow swoony—voice. "What kind of dessert do you want?"

The little girl giggled. "S'mores. Mommy said that's what we'd have."

"As you wish, Vangie."

Be still her heart. David on his own was attractive, but David holding a little girl who obviously adored him? Wow.

Just wow.

Sadie's unruly heart picked up speed again.

Caroline and Leah joined them, saying a brief but friendly hello to Sadie before turning their attention to their brother.

"You guys finished Bible study early." Leah bumped David's shoulder.

"Yeah. Grant was going to hang with Nate until Caroline was ready to head home." David shrugged and set his wiggling niece down.

"What brings you to the square?" Leah stepped to the side as the little girl raced toward the slide.

David sat back down next to Sadie. "Donny's."

"Are you ready for all of us this weekend?" Caroline watched her daughter climb the ladder to the top of the slide.

"As ready as ever. There's not much for me to do. You guys are bringing the sides. Meat's bought, and the fire pit and fairy house have been finished for a few weeks."

Caroline's attention fell on Sadie. "We're all having a cookout at David's on Saturday. You should come. Bring your daughter."

Spend time with David outside of work? With his family who clearly adored him? That would only give her more thoughts to attempt to outrun. Maybe she should take up running as a hobby.

Sadie stood up, brushing her hands down her jeans. "Thanks for the invite, but the store is open on Saturday. I'm going to get Lottie. She's at the library."

"We're going that way, and we'll get her for you. Why don't you come out to David's after you close Saturday? We're meeting for dinner anyway. David built a fire pit, and we're roasting hot dogs."

"And s'mores!" The little girl ran up and climbed into David's lap. He kicked off, swinging slowly.

"Please come," Leah chimed in.

Sadie glanced at David. He'd know how uncomfortable this would be. His brows turned down slightly, and a brief flash of something, maybe hesitation, clouded his eyes. "Of course you should come."

Did David's voice sound flat? That right there was why she couldn't go. "I appreciate that, but—"

"Lottie would have a blast. Think on it. But seriously, David, don't take no for an answer. Come on, Vangie, let's hit the library before it closes. We'll check on Lottie. You stay here and chat." Caroline held out her hand to Vangie, who kissed David on the cheek and jumped off his lap.

Leah lifted her eyebrows at David as if sending him a message, but David just sent an annoyed look back. "I'm gonna go with them. Have fun, you two."

Caroline and Leah walked away, swinging Vangie between them. Apparently, there was no escape from David.

Sadie sank back into the swing and David's knee bumped hers. Her face heated as he studied her.

He was close enough that the lighter brown flecks in his eyes were discernible. How many times had she dreamed about those eyes over the years? Even with a few lines around the outside corners, the intensity of his gaze stole her breath.

"Sorry about them." His deep voice was quiet. Soothing.

"Siblings, right?" Hers could be just as crazy. Demanding information and begging for secrets where none existed. Especially Romee. Okay, only Romee. She couldn't remember the last time she had talked to Anna, didn't even know where her sister was right now. Her job kept her moving around. And her brother? Well, Toby kept mostly to himself.

David's lips tilted upward, drawing Sadie's attention. Nope—not that.

Sadie stood, the gazebo an easy escape. There were no memories of David in a gazebo. His hand moved like he might take hold of hers, but he quickly dropped it before he made contact.

"Wait." His quiet, deep voice sent a chill down her spine. "I'm sorry."

"For?" Sadie sat back down and pushed her swing back gently.

"You were right. I don't have any right to ask you about Jeremy. And I could have..." he seemed to be weighing his next words "handled Costa Rica differently. Better."

"David, I don't think—"

"I know." He held up his hand. "I'm not trying to get you back. You have your life, and I have mine. I just wanted you to know I am sorry for how it went down. And I want...to be friends again.

After all, we do have to work together. It would be nice not to always be—"

"On edge?"

"Exactly."

Sadie nodded and pushed off again. "And I am also sorry. I could have handled Costa Rica better. And a friend would be nice. Lottie adores you."

David matched her pace, swinging next to her. In elementary school, they would have been "married" because their swings were in sync.

Great, why had her mind gone there? She leaned back in her swing, giving it a little more oomph, but David matched her move.

"Do you remember the last time we were on swings together?" His gaze could light her skin on fire.

Oh, she remembered. She remembered everything when it came to David. And that was why she should've gone to the library with Lottie.

"It was the night before our last Christmas." There had been a park near the university, and they'd walked over, hand in hand.

"I'd stuck around school so we could drive back to Heritage together." David stretched his legs out, mirroring Sadie's movements.

"It was cold that night." She'd had her heaviest coat on, and still the air had nipped at her.

David slowed his swing.

Sadie let her foot touch the ground, scraping the dirt enough to stay in sync with him. She shouldn't, but she wanted to know what David would say. Had he ever thought about her after he left?

"I don't remember the temperature." David's voice was barely audible. His cheeks bloomed red.

Sadie stopped her swing. She hadn't been cold that night once David had felt her shiver—mainly because his kisses had kept her plenty warm. She rubbed her damp hands down her pants. Even the memory heated her.

What David didn't know? That she'd returned to that park after their breakup. Sat in the swing. Bonnie had found her there, sobbing.

"Maybe I don't remember that night." Sadie stood up. She couldn't do this again. Memory lane was overrated. "I appreciate the invite to dinner on Saturday, but —"

"I thought we agreed on friends."

Sadie gestured at the swing. "Friends don't walk down romantic memory lane. Friends don't look at each other like…"—she waved in the direction of his face—"that."

"You're right. I'm sorry. I'll be good. Just come."

"I don't think—"

"Mom!" Lottie's voice and running footsteps pulled her attention away from the man in front of her. "We're going to dinner at Mr. Williams's? Did you know he built a fairy house? And I get to see it. Vangie says it's gonna be awesome. And s'mores? I love s'mores!"

"Have you ever even had s'mores?" Sadie walked toward Lottie, a welcome break from David and their past.

Lottie shook her head, her red curls bouncing behind her. "Nope. What are they?"

David's deep chuckle rumbled behind Sadie, and she hated the goosebumps that broke across her neck. He'd moved closer, and she hadn't even realized it.

"They're delicious," he said. "You'll find out on Saturday."

So much for offering an excuse. She hadn't considered that Caroline and Leah would talk to Lottie about dinner. There was no way out now.

Lottie skipped around Sadie to David and latched on to his hand. "Did you really build a fairy house?"

David held up his free hand. "With my own two hands."

"That's so cool!"

David nodded to his truck. "That reminds me. I found something this weekend I thought you might like to see. It's in the bed of my truck."

Lottie's head bobbled up and down. "Can I see? Oh, did you see Otis? The librarian let me read a book to him, as long as I promised to bring the book back before I left. I did."

Sure enough, Otis sat next to the library, looking toward the updated one-room schoolhouse. Sadie had been so consumed with David she'd missed an incredible photo op.

She would not miss out on anything else tonight, so she hurried to catch up to Lottie as she skipped next to David, holding his hand. Once Sadie caught up, Lottie held her hand too, connecting the three of them.

Like a family.

As they neared the back of David's small truck, he let go of Lottie's hand and opened the hatch. He picked the little girl up and set her onto the bed of the truck.

Next to a large, dusty...box. Hadn't she cleaned out enough boxes today?

David peeled it open, and Lottie sat on her knees and looked inside.

"Wow!" Lottie pulled some old newspaper from inside the box.

Curiosity won, and Sadie stepped closer to David. Her arm brushed against his, sending all kinds of mixed feelings over her skin as she stood on her tiptoes and looked into the box. Inside, a good-sized, round clock—probably close to two feet across—filled the entire thing.

Sadie traced the words Heritage, Michigan welded into the metal at the top of the clock. Filigree surrounded the large face where the outline of a familiar building was painted.

"That's the old Manor." Sadie's breath caught. She'd forgotten how beautiful the Manor had been, even in its dilapidated state. But it had been painted on the clock face in all its beauty.

Lottie plunged her small hands into the box and tried to lift the clock. It didn't budge.

David leaned even closer to the box, brushing past Sadie and filling her senses with his clean, soapy scent.

"The clock is pretty heavy. I left it in here to keep it safe."

"It doesn't work." Lottie pointed at the hands.

"Maybe that's why it's not displayed anymore. But I thought maybe you could look into it for your history paper."

Lottie clasped her hands in front of her. "This will be awesome! I'm going to be like Nancy Drew. I'll call it The Case of the Square Clock. Get it? The Heritage Square clock, since that's what this is." Lottie pointed at the square. "But the clock is round?" Lottie giggled at her own joke.

"What if the clock wasn't displayed on the square?" Sadie couldn't help but tease Lottie, whose excitement was contagious.

"Then I'll rename my case." Lottie moved to the edge of the truck and sat down swinging her legs.

David ruffled Lottie's hair as she passed by, and Lottie—who would normally fuss if anyone touched her hair—launched herself at him, throwing her arms around his shoulders. He caught her and carefully set her on the ground.

"Thanks, Mr. Williams. I'm gonna win the contest for sure."

"You will. No one else will have a paper on the missing clock."

"Contest?" How was it that David knew more about Lottie's schoolwork than she did?

"Miss Pimpermill says that the top three projects will be displayed at the fall festival to celebrate the 150th birthday of Heritage. I'm so going to win. Mom, can we take the clock inside?"

Sadie shook her head. "I don't have a place for the clock."

"The back room, Mom. It's clean now. We could leave it there. Please?"

If ever a kid had mastered the puppy dog look, it was Lottie. "If the clock is coming in, it's not coming in that box." Sadie drew the line in the proverbial sand, and she'd die there. No more boxes today.

"Want me to take it in for you?" David pulled the clock out of the box. The back of his shirt stretched tight against his muscles as he lifted it.

Sadie's mouth dried out. So much for the relaxing night she'd hoped for.

Now she had a clock she didn't want, dinner plans she couldn't get out of, and a daughter who had more energy now than an hour ago when they went to the park.

Next time she wanted to relax, she'd take a bubble bath.

On Saturday, laughter rang across his grandparents' property. His nieces ran around the kid-sized fairy house he'd built, and his sisters and cousins gathered around the fire pit.

And yet, David couldn't bring himself to join in. His hands were damp as he wiped them on his jeans. His conversation with Lance from moments ago like flashing neon lights in front of him.

Bring someone with you. Not only did he need to drop everything for a friendly dinner with Lance and Marco next weekend, but they wanted him to bring someone with him?

They'd said they were going to check up on him, be in touch. Lance had even mentioned coming in person, but a dinner? With a plus-one? That's not what David had pictured. They knew he wasn't dating, so why ask for a plus-one? If they wanted Nate to be there, they would have just invited him.

"Vangie, you're it." Lottie's familiar voice rang out as she ran around the yard.

David immediately searched the group and found Sadie talking to Leah. She must have arrived while he'd been in the house, and he hadn't heard her car pull up.

His heart squeezed. More than anything, he wanted to go greet her. Simply stand next to her, feel her soft hand brush his arm as they talked—about their day, the store. Find out how Lottie's history project was going. Anything to be near her and enjoy the calm that surrounded her.

But he couldn't. He didn't have the right.

"You found it. Good." Nate took the fire poker from David's hand—the reason he'd been in the house. He'd completely ignored everything around him as he stood and watched Sadie. "You know, you could go talk to her."

But he couldn't. She was right. Their lives were different. Their futures didn't line up. It was easier, healthier, to keep his distance.

David grabbed the poker back and walked toward the fire. "Lance called while I was in the barn. He and Marco are coming into town next weekend. Want me to meet them for dinner. Are you free?"

"No. Mr. Washburn passed away earlier this week. His funeral will be next weekend. Besides, if they wanted me there, they would have asked me."

David ran his hand through his hair. It had been worth a shot. "You could ask Sadie."

David stumbled and slowed his pace. He didn't want anyone to hear this conversation. "What? No. Why would I ask Sadie?"

Nate slowed next to him. "I could think of a few reasons. I mean, look at you. Are you blushing? What are you, sixteen?"

Great. He'd spent the week trying to keep his growing feelings under wraps, but he'd obviously failed. Maybe he'd been a fool to agree to being just friends with how he felt, but she was right. With him returning to Costa Rica, there wasn't a future for them now any more than there had been before. And the last thing he wanted was to scare her away.

David used his shoulder and shoved Nate, trying to play the suggestion off as a joke. Thankfully, the guys were already talking, and Caroline and Leah had stepped over toward the fairy house to visit with Sadie. "Don't be ridiculous. I'll ask Leah."

"Hate to break it to you, but we'll all be at the funeral." Nate took the poker and moved the logs in the fire pit around.

Austin turned toward them. "Mr. Washburn always liked our roses. One of our first customers."

"Leah and Caroline signed up to help with the meal for the family after the service." Jon confirmed what Nate had said. Too bad he wouldn't be able to bring one of them.

The flames of the fire lapped up the fresh log Grant added.

Who else could he ask? He'd met Seth at the gym but didn't know him well enough to ask him to come along. Mrs. Allen? He'd started painting her kitchen. She probably would come if he asked, but that would be unusual at best.

The guys laughed, and he looked up to see them all studying him. "What?"

Austin crossed his arms over his chest. "Seriously, man. Don't let your pride rob you of a good time. Libby and I almost didn't happen because of mine."

Grant lifted the can of root beer in his hand. "Pride almost kept Caroline and me apart."

Nate slapped David on the shoulder. "Ask Sadie."

David shook his head. It wasn't that simple. "She'll probably be at the funeral."

Nate scrubbed his face and shook his head. "She hasn't been back in town that long. And she was gone for a lot of years. I bet she's not going."

Sadie's head fell back as she laughed at something Leah said. Her shoulders relaxed. Her movements carefree. Something in David's gut twisted—he'd always loved when Sadie had laughed. The sound airy and whimsical. "Then she'd have Lottie."

Austin took a long swig of his Coke. "Guess you're going alone."

Could he though? It seemed everything was a test. A measurement of whether or not he was ready to return to Costa Rica. Lance wanted David to bring a plus-one. He had to figure something out.

Lottie and Vangie skipped up again, holding hands. Lottie had a large, dead leaf in her hand. "When can we eat, Mr. Williams?"

Vangie giggled and pointed at David. "Mr. Williams? Call him Unca David. We all do."

Lottie's large brown eyes looked up at him. A longing flashed there, but it was gone in an instant. "He's not my uncle. I have one of those. Uncle Patrick. I don't want to go visit them."

David knew the feeling of being hoisted on family. Maybe Lottie had those same feelings. "Why's that?"

She shrugged. "They always make me eat all the food on my plate. Aunt Doris always makes me eat the vegetables. And even makes me lumpy smoothies. They're gross and smell like grass. I have to go stay with them next weekend."

"Next weekend? Did you hear that, David?" Austin's elbow nudged into David's side.

Oh, he'd heard all right. But ask Sadie? If she were there, could he get through the meeting without Sadie knowing he was fighting for his job? His calling? How he'd been benched by his mission board?

Vangie tugged on David's sleeve. "When are we going to eat?"

"How about now?" David quickly and easily got everyone's attention, and Vangie offered a quick blessing on the food before the parents helped their kids roast hot dogs.

Everyone dished up their food, and dinner quickly flowed into marshmallow roasting. David hung back as the kids ate their fill of s'mores.

After the parents cut off the dessert intake for their children, the adults took their turns. David hung back until Nate handed him a stick. "Your turn."

Sadie stood next to the fire, keeping her own sugary treat high above the flames as she slowly spun it. David shook his head, his hands trembling.

"Seriously, man up." Nosy Nate. Maybe it would be David's new nickname for his cousin. Besides, he couldn't go over there and let Sadie see his shaking hands.

Before David could brace himself, Nate shoved him toward Sadie. Probably fair payback after earlier, but even so, David still sent his cousin a glare that would have stopped a lesser man. Nate chuckled and walked away.

"Having a good time?" David's voice squeaked a little. Maybe Nate was right. He'd reverted to a younger version of himself.

Sadie's lips tipped up on one side, letting David know she'd heard. She'd left her hair down, the long locks hanging over the front of her green sweater, curling up at the ends. "I forgot how much I always enjoyed being with your family."

David stuck the marshmallow in the fire. It only trembled slightly over the flame. "They are pretty cool. Lottie says she's going to be with her aunt and uncle next weekend?"

Sadie's back stiffened, and she lifted her chin slightly as she looked back toward the fire. "Doris insisted that Lottie visit, and what Doris wants, Doris gets."

David knew people like that.

Bring a plus-one, David.

Lance's voice echoed in his head. He turned his marshmallow above the flame, working the perfect golden color on all sides, and noticed the tremble was all but gone. Like when he worked at the hardware store.

Sadie's arm brushed his as she moved to check her own marshmallow. Heat shot up his arm, settling into his stomach. Her simple touch still had the power to turn a fire into an inferno.

Sadie moved her stick back into the fire, creating space between them. That brief, seemingly accidental touch had sent his mind whirling. Would it be better to let Lance down and show up to dinner alone, or ask Sadie?

David took a breath and let the words flow out. "I have to attend a dinner with my field administrator and executive director next Saturday. They asked me to bring someone…a friend. Would you be willing to go with me?"

Sadie's eyes jerked from the fire to his face. Her eyebrows rose, and her lips formed a cute little O. "Me?"

"We agreed on friends, right?" David motioned to the group. "And everyone is going to Mr. Washburn's funeral. You'd be doing me a solid favor if you could go."

Oh, that was smooth. Real smooth. Silence fell between them. He shouldn't have asked. A solid favor—he really was reverting to an immature version of himself. But before he could correct his blunder, Lottie walked up cradling a bundle of loudly purring fur in her arms.

"Mom, look at how cute she is. Can I take her home?" Lottie stepped close enough to encourage her mom to pet the cat.

Sadie shook her head. "Honey, he lives here with Mr. Williams. You can't take someone's pet."

Lottie's shoulders slumped.

Sadie rubbed a circle on Lottie's back. "But you can play with him here, okay? Just not next to the fire."

Lottie nodded and slowly walked back to the house where Vangie sat on the porch, probably with a kitten in her arms.

Every little girl needed a pet. David stepped closer and dropped his voice. "She can have a kitten."

Sadie's eyes opened wide. "We can't ask for a kitten."

"You're not. I'm offering. They've been inside and raised as pets. I'd like to find them homes before I head back to Costa Rica. If you want one, you can have one. They're old enough to be away from their mom now. Olivia and Nate are taking Cinco. Vangie and Becca have claimed Uno and Dos. Lottie is holding Cuatro. He can go home with you tonight."

"Numbers? Really, David?"

He shrugged. "Easy to remember."

Sadie looked back at the fire, her face unreadable. "Lottie would love a kitten. She's always wanted one, but Jeremy was allergic."

"Then this would be a win-win."

Sadie bit her bottom lip. Finally, she nodded. "Okay. If you're sure the kitten really needs a home. But I need supplies before I can take one home."

The smile that Sadie gave him stole his breath, and his marshmallow dropped a little too close to the flames, its side catching fire. He yanked it up and blew it out. A perfect marshmallow ruined.

"So...next weekend?" David's heart thundered in his ears. But Sadie didn't respond.

Instead, she pulled her roasting stick out of the fire. David followed her to the table with the makings for s'mores. Still Sadie said nothing. He shouldn't have asked. They were finally civil, and he'd ruined it with an invitation to dinner.

David fixed his s'more even though he had no intention of eating the burnt marshmallow. It gave him a little extra time with Sadie.

"I'll go." Her breathy response sent a thrill through him.

David's chest relaxed. "Really? Oh, that's great. I'll pick you up at five on Saturday. We'll have to drive to Grand Rapids."

Sadie nodded and sat down in an open chair between Leah and Libby, carefully nibbling a bite of her s'more.

Nate walked up next to him, chuckling. David handed him the burnt creation. "Don't let it go to waste."

Marshmallow dripped form Nate's mouth as he took a big bite. "Of course not. She said yes."

It wasn't a question. "How can you tell?"

"Her smile. It's a little wider."

Sadie relaxed next to his sister, looking content. There was no difference. There couldn't be. She was the one adamant that they could only be friends. She wasn't going with him as a date, but as a solid favor. He'd made that clear.

seven

THIS WAS NOT A DATE.

A solid favor—that's what David had called this little outing, and Sadie refused to think of it as anything else. Especially considering the silent, hour-long car ride. At least it had given her time to make sure Lottie was okay with Doris.

Outside the restaurant, the lights of the bridge were just coming on. The view through the windows was breathtaking, and the walk to the car promised to be filled with twinkle lights and romance as long as the rain held off. Inside, there were candles, soft string music piped over the speakers, and David's warm arm brushed hers every time he moved. There were four other people at the table.

Four other people pulling them in separate conversations.

"Sadie, dear," Charlotte, Lance's wife, drawled in her sweet southern accent. She set the menu down and rested her chin on her hand. "Tell us how you met our David."

Sadie glanced at David, his strong jaw tense. Stress lines wrinkled his forehead as he talked with Marco, who sat at the head of the table. "We met in high school."

The waitress set water in front of Sadie, and she took a sip.

"High school? Isadora, did you hear that? Why, these love-birds met in high school. And they're getting a second chance at romance. Like in one of those Hallmark movies." Charlotte grabbed the hand of the petite woman sitting between them at the end of the table.

Sadie coughed on her water. Her throat tickled, and she couldn't quite swallow. She coughed again, set her water down and dabbed her napkin at her mouth.

David turned to her and rubbed her back, looking at her with his eyebrows lifted. Her skin burned under his touch. "You okay?"

She nodded, and he withdrew his shaking hand. Was he nervous? At least he hadn't heard Charlotte's comment. He turned back to the others.

"I'm helping Mrs. Allen paint her kitchen. I think she's more lonely than anything. I've had tea with her both times I've been by to work. And Nate has found a few other odd jobs I've been helping with."

Sadie didn't realize David was the man Mrs. Allen had mentioned when she first came in looking at paint samples.

Finally, the tickle cleared up, and Sadie took another sip of water.

Isadora gave Sadie a small nod and slowly extracted her hand from Charlotte's grip. "How did you manage to meet up again after all these years?"

"David is working in my family's—at my hardware store." Sadie slipped her hands under the table. Easier to hide her fidgeting.

"Like in those movies. What did I tell you? Oh, this is such good news. We were hoping for community involvement, but a romance is so much better." Charlotte tucked her hand under her chin again. "Tell us about working with David."

Sadie peeked at David, but he was deep in conversation with

Marco and Lance. Had he told these people they were dating? Did she and David look like a couple?

The waitress squeezed between Sadie and David to set a basket of bread on the table in front of the women and another basket in front of the men. Sadie quickly took a slice of warm bread and then passed the basket to Isadora. Anything to keep from answering the question.

Lance cleared his throat, and everyone at the table looked at him. "David, tell us more about your involvement in the community."

David's neck turned red and his Adam's apple bobbed as he glanced down at the table.

Just dinner her foot. More like an inquisition. For both of them.

David shifted in his seat, his arm brushing against hers once again. His voice was deep, a slight tremble to the undertone. "I've been working at the hardware store with Sadie."

Charlotte bumped her shoulder into her husband's arm. "And she's about to tell us how they met up again all these years later and he swooped her off her feet."

If only the ground could swallow her up. Sadie gestured to David, as his shaking hand moved toward the breadbasket, then back to herself and shook her head. "We're not together."

David's eyes widened, looking at Sadie. Guess that meant he hadn't told them they were together, and Charlotte had jumped to that conclusion all on her own. He pulled his trembling hand back quickly and knocked over his full glass. The water and ice crashed to the table and rushed into Sadie's lap.

Sadie pushed back, but she didn't get out of the way of the water, and it continued to soak her. She sucked in air and pursed her lips. David used his napkin to try and stop the flow of water.

The waitress appeared, handing Sadie a handful of thick, dry napkins, and pointed her to the restroom at the back of the room. Sadie excused herself from the table and hurried to the washroom.

Thank goodness it was empty. She relaxed against the closed door and relished a moment to herself.

Together? With David?

Obviously, the shock that they might be a couple had totally gotten to him. That stung worse than the ice-cold lapful of water.

She closed her eyes and rested her head against the door. It shouldn't bother her that the idea of being with her had upset him so much he knocked his water into her lap. It had been a surprise to her, too. Obviously, they hadn't worked out the first time around.

It wasn't like she hadn't dreamed of his touch, the satisfaction of being with him, his clean, soapy scent as his arms wrapped around her, or the desire of a lifelong partner. She couldn't let the attraction between them bloom into anything more.

She didn't want a second chance with David. Even if her pulse still sped up at his touch. Even if his kindness with Lottie had Sadie dreaming of a family. Even if he still made her heart pound and her breath catch.

She didn't want that.

Couldn't want that.

Not with David.

She had a life in Heritage, with Lottie.

He had a life someplace exotic.

Breathing in a deep breath, Sadie counted to four and slowly let it out. She pressed the button for the hand dryer and worked on her skirt. Thankfully she'd had the foresight to wear black. Small mercies. Too bad she'd left her purse at the table, because it would be a good time to check on Lottie.

"You poor thing!" Charlotte, her Southern accent thick, barged into the restroom. She pulled out several more paper towels and handed them to Sadie.

"That poor young man. He's been through so much already this year, and then to come to dinner for Marco and Lance to quiz him like that. And for me to try and pair you two up. Don't you worry, darlin'. I scolded them something fierce after you left."

Sadie stepped over to the sink and washed her hands, letting the warm water thaw her fingers. "No reason to scold. It was an honest misunderstanding."

"You're entirely too gracious, Sadie darling. This dinner was supposed to be a friendly chat, not an inquisition. Poor David's hands were shaking so bad, it's no wonder he knocked over that glass. And all over you. David has never brought a date to anything. Ever. Lance figured he'd come alone. Or talk Nate into coming since he's been so instrumental in counseling David these past few months."

Sadie gestured for the door, but Charlotte took Sadie's hands into her own. The woman sure liked to touch people when she talked to them.

Charlotte squeezed Sadie's hands. "Well, as much as Nate can. David's shut himself off from everything. But it must not be all that bad if David has you. And you two look so relaxed together. The way he turned to you and patted your back. The way he looks at you—it's the same way my Lance used to look at me. And the way you two steal glances at each other. Mmmm. So cute. I know Lance's hopes soared when he realized that David brought you."

Sadie gently tugged her hands free. Could his conversation be over yet? She'd been caught with her secret glances at David? Of course Charlotte would pick up on all her mixed emotions.

Sadie opened the door and motioned for Charlotte to exit.

Charlotte slowly made her way through the door. "But don't you worry. Those men will be on their best behavior when we go back. Now, are you all dried off?"

Dried off? Hardly. The info dump Charlotte had given was as chilling as her soaked dress. Obviously, tonight was more than just dinner—no matter what David had said.

Charlotte walked next to Sadie as they sidestepped tables

and other patrons. "Your David is a good man. After he almost drowned saving Remy, one of his students, we've all been extra worried about him."

David almost drowned? Sadie missed a step and just about tripped. Charlotte's hand squeezed her arm, steadying her.

"But he's pulled through physically, and we want to make sure he's ready emotionally to return to Costa Rica. We can provide more options if he's led to go a different direction."

Obviously, he'd left out some huge details about his life in Costa Rica. Like almost drowning. Saving a boy's life. That he might not go back. Perhaps she just hadn't asked him the right questions to hear the story brewing under the surface.

No matter what happened in Costa Rica, or before, when they broke up, Sadie wanted to help David. He had stepped in at the store. And with Lottie. He'd made big sales, encouraged her, and helped out wherever he could. The least she could do was help him get through this dinner.

He loved the students, enough to almost die saving them. Like he cared for Lottie. She could see his enjoyment as they studied, as he talked with her. David had a gift.

Sadie's throat tightened, and she blinked back the tears threatening to spill down her cheeks.

David stood and pulled her chair out for her, his breath warm on her cheek as he whispered in her ear. "I'm so sorry, Sadie."

Emotions warred in the depths of his gaze. She couldn't hold this against him. His fingers brushed her back as she sat down, and heat raced down her spine. She wouldn't mind feeling that warmth the rest of the night. "Don't think another moment about it." Because she wasn't furious—it had been an accident—but she was curious.

David needed to go back to Costa Rica, and she'd do whatever she could to support, to encourage, and to help him achieve his dreams.

But when tonight was over, she had some questions. He'd be her captive in the car, and he'd better be ready to answer.

Like...how he almost drowned, and why he needed to report his activities to his mission board.

One thing was crystal clear, though. David had been totally accurate when he asked her for a solid favor. There were no romantic notions in his head.

~

If only David could be back at his grandparents' farm, pretending tonight had never happened. That he hadn't soaked Sadie because of his shaking hands. That he'd had satisfactory answers to Marco's and Lance's questions. That Charlotte hadn't assumed he and Sadie were a couple.

Instead, he sat in Olivia's van. Because even she had thought tonight should be more—a date—and his grandpa's Subaru wasn't as comfortable for a passenger. What did it say about him, that as a grown man in his thirties he didn't even own a car? It had never bothered him before.

"Want to talk about it?" Sadie looked up from her hands. The weight of her stare burned into him.

Not really, no.

The line of red lights ahead blurred and merged together—how could traffic leaving Grand Rapids possibly be this bad on a Saturday night? He blinked and refocused, but the brake lights still glowed in the darkness. They wouldn't be moving for a while. He pushed the button to turn on the CD player. Kid songs would be better than conversation. Anything to fill the void that threatened to swallow the rest of his pride.

An upbeat rhythm filled the car and young voices started singing, "If you're happy and you know it, clap your hands."

He pushed the button again. Nope, he wasn't happy. And the car hadn't moved. Not even a foot.

Silence it was.

"David?" Sadie's hand settled on his arm. It wasn't like he needed the reminder that she was still there.

He really didn't want to talk. Music was a better option. Even children's songs. He turned the CD player back on.

Clap. Clap.

Sadie's hand flew to the power button, cutting off the song.

Well, then.

David racked his brain for a topic, any topic, other than the disaster of the dinner. "Ready for the kitten?"

Sadie sighed, and she withdrew her hand. "Lottie is. Me? I don't know. But we picked up supplies."

The brake lights ahead let up, and cars started moving again. He inched forward, all of fifty feet, and traffic stopped again.

Sadie pulled out her phone and swiped a few times. "Looks like there's an accident up ahead. But GPS says we should only be here for fifteen or so minutes. This is still the fastest route home. So we have at least that long for you to tell me what that dinner was about, because it wasn't just a friendly night with your higher ups."

David hung his head and rubbed his temples. Lance's question about his involvement in the community weighed on him more than the traffic jam, more than the disastrous dinner. He didn't know how to answer Lance. If David hadn't made a single impact in Heritage in the time he'd been there, Marco and Lance were right to be worried about him. He hadn't encouraged anyone. Hadn't helped anyone. Had hardly interacted with his family until they'd forced his hand. And now? Now he sat in a borrowed van with his ex-girlfriend.

Impact? Unlikely. "I was sent stateside a little over six months ago, after an accident, and I haven't been cleared to go back. Partly because they don't know if I'm fit to return. My hands shake, and I've hidden myself away."

"I noticed your hands at dinner tonight. But I've never seen them shake at the store."

David held up his hand between them, letting it shake freely. "I've tried everything to get the shaking under control. They don't tend to shake when I'm at the store. I haven't quite figured out why."

Sadie gently placed her palm against his. Instantly, the tremors stopped, and his hand stilled. Hmm, he hadn't tried that.

The red lights blinked, and David inched forward a few feet. Lightning flashed in the distance. He glanced over at Sadie. Her expression didn't hold pity or anger, only open curiosity.

Something in that look gave him the courage to keep talking even though he pulled his hand away and gripped the steering wheel. "I work at a school for missionaries. Mainly, we work with those new to the culture, who are learning the Spanish language. While the parents are in language class, their children continue doing regular schoolwork as they, too, learn the language. Students come and go on a regular basis as parents move about the region. I oversee the physical education department."

"Lottie has mentioned that."

Of course. Lottie had asked no less than a hundred questions about Costa Rica, his apartment, the classes he taught, what kind of food he ate, about the beaches, and if he had a pet. "I've developed the program from the ground up. Each semester, I take a group of teens white water rafting. The kids look forward to it, and it really does build relationships that last long after they leave the school."

"I bet you love it." Sadie adjusted the air vents away from her.

David shrugged. What was not to love? But no amount of loving his job would save it. "I'm committed to see my work succeed."

"Why wouldn't it?"

The brake lights let up again, and David drove a block before the red lights flashed and he stopped. "On the last rafting trip, one of the teens was...less than thrilled his parents had uprooted his life. Remy had an attitude that wouldn't quit. I knew he might be trouble on the raft, so I made sure he was in mine."

David's throat constricted. Lightning flashed again, and rain plinked on the windshield. The wipers swished, but at least traffic picked up as they passed the accident. "The kid was so stubborn and bitter he wouldn't listen to instruction. He must have loosened the chin strap on his helmet when no one was looking because when he fell out of the raft, it fell off and he bumped his head. Knocked him out and seriously injured himself in the process."

Lightning continued to flash, and thunder rumbled in the distance. Sadie shifted in her seat, turning her whole body to watch him. "So, you jumped in?"

David shrugged. "The raft had gone over Remy, and he hadn't come back up. He needed help."

"Charlotte said you almost drowned."

Almost drowned. He fought back the sting he could still feel in his nostrils, the tightness in his lungs. "The current was stronger than I anticipated. I could reach Remy easily enough, but his shirt snagged a log. When I tried to free him, my foot lodged between a rock and a log on the bottom of the river. I finally released Remy's shirt and sent him down the river since I couldn't get my foot to move. In the process of floating, he bumped his head again. The doctors don't know if his head injury was a result of bumping it when he fell out of the raft or while he floated downstream. If I hadn't gotten stuck, I might have been able to protect him."

"How..." Her question hung in the air.

"The rafting instructor in the second raft saw what happened. He jumped in and freed my foot. But I'd been under for a while. I'm told I responded well to CPR and was talking before they took me to a local hospital. Although I don't remember that part."

Sadie sucked in a breath as she rested her soft hand gently on his arm. He hadn't dated much since Sadie. Hadn't met anyone that made him long for the closeness of physical touch. He'd remained so distant from everyone that he'd forgotten the power of a simple touch. He settled his own hand on top of hers, relishing the feel of her soft skin against his palm. "And Remy?"

David pulled his hand back and gripped the steering wheel. "They airlifted him to the nearest hospital. His head injury caused severe spinal damage. They are hoping he'll be able to walk again." The truth of it threatened to pull him right back under. "I let him down."

Sadie shook her head. "Bad things happen, David. We don't always know why. But it's not your fault. You saved him from drowning."

No. David shouldn't have allowed Remy to go rafting. And because he hadn't stepped up and protected Remy when he needed it, it was possible David had single-handedly derailed God's plan, because he hadn't heard God since. God seemed to still be punishing him by keeping him in Heritage.

Sadie's hand squeezed his arm again, the weight a gentle pressure.

A longing curled into David's system—where the feel of Sadie's comforting hand wasn't so foreign or fleeting, where it was a constant lifeline. Where he had someone who could go through life with him every day. Someone to be there for the highs, the lows, and everything in between.

"David, you know that God moves in ways we can't understand. You know His ways will always be better than what we can imagine."

Her words settled over him. Oh, how he wanted that to be true. But maybe he'd messed everything up. David tightened his grip on the steering wheel. Maybe it was in his blood to mess things up.

He glanced over at her. He wanted to believe her. But how could she offer up these words of kindness, of forgiveness? He'd left her. Shattered both their hearts and walked away from her. But the way she settled her hand on his arm, he wanted her to hang on. But if she did, he might hurt her all over again.

Sadie pulled her hand back and tucked her foot under herself in the seat. "I never thought my life would be what it is today. But I wouldn't change any of it, because I have Lottie. Sometimes life takes many turns to bring us to where we're supposed to be."

"What kind of turns?"

Sadie let out a deep breath and sank back against her seat. David couldn't make out her expression in the shadow of the car.

"I was pretty aimless after we broke up. When Bonnie died, Jeremy asked me to become Lottie's nanny. I never imagined that one day it would lead to marriage."

David's palms stung as he gripped the steering wheel tightly. His breath caught in his throat, and for a brief second, he remembered that feeling of terror as he'd realized he couldn't hold his breath any longer, and he sucked in a lungful of water. My marriage.

His lungs squeezed out the air, painfully. He'd known about her wedding for a while, but the pain gripping his insides, that was new. It shouldn't matter though.

But it did.

Because even after ten years, Sadie still had the power to steal his breath away, calm him with a mere touch, and encourage him with her uplifting words.

"When Jeremy found out about his diagnosis, we talked and agreed marriage might be the best thing for Lottie. You know Machado-Joseph disease doesn't have a long survival rate. We started the adoption process right away. Unfortunately, Jeremy passed away before the paperwork could be finalized. Because of his death, and the continued aftermath of Covid, the adoption process slowed way down. Jeremy left custody of Lottie to me, but now Doris, Jeremy's older sister, is threatening to contest it."

"You're great with Lottie." David turned off the highway and onto Heritage Street to drive into the center of town. A bolt of lightning flashed across the sky, illuminating the road in front of him.

"I try. Lottie has lost a lot. Her mom, her dad, and she never knew her biological grandparents. But at least here, she has my family."

"Your family is pretty amazing. Lottie is lucky. Your parents love big. Even me." David cleared his throat. "Jeremy's parents had passed before I met him."

"His mom passed when he was in high school. His dad while he was a freshman in college. Part of the tension with Doris is because she tried to mother Jeremy. Doris and Patrick were already married with a son when their mom passed away."

David could imagine that hadn't gone over well between the siblings. Sadie loved Lottie though. Jeremy couldn't have picked a better person to leave her with. Sadie worked hard, she loved without reservation, and she cared. It's what made falling in love with her the first time so easy.

And what made getting over her so hard.

"Why didn't you change your last name to Linden? You still go by Hoover." David moved his right hand up and down the steering wheel.

"Honestly? There wasn't time. I had intended to, but between Jeremy's doctors' visits, caring for Lottie, life—it didn't get done." Sadie looked out the window. Her shoulders rounded slightly, visible in the streetlight they passed under. "I did love Jeremy."

His heart stilled. Of course she had. She'd married him. And he'd been a jerk to ask. "He was your husband."

"Yes. But more than that, he'd become my best friend. Jeremy was a good man, a good husband, and an incredible father." Sadie looked down, and her voice dropped. "I didn't love him the way I loved you."

Her quiet words were barely audible above the hum of the car, but she might as well have shouted them at him. He squeezed the steering wheel tighter. Sadie should have had love. The fairy tale. She'd always wanted the happily ever after, the big family, the heart-stopping love. David had thought that described their love, until the breakup.

He turned onto Henderson Road and drove toward the town square. Otis sat as the town sentinel in the center by the gazebo as water splashed around him. David turned on Richard Street, pulled the van behind Hoover's Hardware, and parked. "I saw an umbrella in the trunk when Nate pulled out the car seats. Let me grab it, and I'll walk you to the door."

Relentless drops pelted David as he opened the trunk and found the large, black umbrella. He opened the passenger door for Sadie and held her hand as she stepped out of the van. Then he moved close, so her back brushed against his chest to keep them both under the umbrella.

Sadie's rich, warm scent tickled his nose, reminding him that she wasn't the young girl he'd once dated. She'd grown, matured, faced her own challenges, and he liked it. Liked her scent. Liked the feel of her back under his hand. Liked the woman she'd become.

He just liked her.

They walked up the stairs to the door of her apartment. Electricity shot up his arm. She unlocked the door and pushed it open. David held the umbrella over their heads.

Sadie tipped her face up. The moment familiar, seeming right in a way nothing else had lately. David settled his hand on the soft curve of her waist. Wind swept past him, swaying his body closer to hers. Her hands rested on his chest.

To steady him? To encourage him? To pull him closer?

Maybe it wasn't too late to salvage this night.

Sadie's eyes roamed his face, pausing on his mouth before they bounced back up. Heat climbed up David's neck. If he leaned closer, if he cut the distance between them, would she welcome him?

The golden specks in her hazel eyes mesmerized him. Pulled him closer. He lowered his face, watching for any sign of rejection.

Waiting for her to stop him.

He should pull back, step away. Not slip back into old habits. Except the warmth of her hands on his chest and the feel of her body close to his didn't feel like a habit. It felt right, perfect, and he couldn't—didn't want to—stop. And when she fisted his shirt, keeping him from pulling back, heat pooled in his gut.

The newness, the rightness of this moment, consumed him. He inched forward as Sadie let out a soft sigh. He waited—for her to step back or any kind of sign that she wanted him to stop.

When her eyes closed, it was all the invitation he needed. David lowered his lips, feeling the exhale of her breath on his face.

"Mom!"

Sadie jumped back, the cold breeze almost icy when she dropped her hands from his chest as Lottie walked up the stairs, cradling her stomach, her wet hair dripping down her face as the rain soaked into her clothes. A woman with dark greying hair pulled back in a severe bun carried a backpack and an umbrella.

"Lottie? Are you okay?" Sadie pulled her close, wrapping her in a hug.

Lottie groaned and shook her head. David raised the umbrella higher to accommodate the extra person. He stepped away slightly, so the cool rain pelted his back, keeping Sadie and Lottie dry.

The woman, probably in her mid 40's now that David could see her face better, stopped two stairs below them. "Lottie got sick to her stomach. Begged to come home. I didn't realize you had plans tonight, or I wouldn't have brought her back."

The woman pursed her lips together and looked David up and down.

David stepped back farther from Sadie. He'd been caught with his hand in the cookie jar. Or rather, with his lips centimeters from hers.

He shouldn't still be standing here. He handed the umbrella to Sadie, but she shook her head and looked back to the woman on the stairs.

"Thank you for bringing Lottie home. Doris, this is an old college friend, David."

Old friend. As if the rain hadn't cooled him enough.

Doris snorted. "Right. Keep in mind what's best for Lottie. I know I do." The woman thrust out her hand holding Lottie's bag and marched down the stairs to a dark BMW still running, parked next to Olivia's minivan.

"Mom, I think I'm going to be sick." Lottie rushed into the apartment.

Sadie shot David an apologetic look. "I'm sorry. I have to go."

David hurried down the stairs, his foot slipping on the bottom one. He windmilled his arms to regain his balance and jogged to the van and collapsed into the driver's seat, the rain soaking him as he shook the umbrella out.

His stomach turned, probably feeling much like Lottie's. He'd almost kissed Sadie. He'd never taken kissing lightly, and she was the last woman he'd kissed. He couldn't, wouldn't play with her emotions.

Or with his own feelings. Because after tonight, he couldn't deny that his feelings were not locked securely in the past. They were back and...

Oh no.

He couldn't do this.

Costa Rica. He needed to stick to the plan.

Except...for the first time since he'd returned to Heritage, the drive to return to Costa Rica didn't leave him excited. Instead, he rather hoped he'd be able to stick around Heritage a little bit longer.

What had he done?

eight

TWO DAYS. THAT'S HOW LONG IT HAD BEEN SINCE David dropped Sadie off on her doorstep and almost kissed her under an umbrella in the rain. There was a reason people wrote songs about that. His warm body, his hand pulling her close, the look in his eyes—she would have kissed him, and enjoyed it, if not for the interruption.

For the first time ever, Sadie had been thankful for the stomach bug, because kissing David? That would have been a disaster. Even if they could move beyond all the hurt in their past, there was no way their futures could mix. She'd been honest with him when she told him she'd have followed him to the ends of the earth. But that was ten years ago. Now she had a daughter, a job, a life—and it was in Heritage.

But she was human, and he made her feel...things...she hadn't in years. How could she ignore the way his every touch made her skin burn? How every time he leaned close, she longed to curl into him? How she dreamed about their lips meeting again after ten years of separation?

Her phone vibrated on her desk. Romee. She'd been ignoring her sister since the messages started coming in late Saturday night.

Romee

*gif of a skeleton tapping its fingers. Still waiting for you to tell me about your date.

You can't ignore me forever.

Do I need to show up in your store? Because I can.

Sadie sighed and rolled her head around, stretching her neck. Too bad her sister would make good on those threats.

Sadie

There's nothing to tell.

Except for the way her waist still tingled where his hand had settled, pulling her closer, shielding her from the rain. Nope. Not sharing that.

Romee

Mom says his car idled outside your unit for ten minutes. That's a long time for nothing to happen.

Of course her mom had been spying. Nothing ever got by her when they were children. Nothing would escape her notice now.

Sadie

He walked me to the door in the rain. We were there only a minute or two before Doris dropped Lottie off because she had a stomach bug.

Romee

Poor Lottie.

But a minute is a long time. Nothing happened?

Sadie
Well, he didn't kiss me, if that's
what you're asking.

Romee
That's like saying he's only mostly
dead. Did he almost kiss you?

Sadie
I never almost kiss and tell.

Romee
*gif of little girl squealing and
shaking her fists.

Sadie tucked her phone into her pocket, shaking her head. Romee would report back to Mom faster than—well, she probably already had.

Hopefully, the kiss that didn't happen wouldn't be enough to scare David from coming back in to work today.

But maybe it would be better if he didn't come in.

Food. She needed a snack. Sadie opened the bottom drawer of the desk and tried to pull out her new lunch tote—it matched Lottie's tie-dyed lunch box—but her finger caught on an old ledger, snagging her cuticle.

Ouch. Sadie immediately stuck her fingertip in her mouth. Oh, that hurt. But the cover of the ledger stayed open, and her dad's familiar handwriting peeked out at her.

After shaking her hand, she pulled out the book and flipped through the pages. The yellowed pages were filled with names and numbers. Some of the entries were over twenty years old, and the pencil markings had faded. There was an entry from Dale Kensington. He'd moved out of town years ago. She continued looking through the names.

Every single entry listed someone who took out a line of credit at the store.

She gripped the book to her chest and pushed back from the desk. It was too soon to get her hopes up, but maybe, just maybe, this would help her keep the store.

If these were really outstanding charges, perhaps she could collect a few of them. It would go a long way toward the remaining amount due to the bank. Since paying the bank had wiped out her savings, any extra funds would be appreciated.

The bell jingled, and Sadie stood up. She'd have to worry about this later. "Be right there."

"Just me," her father called back. Well then, she'd get a chance to talk to him now.

Sitting back down, Sadie opened the ledger and studied the names.

"Brought you some lunch. Your mom made soup and thought you'd like some." Her dad set a thermos on the desk and settled in the black plastic chair across from her. "Oh, I know that look. What's up?"

Sadie slid the ledger forward and tapped it. "Don't you think that this is something I should have known about? We have lines of store credit and a massive bill due. You didn't think to tell me about this?"

Her dad bristled. "Those are people in town who needed some help. Those are my friends, and this is between me and them."

"Are you serious right now?" What about her? What about the store?

Her dad nodded. "Yes."

"Who's running this store? You or me? You asked me to come home, to run the store. Have you changed your mind?"

Her dad's shoulders rounded. His wrinkles deepened. She hated fighting with him, and guilt racked her for upsetting him.

"Haven't changed my mind. But these credits weren't given to just anyone. Sometimes things are hard. Those people had big families, medical bills, a burst pipe, a large freeze that knocked out their crops—each person has a story. And while I do run a business, those are my people. And if I can help them out, I will."

"They should pay you back."

"They'll pay when they can."

"This isn't a charity, Dad. This is a business." Sadie shook her head. "Do you trust me to run it?"

Her dad scooted forward and placed his elbows on the desk. "You know I do. It's just...this is not just business. These are my friends."

"Friends who enjoy having a local hardware store. But we can't keep our doors open this way." Sadie let out a sigh. Her dad's jaw ticced. "Why not tell me about this?"

Shaking his head back and forth, her dad stood and paced away from the desk. "I saw those as personal, not business. But you're right, I should have told you about them. I guess I'm having a harder time letting go than I realized. But I trust you to do the right thing."

The bell jingled, and Sadie called out a greeting. "Work calls, Dad."

They walked to the front of the store together, her dad patting her on the back. "I'll tell your mom I gave you the soup."

When Sadie stepped out of the aisle, David stood with a tiny bundle of orange fur pressed against his firm chest, a cat carrier in one hand, bits of cat hair spread across his black T-shirt.

The kitten.

Her dad sneezed. "I'd shake your hand, but I'm allergic. Talk to you kids later." The bell jingled as he left.

David's gaze flickered to the door then back to Sadie. "You okay?

The kitten snuggled deeper into David's chest, and, wow, if it didn't make him even more appealing. Talking about anything other than her mixed emotions toward him would be easy.

"There's so much going on behind the scenes here. You have no idea."

David stroked the kitten's head and neck, making a soft shushing sound. "What can I do?"

She started to brush off the offer, but when she met his gaze, there was a depth of concern she hadn't been prepared for. It wasn't a throwaway statement. He really meant it. Had anyone ever offered to share the load with her? To help her out, not by doing it for her, but coming alongside her?

The tiny orange ball of fur held perfectly still in David's arms, his large, yellow eyes taking in the store. "You really want to help?"

David shifted the kitten so that he held it tightly in one arm. He used his free hand to grip her arm. "Anything you need."

Sadie gently scratched the kitten under his chin. Cuatro looked at her, his big, yellow orbs studying her. No wonder Lottie wanted a kitten so bad. "It's the store. Dad took out a mortgage. I found this ledger full of store credits. Dad says he issued those credits when people really needed help. He doesn't feel right asking them or reminding them."

"You run a business, Sadie. A good one. If people owe the store, it's okay to remind them. Send bills, talk to people."

"That's what I said. But my dad says he doesn't feel right doing that." They weren't running a charity, but it was her business, and the line between honoring what her dad wanted and doing what the business needed seemed jagged. The kitten yawned, his mouth opening wide. He was a cute thing. "What's his name again?"

David stepped closer, his breath fanning across her face. "Cuatro. Ready to hold him?"

David was so close. Close enough to touch, to smell, to kiss. His warm fingertips brushed against her arms as he passed Cuatro to her, the tiny fur ball purring and studying her with curiosity. Could a purring kitten really drain all the fight out of her? She'd heard that petting a cat was good for the soul, but to experience it firsthand...or was it the feel of David's large hand settling on her shoulder?

"I'll...I'll take the kitten upstairs. Show him where the litter box is." Maybe clear her head and figure out how to save the store.

"Do you mind if I look at the ledger you mentioned?" David's gaze never faltered.

"Why?"

"I am serious about helping. You don't have to figure it out on your own. Let me help you."

It would be great to have an extra set of eyes. But what if...There would always be a what-if. Right now, David was willing to be a second set of eyes. Someone to walk with her and help her out. "It's on my desk next to my computer if you want to look at it while I take the kitten upstairs."

The tiny body snuggled closer to her, trusting her, as she carried it up to her apartment. She showed the kitten the litter box and the food and watched him explore his new home, his curiosity winning out. What would it be like to be so trusting in a completely new situation? To have enough faith to explore, to try new things?

Could she have that kind of faith?

Could she go back downstairs and not only allow David to look at the ledger, but talk to him about her ideas and accept his offer of assistance?

The kitten jumped toward the sectional sofa and overshot the arm rest, sliding onto the cushion. Slightly startled with the landing, he sat down and started cleaning his face.

She could take a leap. Invite David in. Maybe with something smaller, less life altering than the business of the store. Like the kitten, if things didn't quite work the way she thought, maybe all she'd need to do was wash her face and try again.

Resolved that she could take a chance on David's offer of help, she returned to the store and found David helping Mrs. Allen pick out another paint color.

Sadie slid into her chair in the office and glanced down at the ledger David had left open. She closed it and pushed it aside. She'd start with something simple.

A few moments later, David settled into the chair across from her.

She pulled her lips in and squeezed them before letting out a breath. Just take the jump. "You wouldn't happen to know anything about webpages, would you?"

David held up his fingers about an inch apart. "I set up the school's webpage."

Of course he did. David could do everything. And he wanted to do things for her. Help her out. "I can't figure out the store website. Could you look at that, too?"

David nodded, scooting forward in his seat. "I'd be happy to."

Those simple words lifted the weight on her shoulders. She slid her computer around to face him. David pulled the computer closer and went to work. His face thoughtful, his thick hair flopping on his forehead. Occasionally, he'd rub his jaw and ask a few questions, but he eventually turned the screen around and showed Sadie a beautiful—could she call a hardware store website that?—layout.

Perfection.

It's just what David did. He jumped in, helped out. Almost like her knight in shining armor. Not that she was a damsel in distress by any means, but when she couldn't reach the top shelf, when the window needed washed, when drywall needed redone, when the website needed finished—David stepped in. He saw her. He saw the needs, and he filled them. Without prompting. Without her asking.

They did make a good team.

She studied the site, and a deep longing she'd buried long ago woke up. The desire to find someone who made her feel safe, seen, protected, valued. Someone who would be here, in the moment, with her.

Love.

Once upon a time, she'd called that feeling love.

She'd had those feelings for David, until he'd shattered her heart. Then she'd set a pipe bomb to her remaining feelings, swept them up and buried them. Until right now, when they clawed up, blooming into a warmth she'd thought she'd never experience again.

But she couldn't give a home to the happiness, the feelings. Costa Rica stood between them.

She could, however, accept his offer of assistance. It saved her from scrolling through her mental Rolodex to find the right person to ask. She could cash in on this lifeline, this phone-a-friend.

No one else offered her that. And she liked it. Liked that he was there to help. Liked that he didn't back away from a challenge. Liked that he wanted to be there for her.

She liked it a lot. Way more than she should.

It had been four days. Four days, and David still couldn't scrub the memory of almost kissing Sadie from his mind.

David picked up a set of heavier than usual weights and held them by his side as he stepped into position for a lunge. The familiar sounds of the gym and guys laughing faded into the background as he bent his knees, letting his back knee briefly touch the mat before he stood up.

David continued to repeat the move, his thoughts drifting back to a certain stubborn, intelligent, hardworking woman at the hardware store. Sadie carried so much on her capable shoulders—far more than she needed to. David had ached to take some of the weight from her. The webpage had been a simple fix, and she'd made him feel ten feet tall, praising his ingenuity.

For the first time since the accident, David could imagine a future. One he didn't have to fight for. One he didn't have to struggle to make happen.

One that included a beautiful woman and her spunky daughter. One right here in Heritage, Michigan.

But that wasn't right. He had to get back—for his students, for his supporters. For his calling.

David switched legs and started another set of split lunges.

"Thought I might find you here." Nate dumped a gym bag on the bench as David finished up this set of lunges.

"Where else would I be? We agreed to be here ten minutes ago." David set his left leg forward again and started another set.

Nate rubbed his jaw and let out a lengthy sigh. "Sorry. It's been a busy day at the church. How'd your dinner with Lance and Marco go?"

Air rushed out as he considered the night. He couldn't call it a complete disaster, because the feel of Sadie's waist under his hand stuck with him. "A mess. I spilled water all over the table, Charlotte thought we were a couple, and I almost kissed Sadie when I dropped her off."

Nate picked up a set of weights and lined up next to David. "Why not kiss her?"

David could think of several reasons. The main one? "Her life is here. We've already established that there's nothing more between us."

"Why not?"

"I have to get back to Costa Rica."

Nate stood up and switched legs in front. Then he continued lunging. "Why, David? Why do you have to go back?"

David allowed silence to fill the space as he did a few reps. "I've done a lot in Costa Rica. I'd like to continue. For my supporters. For my students."

"Your supporters want you to follow God where He is leading."

"That's Costa Rica."

"I believe it was once upon a time. But is it still? It's hard to pivot, but if God is asking you to, the best thing you can do is let go of your personal plans and follow Him."

David paused with his knee on the mat. "Missions work is God's will."

Nate sighed and stood up, turning to face David. "Have you ever stopped to consider that God's will is not one size fits all? It's tailored to fit each person and their unique life differently. God's will is not a specific calling that everyone has to follow in a robotic manner. Finding His will for your life is a daily activity. Every morning seeking God, following Him. God will help you adapt and stretch as you grow and age, if you are seeking Him. For some, yes, it's missions. For others it's being a pastor, or an accountant, or a teacher. Even a shopkeeper."

David shifted his weights so his arms curled up. He held them at shoulder level, spread his feet apart, and started squatting.

Nate continued. "Have you stopped to consider that maybe this accident and subsequent trip back to Heritage might be God setting you on a different path? He can use you anywhere. Look at me, Jon, Seth, Luke—pick any one of us—God has worked in our lives right here. He's using us here. You don't have to cut yourself off from everything you love to follow God. Perhaps He's asking you to change. To follow Him on a new path."

David pushed to standing and placed the weights back on the rack. "God needs people willing to go."

"I'm not denying that. I'm just asking you...have you asked God what He wants for your life today? Because sometimes God wants us to go, and sometimes He wants us to stay."

"He hasn't opened any other doors." David dug through his gym bag and pulled out his water, but even as he swallowed the beverage, he knew that wasn't true. How many times had Lance asked him if he was certain Costa Rica was his future?

David had refused to consider any other option.

Nate set his weights down on the rack and picked up another set. Sat down and started doing some bicep curls. "I've enjoyed having you close. I know your sisters have soaked up all the time you're willing to give them. You keep saying you want to hear God again. But, David, maybe you just aren't listening to what He is saying. And I know you feel God is silent right now, but let me ask you this—if you are only listening for one answer, are you really listening?"

Nate's phone buzzed from inside his gym bag. He dug around until he found it and then blew out a deep breath. "I need to take this. I'm sorry, David. I'll catch up with you later."

David finished his workout routine in silence, Nate's words reverberating in his mind. Maybe you just aren't listening.

Could that be it? Could God be leading him in a path that David didn't want to acknowledge? Had he only been listening for what he wanted to hear?

Okay, Lord. Whatever You want, wherever You want, I'm listening. Even if it wasn't Costa Rica, even if it wasn't the future David envisioned, he'd rather do whatever God wanted. Peace like he hadn't experienced since before the accident settled around him like a blanket he'd left behind in Costa Rica. That's what he'd been missing—the peace that came from living a surrendered life.

David hurried out to his car, flung his gym bag in, and started the engine, but his phone rang before he could back out of his spot. He opened his bag and dug around until he found it. Lance's name flashed across the front of his phone.

"Hey, Lance. Everything ok?"

Lance let out a sigh, and David could picture him loosening his tie. "It was good to see you at dinner last week. Marco and I enjoyed catching up. But...we've been talking to Chris."

Oh no. Lance's hesitation, the catch in his voice. He had something to say, and David could pretty much guarantee he wouldn't like it. "I'm not sure I know a Chris?"

"The young guy who was filling in for you in Costa Rica."

David's stomach squeezed. "Everything okay?"

Lance chuckled. A nervous sound, and David could tell he'd stood up. Probably pacing his office. "Great, actually. He loves Costa Rica. Loves the position. Loves the kids. Has even updated the webpage. Honestly, he wants to stay. Asked if this position could be permanent."

"But it's not. I'm going back." David closed his eyes and relaxed his head against the headrest. He waited for his stomach to drop, for his mind to race a hundred different directions trying to figure out how to keep his position. Instead, peace settled over him like a weighted blanket.

"That's the thing." Lance paused, and his chair squeaked again. He likely sat back down. "We told him the position was his. It's not that you can't go back to Costa Rica. Maybe in a different capacity, but Marco and I have talked, and both agree this is the right decision right now."

Nate's words came rushing back. Are you only listening for one answer? This was a pretty clear answer—Chris was taking his position. Permanently. What could he say?

Lance cleared his throat and took a sip of something. "With the position filled by someone else, it's time to let your supporters know you are changing paths."

David rubbed his chest. Most knew he'd come home after the accident, but if he wasn't going back, he couldn't continue to take their financial aid unless he had a new plan. "What if I go to a different location?"

"If that's the case, you need to make some decisions within the month so you can let supporters know. Some may not continue to support you in a new location, and you may need to find more people to partner with you if you change fields."

The call ended and David sat in the car, letting the now warm air blow on him. He should feel frustrated, disappointed, angry even, not peaceful.

David's mind flashed to Sadie—her resilience, her ability to bounce back, the weight she carried on her shoulders.

He had no future. No plans. No idea what God wanted from him, only what He didn't want from him.

The idea should settle like a pair of shoes two sizes too small, but that weighted blanket of peace didn't budge.

Okay God, I'm ready for whatever You have next.

Nothing.

But maybe that was okay. Maybe part of surrendering was not just letting go of the what but also the when. So, until God opened a clear path, David would stay where he was—in Heritage. Enjoying his family and helping Sadie.

He'd figure out what to tell his supporters soon.

nine

"YOU'RE TELLING ME THINGS ARE COMPLETELY normal with you and David?" No doubt Romee sat in her home music office with a can of Dr Pepper. Her hair was probably in a big messy bun on top of her head as she took her lunch break. "Even after your not-date, you let him into your office? Helping you with the books and the webpage?"

Sadie never should have answered this call as she stepped into Donny's Diner. The tables were filled, and every seat at the counter was occupied. No wonder she'd been told it would take so long to fill her call-in order. Must be the lunch rush. She should have gone back to her apartment, but she was low on groceries. Plus, she had yet to visit her favorite restaurant. The counters had been updated and although the booths were still red, the vinyl wasn't cracked at the corners anymore. But beyond those two things, time seemed to have stood still in the restaurant. Same vintage stools, same tintype ceiling, and same jukebox in the corner.

She'd spent many a weekend close to that jukebox with a stack of nickels and her childhood friend, Fallon James. They hadn't spoken in years, since they both moved away from Heritage. Maybe Sadie should message her longtime friend and let her know she'd moved back. When she came for a visit, they could reconnect.

Sadie inched her way toward the register as she cupped her hand by her cheek, doing her best to filter out the background noise for Romee. "Can we talk about this later?"

Romee huffed. "Fine. But this conversation isn't over. I might even pull in Anna. She knows a thing or two about exes."

Anything but that. "Please leave Anna out of this." Her other sister's on-again, off-again boyfriend, Brock, was—well, Sadie had no idea if he was currently on or off.

"Talk later, sis." And that ended the phone call.

Sadie slipped her phone in her back pocket as the waitress breezed by with a tray tucked under her arm.

"Your order will be right out. You paid over the phone, right?" The waitress placed her order pad in the front of her apron and hurried off.

At least Donny's didn't appear to be hurting for customers. Too bad half of those customers wouldn't walk down to the hardware store and make a purchase today. It would help.

"Two cheeseburgers and fries." The waitress handed Sadie a white plastic bag.

"Thanks." Sadie did a quick check. Two white Styrofoam boxes sat stacked inside the bag. Sadie gave the woman a nod then hurried out the front door and back to the store. She sidestepped Otis, who now sat in the middle of the sidewalk in front of the bank and patted his head as she passed, his warm bronze comforting and smooth. Otis always had a way of making everything a little better. Maybe it was the way his bronze eyes stared at everyone and everything. Maybe, it was just the magic that kept him moving. More than likely though, it was his secret-keeping skills, because there was no way Otis would tell Romee that Sadie had a little extra pep in her step just because she was thinking about David.

Before she could even turn on to Richard Street, her phone buzzed in her back pocket. She scanned the texts coming in rapid fire. True to her word, Romee had started a thread with Anna.

Romee
We need all the details. Tell us what's going on with David.

Anna
I agree. I didn't even know David was back in town.

Romee
Well, if you'd answer your phone every once in a while, you'd know.

Anna
*gif of little girl rolling her eyes.

Sadie shoved the phone in her back pocket so she could open the door of the hardware store. The welcome bell jingled happily overhead. If she told her sisters anything about David, it would open that crack in her heart even more.

He'd stepped in, shared her burden, and opened up to her about Costa Rica. It was all the best parts of their relationship, with a new openness they'd never had before. And it was addictive.

She couldn't dwell on that because he was returning to Costa Rica, so even if he checked off every box she'd ever had for a husband, she had to remember a new box she'd recently added: lived in Heritage. She couldn't uproot her life again. Lottie needed that stability of family, a home, and Heritage provided all of that.

David came up from the back of the store, Nate behind him.

David stopped beside her, his arm brushing hers, sending goosebumps up to her ears and down to her toes. Nate held out a business envelope to her. "I wanted to drop this off. I meant to yesterday but got sidetracked."

Sadie set the lunch bag on the counter behind David, her hands brushing his back. His eyes locked onto hers, and heat raced up Sadie's spine to her neck. Maybe she needed to check the thermostat?

She took the envelope Nate held out and opened it. Inside sat a check. Her fingers tingled.

A check.

It was only a few hundred dollars.

But still—a check.

Nate stood in front of her, his black T-shirt tight across his shoulders, his hands stuffed in his pockets. "I'm sorry it's late."

She hadn't contacted Nate. He was on page two of the ledger, and she hadn't gotten that far yet. How did he know? Did he suddenly remember?

Nate jerked his head toward David. "This guy reminded me."

A check.

It hardly made a dent in the money owed the bank, but someone paid their debt. Someone cared enough to pay off their tab. All because of David.

Nate left and David grabbed the broom from behind the register. Sadie had left it out earlier intending to finish sweeping but just hadn't gotten around to it yet. His biceps tightened as he moved the broom back and forth. Who knew watching a man sweep could be so...sexy.

Sadie pulled out her phone.

_____

Sadie

Ok. So maybe I'm in trouble.
The man steps in to solve
my problems. He sees them
and jumps in to help without
being asked.

And he invades my personal
space. And...I like it.

*Grimace emoji.

Romee
I KNEW IT! You still like him.

Anna
*gif of Ariel nodding her head to Prince Eric. Yeah, she does. She always has.

Romee
*gif of Superman flying. David's always been her kryptonite.

Sadie
Not helping. What do I do? He's leaving.

"Is it okay if I start eating?" David's deep voice interrupted her text.

She shoved the phone into her back pocket. Had he seen their texts? She'd been standing here texting like a dolt while David had swept the floor and put the broom away. Yikes.

He stepped closer and reached for the lunch behind her.

"I talked to Lance last night." David leaned closer. His breath, smelling of peppermint, whispered over her face.

Her stomach squeezed. This was it. The he's-leaving-for-Costa-Rica conversation she'd been waiting for. She gulped. "When are you going back?"

"I'm not sure. They've hired someone to fill my spot."

It was like time stood still for a moment, until Sadie's heart slammed against her rib cage. "You're not going back?"

"I'm not sure what my future holds. But I'll..." His words trailed off, as his eyes dropped to her lips. If she tilted her chin up just so, she could meet him with a kiss. And it would be...delicious.

"You'll...?" Sadie kept her chin tilted down, needing David to finish that thought.

"I'm...not sure anymore. Maybe..." David's thumb tilted her chin up.

"Sadie." Her name on his lips. A caress. "Have dinner with me?"

Like a date? With David? Warning bells sounded in her head. She blinked and dropped her gaze. Danger. Danger.

Or was it? He wasn't leaving.

He. Wasn't. Leaving.

She met his gaze again—the hope and promise buried within warmed her from the inside. That might be an entirely different kind of danger.

The bell jingled and Sadie tried to jump backward out of David's grasp, but she stepped into the counter. How had she totally forgotten where she was?

David sighed, stepped back, dropped his hands, and ran one hand through his thick, auburn hair, his biceps flexing. Holy Batman, she needed to keep her mind in the moment and off his mouth-watering muscles.

"Didn't mean to interrupt." Her mom's voice broke the last of the fog surrounding Sadie.

"It's always good to see you, Dawn." David offered his hand to her mom, but she batted it away and hugged David.

When her mom stepped back, she eyed Sadie with a knowing look. The weight of her accusation didn't need to be voiced. "I, um, Nate stopped by." Sadie held up her empty hand. Where had the envelope gone? David bent down and retrieved it off the floor and handed it to her. Sadie nodded. "Nate paid off his tab."

Her mom's perfectly shaped white-blonde eyebrow lifted, looking between Sadie and David. Sadie studied the floor.

"Sadie, honey, I brought some cookies for you and Lottie. Want to take these back to your office?" Her mom's normally honey-sweet voice held an unarguable edge of stone to it.

Sadie took the cookies and walked to her office. She pulled out her phone and sent a message to her sisters.

Sadie

Things feel different.

David said they gave his job in
Costa Rica to someone else.

Anna

He's not going back?

Romee

Girl, it's time to move in on
that. Strike while the iron's hot.
*flame emoji.

Sadie

There will be no striking.

Anna

Don't you want to strike?

Sadie

Maybe? I mean, if he's staying
here. Does that change things?

Romee

*gif of Jimmy Fallon fist pumping.

Anna

Only if you want it to.

Sadie

He asked me to dinner.

Romee

Way to bury the lead.

Anna

What did you say?

Sadie

I haven't yet.

Mom sort of interrupted.

Romee

Again, bury the lead, why don't
ya? I'll message Mom.

Anna

You know she will want
to know too.

But seriously, do you want to go?

Did she want to go? The overwhelming yes settled in her soul. If it meant that there might even be a chance for a future with David, she wanted to find out. Her heart did a tap dance routine in her chest.

Sadie

I'm going to say yes.

Romee

*gif of Michael Bublé saying "You
got this."

Anna

*gif of Jennifer Coolidge eating
cake saying, "You go, girl."

Sadie tucked her phone into her pocket and grabbed a peppermint from her desk drawer. If David invaded her space again, hopefully she wouldn't have coffee breath.

Her mom's low voice floated low through the hardware store. "Be careful with her, David."

"I will."

"We love you like you're our own son. But when you left last time, you broke her."

145

"I know."

"No, I don't think you do. I have never seen her like that. Frankly, it scared me, and I don't ever want to see her like that again."

Way to scare him off before things even get started, Mom. Sadie coughed, and the conversation changed as she stepped out of the aisle. Her mom's open expression welcomed Sadie, hiding the fact she'd just given David a warning speech.

"Dinner tonight? I made a pot roast. It's your favorite, hon. David, you're welcome, too."

"You know I can't turn that down." Sadie's phone buzzed again. A reminder her sisters would want an update.

David shoved his hands into his jean pockets. "I appreciate that, Dawn, but I'm playing soccer with some of the teens tonight."

Opening the door, Sadie's mom gave her a knowing look. "I'm going to run. Your sister has been messaging me non-stop for the past few minutes."

Of course she had. Romee would wheedle every little detail out of their mom.

The bell jingled again with the shutting of the door, and the store descended into quiet.

"I'm sorry you haven't gotten a chance to eat your lunch." Sadie stepped toward the counter and pulled out a Styrofoam container from the bag and held it out to David. "Probably cold by now."

David took the container and set it back down on the counter then intertwined their fingers. "I'd rather have an answer. My question was sincere. Dinner with me?"

Sadie swallowed. This was it, the moment to decide. "Yes."

A sweet grin lit up David's face. "I'll pick you up Friday night. Will that work?"

"After the store closes."

"It's a date then." David picked up his lunch and headed to the back room.

Sadie turned, and next to her lunch sat the crinkled envelope with the check inside. One check. One payment due. A start. With David's help, she might save the store.

But her heart might be a lost cause.

It was just dinner, and he was acting like this was his first date.

In some ways, it sort of was. David's sweaty palms squeezed the steering wheel as he parked next to the hardware store, reminding him that it was more than just a dinner with Sadie. Forgiveness and perhaps—hopefully—a second chance.

Reservations made. Check.

Nice clothes. Check.

On time for dinner. Check. Maybe even too early.

A quick walk to the gazebo would blow off some of the energy coursing in his veins and kill a little bit of time. David stepped out of his grandfather's truck, shook his hands, and walked to the front of the hardware store.

Otis guarded the playground, near the slide. Lottie sat on her knees next to him, scribbling back and forth on a piece of paper on his hip.

What on earth was she doing? David crossed the street to her.

Lottie leaned back on her heels and held the paper up to the setting sun. "I will figure your secrets out, Otis. You might think you can keep them hidden from me, but I will figure them out."

David stepped closer to see what the paper held. A blob of scribbles. "That mystery is as old as Heritage itself or at least close."

"Look what I found." Lottie held up the paper. But the scribbles didn't look like much. "Did I tell you I opened the Heritage Square clock face?"

David shook his head.

"Well, I watched a YouTube video about repairing clocks. It didn't help me repair it though. The inner parts are all bronze, like Otis here. And inside I found a logo for a watchmaker. There used to be a manor on the square, and it was built by an old watchmaker. The logo in the clock looked like this." She rattled the paper. "Well…sort of. The one in the clock has lots more details. Maybe the builder of the clock and Otis have a connection." Lottie traced the blob of scribbles with her fingers.

David watched her. He squinted and tilted his head—nothing. He couldn't figure out how she saw a logo. "Where'd you find it?"

Lottie pointed to a spot on Otis's back side. David ran his fingers over the section. Smooth. Except…were there a few shallow ridges? Those could be nothing more than scratches due to wear and tear. If there had been a logo there, it had long ago been rubbed smooth.

"Lottie!" Sadie stood across the street, a bag in hand, her purse over her shoulder. Her hair was down, hanging in loose waves, and she wore a maroon sweater with a white vest, jeans, and tall brown boots.

Stunning.

"Oh! Time to go! I get a sleepover with Aunt Romee tonight. Don't tell Mom, but we're going to watch a movie about a big shark and eat popcorn." Lottie ran across the street, and David followed.

Sadie hugged Lottie before she dashed off to the Hoovers' house and threw open the front door. Romee came to the door and waved at Sadie. Must be a signal, because she turned to David then and shrugged her purse on her shoulder. Her cheeks flushed as she offered a small wave.

"You look, uh, really nice." Wow. Nothing awkward about that. He gestured toward the truck. Maybe he should have asked Olivia to borrow the van again.

He opened the truck door and closed it after she settled in the passenger seat. He flexed his hands as he jogged around the car. They'd make their reservation in Ludington, no problem.

Thirty minutes later, David slid into the black booth across from Sadie at Cafe d'Amour. The white linen tablecloth, pressed to perfection, lined the table. A single red rose sat next to a floating candle. Soft string music floated through the restaurant, barely drowning out the murmur of other guests. Private and cozy—just like the reviews online said—but also romantic.

Sadie studied the menu, her long hair hanging over her shoulder. She pulled her lips in and let them out with a deep breath. The barest hint of a smile curled her lips up, even though she continued to study the menu. "Are you going to stare at me all night?"

"If I say yes, will that make you uncomfortable?"

Finally Sadie looked up, her hazel eyes searching his, all traces of teasing gone, and her cheeks turning a lovely shade of pink. Breaking eye contact, she picked up her purse and pulled out her phone. "You're incorrigible."

She tapped away on her phone and then set it down face up.

"Expecting a message?" David pulled his hands into his lap.

A nervous chuckle escaped Sadie. "Honestly? No. But I'd really love to hear that everything is okay. With Romee watching Lottie tonight, I just want to make sure I'm available if something comes up."

"Is it hard to leave Lottie?"

Sadie let out a small sigh. "It's just, what if something happens and Lottie needs me—I won't be there. Her emotions have been a little volatile lately, and I just want to be there if or when things finally come to a head."

"Romee is there."

Sadie scoffed. "That's just it, though."

There was a story behind that. Sadie looked down to pick at her cuticle.

"It's just I've always felt a little responsible for Romee—for all of my siblings, really. As the oldest, it was always my job to take care of everyone. And one night...well, I stepped out of the kitchen to talk on the phone, and Romee started a fire trying to make grilled cheese. Mom and Dad were furious. What if she'd lit the whole kitchen on fire instead? They reminded me that there wouldn't have been a fire if I had been there. There wouldn't have been any smoke damage. What if something like that happens with Lottie? What if she needs me and I'm not there?"

"Is that why you're so controlling? With Lottie? With the store? Because, if you step out, you think it all might go up in smoke?" David took a sip of root beer as he watched Sadie glance at the phone again with a nervous laugh.

"It might. Life's proven that over and over. When I'm not in control, when I don't know all the details, when I can't plan for all the contingences in life, I get blindsided and things go south. Even when I went to dinner with you last time, Lottie got sick. And look at the store. I jumped into being the proprietor because of Dad's accident. Granted I needed a job, but still, I jumped in without all the details." Her phone vibrated on the table and lit up. Sadie pounced on it, reading a message and quickly responded. Her shoulders relaxed, and a small smile spread across her face.

"They look happy." Sadie turned the phone around to show David a picture. Romee and Lottie filled the screen, both holding big forkfuls of mac and cheese, their mouths hanging open like they were ready to shove that food in.

Sadie placed the phone back on the table.

No wonder she seemed to carry so much on her shoulders. Did she not share any of her load with God? His heart pricked. He'd been doing the same thing though. By refusing to listen to what God was saying, by only considering Costa Rica as his future, he'd been playing the control game. "How do you bring God into the equation?"

"What do you mean? He's there with me."

Of course He was. "I guess. I mean, I've been doing something like that, too. With Costa Rica. Just asking for one answer and not wanting to hear anything else. Are you doing that? Just asking Him to bless your plans? How does His direction, His wants, come into play?"

"I listen." Her voice oozed with defensiveness. "But I've also learned how to manage on my own. Make plans and move forward. It works for us."

It didn't leave a lot of room for trust. But wasn't that what he was doing right now? And God had suddenly "unblessed" his path back to Costa Rica. Maybe Nate was on to something about God's will being something he needed to seek daily.

The waiter came and took their orders, leaving a breadbasket on the center of the table. David lifted his hand off his lap, but his fingers shook. No way would he chance knocking over her glass. Again. He laced his fingers together below the table. "Is it really working for you?"

Sadie lifted one shoulder. "I mean, I have Lottie. That's the biggest blessing I've ever gotten. But the path here has been bumpy. And it's not final until the adoption hearing in a few weeks. But I have planned for everything, so it should be fine."

He opened his mouth to question her further, but she tilted her head back and a nervous laugh bubbled out, and her cheeks turned that beautiful shade of pink. "This feels an awful lot like a first date."

David glanced at the breadbasket and her water glass. "First date jitters and all."

"The view is a little different this time." Sadie studied him, her gaze wandering from his hairline down to his shoulders.

The view had changed. She was even more beautiful than when they were younger.

"I look more and more like my dad." David slowly reached for a slice of bread when Sadie picked up her water for a drink. He set the bread on his plate, buttered it, and took a bite.

Sadie's teasing glint turned serious. "In all our years of dating, you've never mentioned your dad."

The bread sat on his plate. The first bite had been delicious, but it didn't hold any more appeal. "Probably because I don't like to talk about him."

Sadie stretched her arm across the table and squeezed his hand. Her warm, soft skin gentle and soothing. "Why?"

Her thumb made small circles on his hand, and he watched the movement. It would be easy to change the subject, and she'd let it drop. He released a breath.

If there would ever be a future between them, he had to start opening up, let her in. Talk about the things that shaped him. Sadie must have seen the resignation on his face, thinking he was shutting her out. She nodded sadly and slowly pulled her hand away.

But he stopped her movement by placing his hand on hers.

"That summer that Leah and Caroline went to stay with Nate's family, Mom and Dad were traveling. It was the summer before my senior year of high school. I stayed home for my summer job, and one day, a woman came by the apartment looking for my dad. She'd looked him up and found our address. When I asked how she knew my dad, she was surprised. Didn't seem to know he was married. She didn't say anything explicit, but I could read between the lines. She was my dad's mistress."

The waiter came and set their meals in front of them. They sat back, but as the waiter left, Sadie pushed her plate to the side, offering her hand. David intertwined their fingers again, and Sadie held tight. "I'm so sorry, David. I can't imagine."

David looked down, the memories coming fast. He gripped Sadie's hand, like a lifeline. He didn't like to walk down memory lane because the memories liked to pull him in, but with Sadie's hand in his, he had someone to ground him. "I debated if I should tell my mom. She'd been so excited to travel with my dad. The trip was to help them reconnect."

David could still see the haunted expression the confession had put on his mom's face. It had never left. "Mom was devastated when I told her, and I vowed never to think or talk about my dad again. But even so, there are times when I wish I wouldn't have told my mom."

"You can't say that. She needed to know."

"But if I hadn't told her, maybe they wouldn't have split. Maybe she wouldn't have gotten sick. The doctors said it was a virus, and her body just couldn't fight any more. But maybe if my dad was there, she would have had more reasons to live. More reasons to fight."

Sadie's hand tightened. "I think she would have wanted to know. Could you imagine the pain she would have experienced if she found out your dad was cheating and that you knew? You did the right thing."

David studied their hands, interwoven together on the table. A team, and one he wouldn't mind being on long-term. "I don't know what the future holds, Sadie. Without a spot to return to in Costa Rica..."

He had a few weeks to make a decision, and he needed to let his supporters know what he was going to do.

Sadie sat back in the booth. The lights behind her highlighted the colors in her hair as it hung over her shoulder. "So, you're working unpaid at Hoover's because..."

"The mission board wanted me to be involved in the community." But now? He wanted to be there for Sadie. Help her make a go of the store.

"If you're staying, you're going to need a paying job. I can't do that right now. You've seen the books."

"I'm not asking you to pay me. I'd like to continue on at the store. Maybe I could help you get the numbers back into the black, and then we could reconsider a paid position? Maybe you could pay me for a season then?" If he was still in Heritage. Not that he knew where else he would go. But he'd like to see how things worked out with Sadie. See if he could have a future here. "What if we plan a grand reopening? Perhaps for the weekend of the town festival. We could start advertising now—putting flyers in the windows, on the community boards around town, and even online. We can tell our regular customers, and it will be a Hoover's-has-new-management celebration."

"You know, it might work. That's just before I pay the bank the final payment. Maybe it could help push me over the top to have enough. Especially if people pay their tabs."

"Whatever you want to celebrate. I'll be there for it all." For Lottie's adoption, for meeting bills, for a grand reopening. For coffee over breakfast—Okay, maybe he was getting ahead of himself. That was too serious. He had a little time to pray about things, figure out what direction God wanted him to go. Until then, he'd like to continue to explore whatever was happening between him and Sadie. Maybe it was a second chance. Maybe it was God opening doors. Maybe it was David healing wounds he'd left in his wake.

Or maybe, just maybe, it was a chance for a new beginning.

ten

IF ONLY THE BEAUTY OF HER MOM'S SCRIPT AS she wrote out accounting problems could change the ugly bottom line in the red ledger. Sadie sat with her mom at her parents' house, looking over the books.

Her mom tapped her pencil on the table. "It's not that bad, really. We have three outstanding lines of credit that have now been paid in full."

Sadie closed her laptop. "True. And with those checks, we have almost a quarter of what we still owe the bank."

Her mom squeezed Sadie's hand. "And that's something. Closer than your dad has ever been. Between David's big sales and the checks coming in, I think we have a chance of making this deadline. And the grand reopening over the weekend of the fall festival? Genius."

All thanks to David. He'd made flyers and posted them all over town yesterday. There had already been a lot of buzz about the event. "You're not just saying that."

Her mom straightened her papers. "You know I wouldn't. I don't give false hope."

That she didn't. Her mom had been the one to tell Sadie to move on after David broke up with her. She'd been the one to tell her to hang on after Bonnie died, and she'd been there when Sadie had cried after Jeremy's death.

Her mom hadn't asked about dinner yet, but Romee had sent several texts and even brought Toby into the group messages. Now she had all of her siblings wanting details.

Her mom placed her elbows on the table and tucked her hands under her chin. "Please don't make me ask about your dinner."

Moms must have mind-reading abilities. Hopefully that would kick in when she was officially Lottie's mom. Sadie could hope.

"It was..." Dreamy. Romantic. Fun. Sadie stretched her fingers, remembering the feel of David's larger, more calloused hand on hers. "Educational. We talked about things we've never talked about. Maybe even hinted about a potential future."

"Good. You guys never were great communicators, and that's an important part of successful relationships. Be careful, honey. You've always loved that boy, we all did, and I only want you to be happy. David has grown into an incredible man. But be careful with your heart, because he shattered it once. And also, guard Lottie's. She talks about him a lot."

A good point. How could she protect Lottie, her own heart, and explore the possibility of a future with a man she'd once loved? Might still love. For now, they were friends who were exploring a potential future. No strings attached. Maybe that's why they hadn't kissed goodnight.

Sadie's phone vibrated on the table, and she picked it up. "Oh no. Mom! I totally forgot about my appointment with Meredith. My house is a mess."

"Lottie's social worker? You better run."

Sadie swiped the phone to answer. "Hi, Meredith. I'm across the street, and I'm on my way over. I'll be there in a jiffy."

Her mom waved her hand over the papers on the table. "Leave this. I'll bring them over in a while. You take care of Meredith."

Sadie hurried out of the house, straightening her shirt and hair as she jogged across Richard Street from her parents' house to the hardware store. She could see her dad and David through the glass talking with Colby Marc at the register. Colby and Madison had recently returned from a tour. She hadn't seen them since she moved home, but her mom had told her all about how the singer had moved to the small town and fallen in love with one of Heritage's very own girls.

She pulled up the group chat with her siblings. She needed to know someone would have her back, that they'd pray for her and support her. The group chat may have formed recently, but it had become something Sadie loved. She typed in a quick message and fired it off.

_____ Sadie
Forgot meeting with social
worker. My house is a mess!
Prayers needed.

Romee _____
You're a neat freak, it can't be
that bad. *Praying hands emoji.

Anna _____
What's that? A cereal bowl in the
sink? Oh no. *Shocked emoji.

Toby _____
I still don't know why I'm here, but
you've got this. Prayers.

Sadie tucked her phone away and fluffed her hair one more time as she walked around the back of the building and found Meredith

Coldbrug leaning against her silver Camry. "I'm so sorry. I let time slip away from me."

Meredith extended a welcoming hand and a warm smile that helped calm Sadie's racing pulse. "No worries. Things happen. I'm a little early."

Sadie glanced at her watch. Meredith wasn't early, but Sadie appreciated the gesture. Meredith had been a blessing since the court assigned her to Lottie. Always put together, the tall woman had an easy smile and a laid-back demeanor that quickly put Sadie at ease. Today she had her thick, white-blonde hair pulled into a soft Dutch braid and her burnt orange blouse tucked into black wide-leg pants with round ballet flats peeping out of the hem.

"Come on in." Sadie jogged up the stairs. Please, Lord, let the place not be as dirty as I remember. Sadie unlocked the door and pushed it open.

A welcoming, homey scent greeted her—at least the Gain-scented plug-ins were working. Sadie slipped off her shoes and did a quick once over. Breakfast dishes sat on the kitchen counter, and the pan she'd scrambled eggs in was still dirty on the stove. Blankets and pillows were strewn across the sectional sofa, and the Heritage clock was spread across her dining table in disarray. At least the boxes were all unpacked and gone. And hopefully, Lottie had made her bed this morning. Sadie hadn't checked.

"Would you like some coffee?" Sadie stepped into the kitchen to block the view of dirty dishes.

Meredith studied the apartment as she shook her head. "Just a glass of water if you don't mind."

Sadie filled two glasses with water and headed toward the sofa. "Sorry, it looks a little lived-in today."

Sadie picked up the throw blanket and folded it, making room for Meredith and trying to tidy up.

Meredith sat, placing her over-the-shoulder bag on the floor, and took a drink of her water. "Honestly? It's nice to see you settling in. The clock on the table has me mystified though."

Sadie hugged a throw pillow as she settled in next to the armrest of the sofa. "That's part of Lottie's history project. She's determined to see if she can get it working again. The number of YouTube videos we've watched..."

"Tell me how you're settling in after the move." Meredith opened her bag and pulled out a manila folder.

Leaning back, Sadie relaxed as much as she could "Lottie and I are comfortable here. Eventually I'd like to purchase our own place, but being so close to my parents and the store has its perks. And Lottie has made friends with a little girl, Lucy, who lives not far from here."

Sadie set her water down, her stomach in knots. She couldn't quite put her finger on it, but something wasn't right.

"Your parents live across the street? Lottie mentioned being able to visit regularly." Meredith glanced at the folder in her lap, but sipped her water, hiding any reaction Sadie could decipher.

"They do. And Lottie does check in over there often. My mom always has a cookie for her. Plus she's taking piano lessons from my mom, so she goes there to practice."

Meredith set her glass on the table. "Your setup is fantastic. This is just what Jeremy wanted for Lottie."

Meredith had met with Jeremy before he passed, when he and Sadie had started the adoption process. Over time, Sadie had been so thankful for Meredith in their life, keeping them focused and the process moving forward.

"He would have. But I sense a but from you. What's up?"

Meredith opened the folder on her lap and pulled out an official-looking document and handed it to Sadie. "Doris and Patrick have contested the adoption and petitioned for custody."

Words swam on the pages. Sadie blinked, trying, and failing, to clear her vision. Contest the adoption? Doris had threatened this.

But why now? Because Sadie had missed one phone call? Because Lottie came home with a stomach virus? Because David had been at the front door when Lottie came home?

"What can I do?" Sadie laid the paper in her lap. She'd have to read it later. Her throat tightened and she picked up her water glass, hoping maybe a sip would ease the tightness in her throat. It didn't.

"What you're doing—you have a steady job, a great apartment, and family surrounding you. You have the father's wishes behind you. You have Lottie in school, where she's thriving. She's participating in piano and ballet. I talked to the school today, and they said you requested Lottie's grades be sent in before the court date. You have crossed every t, dotted every i. I can't imagine the court not ruling in your favor. It's unfortunate that Doris and Patrick would contest, but I think you can work through it. Make sure your lawyer knows."

"What if—"

Meredith squeezed Sadie's hand. "Don't go there. You are prepared. Lottie loves you."

Sadie blinked quickly, but the tears ran down her cheeks. "And I love her. I can't lose her."

Lottie burst in the front door huffing, like she'd raced up the stairs. She threw her backpack on the floor and grumbled a bunch of unintelligible words. Then she kicked off her shoes and slammed the front door. "I hate it here. I wish we never moved here."

Sadie stood and rushed to the kitchen, blinking to clear her eyes as Lottie yanked open the refrigerator and grabbed the milk. Sadie took the milk from her and poured her a glass. Then she knelt in front of Lottie. "Hey. What happened?"

Lottie sniffed and chugged her milk. Then placed the glass in the sink with a bang. Sadie stood as Lottie stormed out of the kitchen. "Lucy was sick today. Tommy said my clock project was stupid and that there was no clock in the square. Jack said I made up the clock and that a paper on Otis would be way better. But I want to be different. Then I got my spelling test back. I missed 'frightened.' I know how to spell 'frightened.'"

Sadie followed her daughter as she headed toward her room. Lottie crossed the threshold and spun around. Her faced turned red as she hiccupped. "F-R-I-G-H-T-N-E-D."

The door slammed, echoing through the quiet apartment. It wouldn't do to tell Lottie she'd left out an e and really hadn't spelled the word correctly. The storm had finally hit, all the volatile emotions colliding. A tiny meow sounded from within the bedroom. Maybe Cuatro could calm her down.

Meredith cleared her throat, and Sadie hung her head, rubbing her forehead. Of course the social worker was here to see this. And no, Lottie hadn't made her bed today.

Sadie inhaled and exhaled before turning to face the ever-professional social worker. "I'm so sorry about that."

Meredith stepped forward. "You handled that like a champ. Kids have bad days. Do you mind if I talk to her?"

A sad chuckle escaped. "As long as you don't correct her spelling."

Meredith knocked on the door. "Wouldn't dream of it."

Lottie hollered an unfriendly, "Go away!" To which Meredith opened the door and peeped her head in. The nine-year-old brightened at the silly face and strange voice Meredith used as she stepped in the room.

Certain Lottie was in good hands, Sadie slipped back to the sofa to look at the paperwork.

She skimmed the words. Doris and Patrick wanted custody, claiming Sadie wasn't a disciplinarian and that she was unorganized.

It was a nightmare come to life.

But Meredith said Sadie had a lot going in her favor. She'd keep it that way. A happy little girl, glowing grades, well-adjusted with piano and ballet lessons. Not to mention Sadie had a support system in place with her parents across the street. They had a great apartment and the store—if she saved the store.

She would save the store. She had to.

Please, Lord, I try not to ask for much, but I'm asking for this. Let me keep Lottie.

Sadie had tried praying when Jeremy was sick, but it's like her prayers had gone unanswered. After his death, what little trust she still had disappeared. How could she let go and trust after God took Lottie's dad? Her best friend and husband? But in this moment, she could only hope that the Good Lord would hear her. That He would indeed step in. Because she needed all the help she could get.

Please.

⌐

Four hundred dollars and fifty cents—David ran the total in his head again just to make sure. It wasn't huge, but at least it was something. A bigger day than they'd had all week, and two more people had dropped off checks to pay off their lines of credit.

The sun sat low on the horizon as David slipped the key into the door of Hoover's Hardware to lock up. Children laughed as they played at the playground in the town square. And a game of soccer looked like it was in full tilt beyond the playground.

David checked his watch—five-thirty—he could probably join in before he made his way to the gym. Otis still sat by the playground, surrounded by children climbing him and sliding down his back.

The date last week had been great—or so he'd thought. He hadn't kissed her goodnight, but he'd wanted to. They'd talked—a lot. About important things. Maybe he'd misread all the signs. While things had been great in the store—larger than average sales, people paying their tabs—Sadie seemed...off. Distracted. Upset. She hadn't said what had happened, but David could see it in her shoulders, in the worry lines that had appeared. She put on a good face, but when she thought no one was looking, it was clear to see—something was wrong.

"Hi, Mr. Williams!" Lottie waved wildly and skipped toward him. "All done with work? What are you doing now?"

"Maybe joining that soccer game over there." David gestured to the square.

Lottie shook her head, placing her hands on her hips. "You need dinner. Come with me!"

Dinner with Sadie and Lottie? That was a big step. David glanced around. Dawn, Sadie's mom, stood on her front porch watching. Lottie must have been over there. He waved, and she did too.

"You can't say no, Mr. Williams. Mom's making spaghetti. It's my favorite." She spoke with just enough nine-year-old sass that David let her pull him up the stairs to Sadie's apartment.

"Spaghetti was your dad's favorite too. Every Friday night in college, he'd make a big batch in the dorm. Made the whole floor smell like garlic and oregano." David's stomach rumbled.

"And garlic bread?" Lottie slowed down as she looked back at David. "Daddy loved garlic bread."

"Of course. I always brought ice cream. A couple of the guys would bring pop or something. Your mom came too." David paused. Both Bonnie and Sadie had joined in those dinners.

"That's why Mom makes spaghetti on Fridays, but we don't have it every Friday." Lottie flung open the front door, and David was met with the overwhelming smell of garlic, oregano, and yeast—all the delicious scents of his memories. There was nothing quite as appealing as a homecooked meal. "Mom, I brought company."

"That's great, Lottie. Hi, Lu—" Sadie's words died as she stepped out of the kitchen. She had changed since she left the hardware store, and now she wore black leggings, which only highlighted her shapely legs. Her oversized maroon sweater hung off one shoulder—her soft, freckled shoulder.

"Hi, David." Her cheeks flushed a becoming pink, and she stepped closer to him, like she was glad to see him.

He stepped toward her, but Lottie spoke and reminded David they weren't alone.

"I'll go get Cuatro. He'll want to see you." Lottie skipped off toward the hallway.

Maybe he should have said no, because the moment Lottie left, Sadie's shoulders tightened, and the stress lines appeared again.

David leaned against the doorframe of the kitchen, watching Sadie as she moved about. Comfortable, confident, adorable. "I can go. I don't need to stay." But if she turned him out, he'd be making spaghetti at home, because the aroma of the cooked meat, garlic, Italian seasoning... Mouthwatering.

"It's fine you're here. I just would have made something nicer if I'd known. But if I remember correctly, you liked spaghetti, so make yourself at home." She dismissed him with a wave and stirred the sauce on the stove.

He made sure he spoke low so Lottie didn't hear. "Maybe it was just you I liked."

Sadie didn't respond, but by the way her neck reddened, he had no doubt she'd heard. He settled into the sofa. Or at least he tried. He pulled an oversized pillow out from behind him and settled against the blanket arranged behind it. At least she didn't have a gazillion pillows on the L-shaped couch.

His gaze drifted to the photos decorating the wall in a collage. He paused at the one of Bonnie and Jeremy holding who he could only assume was a newborn Lottie. There was a picture of Bonnie and Lottie at a lake, and another of Jeremy, Sadie, and Lottie at what looked like the same lake. His friend and his girl. He wanted to hate the picture, but he couldn't bring himself to. Instead, he was thankful they'd been there for each other during that season. They'd needed each other. For support. For comfort.

Lottie stood behind him and touched him on the head, then she crossed to the dining table and set the kitten on the table next to her.

"Mr. Williams, look." Lottie sat on her knees in a padded, navy pleather chair at the table, holding a flashlight over the old Heritage clock.

He stood up and joined her. "How goes the work on the clock?"

"I really think there's something in there. I think that's why the clock doesn't work. Although, how something dropped into the gears..." Lottie's tongue stuck out as she stilled and shined a flashlight into the clock open in front of her.

David peered into it. The insides were brass, similar to Otis. No wonder Lottie had tried to connect the two. And the gears all seemed to be in perfect order.

Lottie picked up a pair of tweezers and reached into the clock, squeezing past gears. David flexed his hand—there was no way his would fit in there.

Leaving Lottie to work, David stepped into the kitchen and immediately into Sadie's personal space. Wow, talk about a tiny room. "Can I help?"

"In my huge kitchen?" Sadie stretched her arms out and bumped him then gently pushed him out. "Thank you, but I've got it."

Sadie stepped out with him, her eyes landing on Lottie. A contented expression flashed across her face briefly before she pulled in her bottom lip and the wrinkles in her forehead deepened.

As David stood next to Lottie, Cuatro stretched up on his hind legs and put his front paws on his arm. He picked him up, and he snuggled into his chest. Cuatro had grown since he'd dropped him off a little over ten days ago. David scratched under the kitten's chin, and he purred, lifting his head so he could find the perfect spot.

Sadie watched him as she carried three glasses of ice water to the table, the weight of her gaze heavy, endearing. Time seemed to stand still.

David smiled. Hopefully, more smolder than goofy, but it must have worked, because Sadie's forehead relaxed.

She set the glasses down and turned to David. The spicy scent of her shampoo filled the space between them, and heat built in his chest as she stepped closer. He could reach out and touch her.

Except small paws pushed off David's chest, forcing him to step back.

He'd completely forgotten he held the kitten in his arms.

David tried to catch the cat, but the small ball of fur star-fished in midair only to land next to Lottie on the table, knocking one of the glasses of water over. Ice and water splashed, and Cuatro jumped out of the way, spraying water over Lottie and David.

Lottie jumped as the icy liquid coated her arm, and she dropped the flashlight and tweezers she'd been holding into the clock.

"Oh no!" Lottie's wail could raise all the alarms. She stood up quickly, knocking her chair over. "Cuatro! Look what you made me do."

She reached into the clock and picked up the flashlight, shining it inside the clock again.

"I dropped the t-t-tweezers into the clock. It will never work now." Lottie threw the flashlight on the floor, ran down the hall to her room, and slammed the door.

David picked up Cuatro and set him on the floor then retrieved the flashlight. The kitten quickly ran down the hall, heading into another room.

Sadie slipped back into the kitchen and returned with a dish towel and started cleaning up the spill. "I'm so sorry about your shirt."

David looked down at the water splotches across his chest. "I'd say we're even now, but this is only a few drops compared to the entire glass I dumped in your lap."

Sadie didn't laugh, but she nodded as she scooped the ice back into the glass. "Perhaps you're right."

David righted Lottie's chair and moved the clock, making sure there was no water underneath it. When they'd cleaned up the mess, David followed Sadie to the couch where she sank into it.

"I'm sorry." David sat next to her.

"Not your fault. Lottie's been having a lot of meltdowns lately," Sadie mumbled as she sank deeper into the corner of the couch, pulling her knees up to her chest.

"I probably didn't help matters. We talked about Jeremy on the way up. Grief can be difficult for anyone to handle. Especially a nine-year-old. Little things will trigger the pain." He placed his arm around Sadie's back and pulled her closer. She nestled into his side like she belonged. A comfortable silence lingered between them, until she inhaled, and her shoulders shivered.

"It's just so much more than that." Sitting up, she wiped at her face. "I'm sorry. I didn't mean to do this in front of you. There's just so much going on, and sometimes it's hard to hold it all together."

She scooted back, and the wall she'd built between them this week started coming back up. He had to stop it. He rested his hand on her upper arm. Rubbing up and down slowly. "You have a lot on your plate with the store. The grand reopening, the money due, and you're a single mom. You're allowed to feel overwhelmed. To ask for help."

Sadie let out a strangled laugh. "If that's all it was." She brushed at her cheeks again. A moment passed—it could have been longer—but he waited. His chest squeezed as time ticked by. He wanted her to open up. To let him in, but he couldn't force it. Couldn't make her want this relationship. Then, "I found out Doris and Patrick are contesting the adoption."

"What?" That couldn't be.

Sadie leaned back. Pulled her feet up, placed her arms on top of her knees. Lowered her head. She'd opened up but then physically backed away. David gently pulled her leg toward him.

Sadie's glassy eyes looked at him. His hand tightened on her calf. "This is garbage. They shouldn't contest your adoption. Do they have brains? Eyes in their heads? I've only been working at the hardware store for a month, and I know you are an incredible mother."

Sadie inhaled a shaky breath, and David ran his hand up to her knee and back to her ankle.

The muscles in her legs relaxed as David continued to run his fingers up and down. "I called my lawyer. He's not worried. Says it's an open-and-shut case. Not only do I have Jeremy's written wishes, but I have a job, a home, a support system. Lottie is thriving here. But, David—"

"No buts. None. Don't go down that path. You are a fantastic mother. The best that Lottie could have." David rubbed his hand up and down her calf again, the soft material of her leggings like butter.

Sadie relaxed under his touch, even as she shook her head and wiped her face. "I'm not Bonnie. She was such an incredible mother. Confident, calm, loving."

"And so are you. You might not be Lottie's birth mom, but you will make sure that little girl grows up knowing that not only did her birth parents love and adore her, but you do, too. Look at these photos on the wall." David gestured to the photos on the wall behind him. "Look at all the people who love her. She will grow up knowing that kind of love."

Sadie closed her eyes and let her head fall back on the couch.

"Thank you." Sadie lifted her nose in the air and sat up. "Do you smell that?"

David inhaled. "Smoke?"

"Oh no!" Sadie scrambled to her feet and raced to the kitchen.

David followed right behind her. Light gray smoke filled the air and Sadie pulled a dish towel out of a drawer and waved it in the air.

David opened the front door, and a breeze rushed in. Sadie turned the air vent over the stove up and opened the oven door.

The garlic bread sat on the cookie sheet, completely charred. She pulled it out and set it on the stove. A nervous laugh hiccupped out of her.

Not good. David shoved his hands in his pockets, unsure what to do. Comfort her? Hug her? Escape out the front door?

"This is rich. I can't even cook dinner...how on earth am I supposed to care for a little girl? Maybe Doris is right? I mean, the store is crumbling, and if I fail, I lose everything. My home, my job, my income, my savings." Sadie pinched the bridge of her nose. Laughter and tears mixed together.

David wrapped his arms around Sadie, pulling her into a tight hug. She clung to him as her breath puffed on his neck. She snuggled closer, her breath calming, evening out, and her body relaxing.

Was this what home felt like? Because in this moment, David could see a future, different than anything he'd imagined before, but one where he could step in and support this incredible woman. Where he'd have the right to offer her comfort like this and so much more.

"I'm here, Sadie. Whatever you need." It was lame. Her entire life hung in the balance. What could he really offer her? "Seriously, just say the word. More hours in the store? Consider it done. A written recommendation? I can do that. The tweezers out of the clock? I'll figure out how to get it working."

Somehow, he'd solve the clock problem. Someone had to know something about clocks. He'd ask around.

"For right now"—Sadie tightened her hands around his back—"this is enough."

David closed his eyes and rested his cheek on the top of her head. He could stay here as long as she wanted. He didn't want to be anywhere else.

Eventually, Sadie stepped out of his embrace. She wiped her face once more with a nervous chuckle. "I'm sorry about that."

"Don't be. Not with me."

She turned away from him and dumped the bread in the trash. "What now?"

"We could make more bread." David eyed the loaf of fresh bread.

"No, I mean for you. If you aren't going back to Costa Rica, then what will you do next?"

Wasn't that the question of the month? "I don't know."

"You could stay?" She held his gaze. "In Heritage."

With her?

It wasn't the time to ask. Especially after tonight. The time he'd spent holding her in his arms, comforting her—it sure made staying in Heritage appealing.

Sadie started filling a plate with spaghetti and topped it with meat sauce and then handed it to David. "I'm sure your sisters would love to have you stay. Free babysitting and all."

"Free babysitting?"

"Please tell me you take the kids sometimes. Come on, Uncle David, step up." She held out the plate.

Maybe it was time to think about Heritage as home and the potential future here.

He accepted the plate full of spaghetti, sans garlic bread, a shy smile on Sadie's face—Heritage might have some perks he hadn't considered before.

eleven

"I DON'T UNDERSTAND WHY WE HAVE TO GO." LOT-tie's whine could shatter glass. And it had been nonstop since Sadie had convinced Lottie to pack up the dolls to go to David's to play with Vangie, rather than play at home together. Not to mention that she'd answered the same question five times already. Not even reminding Lottie about the kittens left at David's place had stopped the questions from coming. Over and over.

But when David called with panic in his voice, Sadie had felt a smidge of guilt. After all, she had cajoled him about babysitting his nieces just two nights ago.

When she'd asked if he'd consider staying in Heritage, he hadn't shut down the option. He also hadn't enthusiastically said he wanted to stay with her. Not that she was ready for that, but maybe she wanted to know if it was a possibility.

At least David had called after she had made the reservations to go stay at the lake house that Jeremy loved after the adoption hearing. "You know we can take the dolls on our trip and have a few days just you and me to play."

That seemed to do the trick, because Lottie grabbed Sadie's seat and shook it. "I can't wait! We'll get to see the leaves. Daddy loved the colorful leaves."

Fall had always been Jeremy's favorite season. Lottie had mentioned the leaves several times lately, and visiting the lake house would give them time away to enjoy some fall foliage and a way to celebrate the adoption.

"Look, Lottie. We're here." The car bounced along the dirt driveway until Sadie parked in front of the old farmhouse. "Maybe Mr. Williams will still have a kitten you can play with."

"I'm really good with the kittens, Mom."

Sadie opened the car door and was met with the cries of a baby—maybe two—and blaring music. The noise intensified as they jogged to the front door. Vangie, her long hair loose and tangled around her face, pushed open the screen door to let them in. As soon as they were inside, she ran back to the couch and jumped up on the cushions, singing. Becca sat on the floor, crying. Snot ran down her face, and her cheeks were tinged red.

Lottie let go of Sadie's hand and ran to jump on the couch with Vangie.

Sadie shook her head and stepped away. She turned the volume of the music way down. She picked up the toddler on the floor. The little girl instantly buried her face in Sadie's sweater. The snotty-clothes phase wasn't one Sadie missed, but Becca's sobs turned into quiet, shuddered breaths almost instantly. "Lottie, why don't you show Vangie the dolls you brought."

A quick cheer sounded, and the girls sat on the floor while Lottie opened her backpack. The toddler in Sadie's arms snuggled closer.

David walked out of the kitchen, a bottle in hand, and a very angry, very loud baby in his arms. His hair stood up straight.

The little girl snuggled into Sadie as she walked toward David.

David silently pleaded for help. The guy was out of his comfort zone. "I might blame you for this. I shouldn't have offered to watch the girls. I don't know anything about babies."

"You can do this."

He shook his head. "You had this room calmed in seconds. I couldn't calm Becca and Isabella at the same time. And Isabella won't take her bottle. I don't know what she wants. I checked her diaper. I've walked and bounced and snuggled and changed positions. Nothing has helped."

Sadie ran a hand down the back of Becca's head. "Where's Isabella's Binky?"

David blinked. "Her what?"

"Her pacifier?"

"Oh! In her diaper bag." David handed Sadie the bottle and hurried from the room. He returned with a pink pacifier and a still screaming baby. "She won't take it."

"She's too worked up. Put it in her mouth and hold it for just a second. See if she will start to suck on it." Sadie watched as he did as she instructed, lightly holding it in place. Then the baby calmed as she sucked on it.

The room quieted, and David's wide shoulders relaxed. The same shoulders that had held her and comforted her Friday night.

David stepped closer, his clean scent mixing with baby powder, his shoulder bumping Sadie's. "Thank you. I don't know what I would have done without you. I told my sisters I'd be happy to give them a date night like you suggested, but I didn't expect for everyone to fall apart at the same time. You saved me."

"I didn't do much." Sadie shifted Becca to the other hip.

"Don't downplay it. Without you being here, Isabella would still be screaming. Becca would still be in tears, and Vangie would continue to turn the volume of the music up even louder because she couldn't hear it over the cries of everyone else. I might've even joined in the sobbing before long."

David sat on the couch, and Sadie handed him Isabella's bottle back. "She may want this now that she's calmed down some. Babies won't always take a bottle if they are too worked up, especially if she normally nurses."

With a hesitation in his motions, David tugged the Binky out of Isabella's mouth and quickly replaced it with the bottle in hand. Sucking noises filled the blessed quiet.

David motioned, and Sadie sat next to him. Becca uncurled herself from Sadie to crawl over to David and snuggled into his side.

Sadie ran her hands down her sweater, noticing the stains Becca had left. Thankfully, they'd wash out. With the older girls happily playing on the floor and Becca snuggling David, Sadie excused herself to freshen up. Just before she left the room, she turned back and snapped a picture of the happy group. David's sisters would want to see this.

So would hers for that matter. She sent it off.

> **Romee** _____
> *gif of Bugs Bunny with heart eyes.
>
> Girl, that looks serious. Are you practicing for the future?

> **Toby** _____
> I don't understand why you'd send this to me.
>
> Clara says awwww.

Sadie tucked her phone in her pocket and stepped into the kitchen to scrub at the spot on her shirt and then wash her hands before returning to the group, where she found David with his back against the couch, his legs stretched in front of him, with Isabella nestled in her blankets resting on his thighs. His bare feet stuck out in front—there was something in his pose that made the moment feel casual, yet intimate. Becca sat on one side of David, holding one of Lottie's dolls. Lottie sat on David's other side, her back against his side. He had his arm around her shoulder. Vangie sat in front of Lottie as they played with the dolls.

The picture of perfection. Sadie pulled out her phone again and snapped another picture. Who wouldn't? Besides, Leah and Caroline would eat this up.

And she'd want to see this picture again, more than just in her dreams. She'd want to remember that for a few brief moments in life, David Williams had needed her. That they'd come together as a team outside the hardware store.

David looked up, the look on his face doing funny things to her insides. Longing for this kind of moment, for a home, a husband who looked at her the way Jeremy had always looked at Bonnie, for children of her own...it struck with a ferocity that took her breath away.

Sadie had given up the dream of a big family when Jeremy had been diagnosed with Machado-Joseph disease. But David watched her with the same kind of look Jeremy had in his eyes when he talked about Bonnie. Sadie would give up all her Sunday afternoon naps to have moments like this—maybe even in this house, with this man.

"Thank you." David mouthed the words to her, but she shook her head. She hadn't done much. Quieted anxious children. He'd kept them calm, made them happy, and loved them.

"Come play, Mom." Lottie patted the floor next to her.

Sadie's throat tightened, but she nodded and made her way over to the girls, sitting across from David, her back to the loveseat. She stretched her legs out, and David's bare foot tapped her ankle.

Feet were supposed to be gross, hairy, smelly things. Not a conduit that could turn a simple touch into something so cozy. So affectionate. So...intimate.

Becca stood up on wobbly legs but quickly waddled to Sadie, plopping on her lap. The little girl snuggled into Sadie, still brushing the doll's long black hair.

A few hours later, when Caroline and Leah returned, the girls were all asleep. Lottie and the kittens—Tres and Cinco—included.

The house was blessedly quiet.

"Oh my!" Leah whisper-yelled. "Look at how cozy you are."

Grant and Caroline walked forward and carefully picked up their girls.

Leah packed up the diaper bag before returning to take Isabella from David. "Did you guys enjoy practicing for the future?"

Sadie rubbed her cheeks to hide her humor. She didn't need to encourage Leah, but sisters all thought alike.

David just shook his head, saying something to Leah as she picked up the baby, which made her laugh. Thankfully, they were able to leave without waking Lottie. She must have really worn herself out playing with Vangie this afternoon.

David and Sadie walked his sisters to the front door and waved goodbye from the porch while Lottie slept on. After his sisters' cars drove out of sight, David wrapped his arms around Sadie's waist and pulled her into a hug.

His clean, masculine scent, his hands splayed on her back—completely captivating. Sadie relaxed, savoring the feel of David's warmth pressed against her.

"I couldn't have survived today without you. Thank you." David's soft, deep rumble rolled through her body.

"There were a few bumpy moments, but it ended strong. You were great with the girls. Lottie, too." Sadie stepped back, needing space. Because this barefoot man had held a baby all afternoon while playing dolls with three little girls until they had all fallen asleep. And she liked it. Liked him.

But David didn't let her go far, his hands tightening on her waist, stopping her retreat.

"It ended strong because you were here. You helped. You always make things better." David's hand cupped her cheek, his calloused palm steady as she leaned into it.

David bent down slightly, resting his forehead against hers. She enjoyed his closeness. His clean scent mixed with baby powder and caramel candies. His familiarity, the newness of the situation, the excitement of his touch.

Slowly, Sadie lifted her hands and rested them on David's chest. It had become so solid. So strong. The kind of constant strength that could support a girl. A family.

"Sadie?" David's breath tickled her face.

"Hmm?" She couldn't quite find words to say.

"If you keep touching me like that, I'm going to kiss you."

Sadie's hands stilled.

What had she been doing?

Her hands on his chest twitched and itched with the desire to move. Again.

David dipped his head to make eye contact as heat climbed her neck. "I'd like to. Okay?"

Okay? It might not be okay if he kept looking at her like that. Her heart picked up speed, and her breath turned short and shallow. If he looked at her like that much longer, she might kiss him. Sadie lifted her face up toward him and hummed agreement.

She closed her eyes in anticipation. David's gentle breath heated her face for a heartbeat, the desire to close the distance almost overwhelming. But this moment couldn't—shouldn't—be rushed. A shiver raced down her spine as she waited.

His body leaned closer still, his nose brushing against hers. It would be so easy to close the gap. Instead, she let the intensity of the moment build. A warm hand slid down her back, tucking her even closer.

Finally, finally, David's lips pressed against hers.

Fireworks exploded behind her eyes. Her body trembled, relishing the gentle pressure of David's hand on her lower back and the one on her face. His touch was featherlight, like the pressure on her lips.

Kissing David was better than she remembered. Better than she dreamed...because after the almost good-night kiss on her doorstep, David's kisses had a starring role in her dreams.

In that moment, the front porch faded away, the concerns of the day gone, worry over the store and money nonexistent. There was only David. The feel of his lips as they moved against hers. He tasted of root beer and caramel candy. Delicious and sweet. The tender exploration of her mouth made her feel treasured and... loved.

She kissed him back with all the longing the day had built up. With all the hope of a future, of a family, of love, and of home.

David pressed her closer, erasing what little space remained between them. A wave of electricity coursed through her body. His fingers wove through her hair as he deepened the kiss. His strong arms familiar and reassuring, new and exciting. His hands confident, and achingly tender.

Sadie slid her arms from his chest and around his neck, running her fingers up into his hair.

A moan escaped from David, and he slowed the kiss, gently moving to Sadie's jaw and up to her ear. He hummed a sound of appreciation that caused goosebumps to race over her skin. She shivered as he worked his way back to her mouth, gently kissing her lips. Once. Twice. A third time he lingered, before he loosened his grip on her back.

Thankfully, he didn't let go, because Sadie's legs wouldn't hold her up.

David's fingers gently moved down her neck, to her shoulder, and then her arm. "Wow."

That wow had stuck with her. Because thirty minutes later, as Sadie tucked a still sleeping Lottie into her own bed, she could still feel the effects of the kiss down to her toes. Wow, indeed.

She pulled out her phone and saw a bunch of messages she'd missed from her siblings.

Anna
_____

Brock and I broke up today. I
think it's for good this time.

Toby
_____

Good. He's a loser and you can
do better.

Romee
_____

Ouch, Bro. Way to speak your
mind there.

I'm sorry, Anna. Even if Brock
is a loser. Toby's right, you can
do better.

Anna
_____

This time I'm not taking him back.
Leopards don't change their
spots, neither do guys.

Toby
_____

Hey now, we're not all bad.

Anna
_____

*Gif of a little girl sticking out
her tongue.

Anna
_____

Sadie, let this be a lesson to you.
Don't follow in my footsteps.

Sadie tucked her phone away. What could she say? She didn't
want to share her happiness when Anna was hurting. But what if
Anna was right and heartbreak was the only future they had? But
they'd talked things through. The heartbreak in their past was both
of their faults, and they weren't the same people anymore. They'd
changed, hadn't they?

Sadie touched her lips, the heat of David's touch still warming her skin. Anna had to be wrong. There was no way he would kiss her like that if heartbreak was their future.

David's truck bumped down the dirt driveway of Chet Anderson's house Monday morning before work, the old clock carefully packed in a box secured in his truck bed. Hopefully, Jon hadn't given David bad information, or this trip out to see if Chet could fix the clock would be a complete waste of time.

Thoughts of yesterday's kiss with Sadie still stole his breath and left him wanting to find reasons to do that again. Hopefully, coming through with a repaired clock would earn him some brownie points, and maybe a few more of those kisses.

David's truck bounced to a stop in front of a farmhouse that had seen better days. The fresh paint and fairly new shutters couldn't hide the age of the place. A shack of a barn with a large barn door sat next to the house. Jon had told David that if he wanted something from Chet to bring biscuits and gravy. Thomas had accommodated the request and placed the order in a to-go container.

David held the to-go breakfast and knocked on Chet's door. A bunch of grunting, banging, and grumbling came from within the house before the older man opened it. Chet's wild gray hair stood up on end, and the man looked over David's shoulder at his truck. He held out his hand and gestured for the food. "Why'd you bring me this? What do you want?"

David handed over the container. "Jon said you might know how to fix an old clock."

Chet opened the takeout box and nodded. Then closed it tight, raising an eyebrow at David. "Why would Jon think I know anything about clocks?"

That was the question of the day. "I have no idea. But I don't know anything about clocks, and Jon didn't have any other suggestions, so I figured I'd hunt you down."

Chet narrowed his gaze at David then looked down at the biscuits and gravy. "Since you brought me my favorite meal, I guess I'll take a look. Take it to the barn over there. I'll set this down and meet you in there."

That was Chet. Gruff and to the point.

David backtracked to his truck to retrieve the clock and returned, letting himself into Chet's barn, which was surprisingly neat. A large workbench sat on one side, filled with an assortment of tools that would make any hardware store owner proud. Sadie would love this space.

David set the box on the bench next to a collection of little tools he'd never seen before. The area was practically dust free.

Chet ambled into the barn and used the workbench for support. "Tell me about this clock of yours."

"I found this in my grandpa's barn a few weeks ago."

Chet tapped the side of the box. "Take this thing out of the box for me, will ya?"

David pulled the clock out and set it down.

Chet scratched his chin. "It rattles."

David nodded. "Yeah, about that. Lottie was looking at the gears, but she dropped her tweezers inside. We can't get them out. And Lottie's pretty convinced one of the gears is jammed."

Chet grabbed some magnifying glasses and some tools wrapped in leather that he spread out next to the clock.

"You don't have to stand there and watch me. You'll make me nervous."

David backed up, and Chet expertly opened the clock as he whistled like it was any other day.

"Do you see the watchmaker's logo there?" David stepped up to the workbench. "Lottie says she found a similar marking on Otis, near his back side. I couldn't see it when she showed me, but she's convinced they're connected somehow."

Chet didn't even spare David a glance, simply continued using sharp-looking tools David had never seen before to twist and test each gear. "You wouldn't happen to know if they were connected—the clock and Otis?"

"Don't know. I don't reckon I've seen this clock in person. Seen pictures but not the actual thing. How'd it end up in your grandpa's barn?"

"That's a mystery that will continue, I suppose."

"Like Otis." The man harrumphed. "So, tell me. What's going on between you and Lottie that you're here with the clock and not her."

"Nothing is going on. Lottie's nine." David shoved his hands in his pockets and took a step backward.

"So, this is about her mother." Chet stood up and pushed his glasses on top of his head, his older eyes squinting at David.

"I offered to help. Sadie's got a lot on her plate."

"Sadie? I've heard that name recently. Is that Gary's girl? She got married."

David nodded, and when Chet glared at David, he held up his hands. "She's widowed now."

Chet hummed. "Sorry to hear that. I take it you're helping out, hoping to fill her late husband's spot."

David hadn't anticipated that being thrown out. Fill her late husband's spot? Way to make it sound morbid. Marriage, though... he hadn't actually thought that far ahead. Stay in Heritage? Sadie's words, the look in her eye, the way she'd kissed him last night— he'd like it to be in his future. Not that he'd admit that to Chet.

"Sadie and I share a history. I'm here now and can help. That's what I'm doing."

Chet took David in, watched him, like he was measuring David's words. Uncomfortable though it was, David stood his ground. Didn't break eye contact.

Chet must have found something though, because a rough smile broke out across his face. "I'll call you when I'm done. I don't like working with people staring down my back. And you better figure out a way to tell that girl you love her."

David took a step back. Confess his love? "It may be too soon to call it that."

"Look, David, I may be old, but I'm not dumb. I've got eyeballs and ears. You wouldn't be here if you didn't love her. And it's about time, boy. You've been running from love for as long as I've known you. Now git. I got work to do."

"Thanks, Chet." David didn't know about running from love, but he'd gladly 'git' from this conversation.

"David?" Chet's voice rang out as David stepped outside the barn.

He poked his head back in. "Yeah?"

"Don't go hurting that girl again. But as I see it, if you're to put this much effort into helping her daughter out, there must be more going through your mind. If Sadie makes you happy, don't bungle your chance with her. You hear me, boy?"

David knocked on the barn door. "I hear ya."

Then he hightailed it for his truck. Because no matter what else Chet had to say, he was right. There were feelings involved. Strong feelings he wasn't ready to name.

David tossed the truck into reverse and hurried over the bumpy road. He had a job to get to, and Sadie would be waiting for him.

twelve

THREE DAYS WITHOUT A SALE.

Could that even be real?

Sadie stood inside the empty store. The floors practically glowed after she mopped them, not a single dust bunny or cobweb could be found, but even with satisfaction of a job well done, the looming bank deadline flashed in her mind like a blinking neon sign.

Outside the store, children played across the street. A huge soccer game that David had watched through the window. When a couple of teens had stopped by to see if he would come play after he finished, Sadie had pushed him out the door. With no business, and the store clean, there had been no point in making him stay cooped up inside.

David passed the ball to someone who shot and made a goal. The two high-fived and a small celebration took place.

This could be life—in five years. Ten even. Working the store together, enjoying life together. The key word: together.

Maybe even a few kids of their own.

Lottie played on the playground, running with Lucy around the swing set in what looked like a game of tag.

Sadie settled onto a stool behind the register, pulled her phone out, and opened the group chat with her siblings. Funny how they'd never had a group before, but since they'd started texting, it had become so easy to share things with them.

Sadie

Three days without a sale.

Romee

Good thing you've got eye candy working for you.

Anna

Or not. Remember he broke your heart once. He can do it again.

Romee

*gif of the witch from Princess Bride shouting "Boo!"

Don't be such a spoilsport, Anna. Besides, you haven't seen David after all these years. *hot emoji.

Toby

Gross. I did not need to know that.

Sadie

We've both changed. Things are different now. But that's not why I messaged. Focus on the problem—no sales.

Romee

*gif of two penguins wearing hats saying, "I'm sorry."

Anna
_____

I can place an order. One
hammer, please.

Sadie tucked her phone away. Obviously, they wouldn't be able to help with sales, but it did help that she could talk to them.

The welcome bell jingled, and Sadie's breath caught—could it finally be a customer? She turned toward the door. Nope, not a customer, just her mom.

"Oh, don't look so thrilled to see me."

Sadie stepped out from behind the register and hugged her mom. "It's not that. It's just been super slow today."

Her mom shook her phone. "I heard. Anna said she needed a new hammer and I had to come buy it right now. Right now. She was very emphatic."

Her mom's phone chimed as a message from Anna popped up. After opening the message, she typed a response to Anna while Sadie went and picked up a hammer—the one she carried to appeal to women—a pink floral grip on the handle and pink metal for the head.

"Here, let's send photographic evidence you're here." Sadie pulled out her phone and stepped close to her mom, holding the hammer between them, and snapped a selfie. She sent it to her siblings.

_____
Sadie

Finally made a sale after three
days. Thanks, Anna. *laughing
emoji *golden heart emoji.

Anna
_____

I'll pay for shipping. Just have her
drop it in the mail for me.

Sadie chuckled. Even with her broken—and slightly bitter—heart, Anna was trying to help out.

Her mom walked toward the register and pulled out some cash.

"I can't believe she really wants a hammer." Sadie chuckled as she handed her mom her change.

"You've been busy in the store even if you haven't made a sale." Her mom looked around the shop.

"Until a few hours ago. Now I'm just watching Lottie at the playground." Sadie's cheeks heated as she motioned outside. Of course, her mom would see the bigger picture.

Her mom turned to look out the window and then bumped Sadie's shoulder. "Or David playing soccer."

"It doesn't hurt. He's so good with those teen boys."

"I ran into Hannah at the grocery store yesterday, and she was telling me David's been helping Jimmy out at the gym, too. Her son just adores David. I wonder if he could be content working with the kids at church?" Her mom's voice trailed off.

The church had grown since Nate took over as pastor. And the youth group had grown, too. Maybe David could help out there. Maybe he could be happy in Heritage.

With her.

Of course, she came as a package deal with Lottie included. But so far, David had worked well with Lottie, and the girl clearly adored him.

David stopped the ball with his foot and then kicked it to another teen. She really should learn the teens' names, but with no teen volunteers in the store, she hadn't needed to. But if David stayed around, she could help out with him. Be a team, not just at the store, but in life. In service. David ran forward, and then the kid passed the ball back to David, but David slid, his leg going out from under him, and he rammed into Otis.

Sadie's breath caught. That had to hurt.

"Oh dear." Her mom brought her hand to her mouth.

Sadie waited for David to jump up, shake it off. But instead, the boys ran over and knelt in front of him. Lottie jumped off the swing and ran over to David, too.

"Honey, why don't you go check on him." Her mom propelled her toward the door. "I'll watch the store. If you think you need to take David to the doctor, send Lottie back here, and I'll get her to ballet and have your dad close up shop. Now go!"

"Thanks, Mom." Having support made such a difference. The bell jingled as Sadie pushed open the door and crossed the street. The teen boys backed up as she jogged closer and knelt next to David. His brows crinkled even though he laughed at something one of the guys said. His face had lost its usual color, and his shoulders were rigid.

Lottie sat next to him and patted his shoulder. "It's gonna be okay, Mr. Williams. Otis is fine. See? He doesn't even look sore."

Be still her heart. That might be the sweetest and craziest thing Lottie had ever said.

Lottie stood up and Sadie gripped her hand. "It's time to get ready for ballet. Oma is in the store—can you run see her?"

Her daughter kissed her on her cheek and skipped off to the store.

She lowered her voice and leaned in close so the teen guys wouldn't hear—since he was putting on such a casual face in front of them. "You okay?"

He shook his head slightly, but his resolve was clear. "Can you help me stand up?"

She nodded as she stood and offered him a hand. She pulled him up as he balanced on one leg. He turned to the guys and offered his fists. Several of the boys bumped knuckles, or whatever they called it, and David waved them off, telling them he was fine and that he'd just sit out the rest of the game. All while balancing on one leg.

The guys ran back to the game, and David's entire demeanor changed. His shoulders fell, and the pain he'd been hiding from the guys etched across his brow. Sadie slid her arm around his waist to support him as he hobbled off the field.

Sadie got him to her car, which she'd left on the street earlier. "Let me take you to the doctor and get that checked."

David shook his head. "If I take some time, maybe some pain meds, it will be fine."

"Don't be like that. It hurts bad enough you needed me to help you cross the street."

"Lottie—"

"Mom's in the store, and she'll take care of Lottie. Dad's going to close up tonight." Sadie knew the moment he decided to go along with her request because he relaxed and gave a single, short nod. She opened the passenger door for him. "Let me go grab my purse. I'll be right back."

When Sadie returned to the car, David sat with the door open. His face was even more pale than before.

She closed the passenger door and jogged around to the front of the car. A short while later, she pulled into the ER parking lot, thankfully finding a spot right next to the door. She looked over at David sleeping. She placed her hand on top of his and squeezed.

He inhaled as his eyes fluttered open. "I'm sorry, I didn't mean to fall asleep."

Sadie brushed his hair off his forehead. "You needed it. We're here now. Do you want me to go get a wheelchair to get you in?"

David shook his head. "No. I'll walk."

To say he was stubborn would be an understatement. Sadie tucked herself under his arm, and with her help, they managed to make it into the ER. Thankfully, the afternoon was slow, and they were seen quickly.

David sat on the exam table in the room they'd been placed in after he'd been taken for X-rays. She pulled the hard, plastic chair next to him and sat down. He offered her his hand, and she quickly interlaced their fingers.

Warmth radiated up her arm as his thumb circled the back of her hand. He'd held on to her since they got here, except during the X-rays, giving Sadie as much comfort as she hoped she could offer him.

"Hey, now." David tugged her to standing and guided her in front of him. She stepped between his knees and his arm wrapped around her waist, pulling her a little closer. "Thank you for bringing me to the ER and staying with me."

Sadie relaxed in his embrace, his warmth seeping into her frozen body. ER rooms always ran so cold. She inhaled David's clean, soapy scent, happy to block out the sterile fumes.

"I'm sorry, David." His hand ran down her spine and back up, stopping between her shoulder blades, pressing her close.

"Not your fault." His hand slowed and pressed her closer still.

"No. It's not my fault you tripped over the town's lovable statue."

David shook his head. "I hardly tripped over Otis."

"Then what? Your own foot?" Sadie let her arms rest on his shoulders, her hands playing with his thick hair at the nape of his neck.

"Not my finest move." He puffed out a small laugh.

"I'll say."

"Hey now." David pushed her back a little as he brought one hand to his chest. "You wound me."

"You do that to yourself."

He tucked a loose strand of hair behind her ear. Sparks fluttered across her skin, and her breath caught. "Sadie...I want..."

Me. Say it, please. She held her breath, waiting for his next words.

Silence stretched between them as he studied her. A million possibilities, but they'd made promises the first time around. The pain of those broken dreams was almost more than she could bear the first time. Maybe it would be better not to say things that would make another break up even more painful. "Let's not make promises, instead, let's enjoy today."

David shook his head. "I can't do that."

He tugged her a little closer, and she melted against his warm frame. Buried against him, she let a little bit of her fear slip out. "I'm not sure what you mean. Why can't you?"

A deep rumble sounded in David's chest. Great, she'd made him laugh. She pushed off him, but David caught her hands, keeping her close. "Because you are strong. Independent. A single mom. You've taken over your family business. You have come through the fire, and you're even more irresistible than I remember. I'm not playing around, and I want to make sure you know it." David cupped her face, his fingers tangling into her hair, his thumb brushing her cheek. His eyes darkened and dropped to her lips. Oh, sweet mercy.

"What are you saying?" She held her breath. David pulled her closer still, and the heated look he gave her warmed her from the inside out.

A knock sounded and Sadie jumped back.

"I'm here. For you and with you. We'll talk more later." David winked at her. "Come in."

Sadie sat back in the plastic chair next to him. She slipped her hand into his. She might not know what the future would hold, but he was here. Right now. Could this moment be enough? If she didn't at least try, she'd never know.

The doctor opened the door and walked in, reviewing David's file.

"Hello, David. I've got the results of your X-ray."

David's ankle protested as he shifted on the chair at his kitchen table a few hours later. His foot was propped up on a pillow with an ice bag on the chair in front of him. At least it wasn't broken.

A simple sprain. The trip to the ER had been a total waste of time—except the time with Sadie hadn't been a waste. He'd told her he wasn't playing around, and he meant every word. The doctor had wrapped his ankle and gave him some pain medication and anti-inflammatories—since his ankle had swollen up to the size of a small melon.

Sadie had stopped for takeout next to the ER, but it had cooled off on the drive home. She stood at the stove, heating things up again.

"You could just microwave it," David said, his stomach rumbling. Lunch was hours ago, and he would have eaten dinner cold.

Sadie shook her head and threw him a playful look. "I'll have you know, that after we finished college and I moved to Grand Rapids, I became a whiz at reheating my Chinese takeout. Don't mess with my skills. Besides, you're finally home. Chill, okay?"

She turned back to the skillet, and David couldn't deny the sweet and tangy scents were making his mouth water. But stale bread sounded appetizing at this point.

His phone rang in the other room, and Sadie put down the wooden spatula she'd found next to the stove. "I'll go get that for you. Don't move."

David yawned. What a day. The pain medication was working, and his bed called to him. Not that he'd give up this time with Sadie. Especially since she hadn't pushed him away when he'd told her he wanted more.

His stomach rumbled again. He wouldn't give up the food either.

Sadie walked back in with his cell still ringing. Lance. The call went to voicemail before David could answer.

"You can call him back." Sadie picked up the wooden spoon and started dishing up the chicken chow mein.

Not with food coming. Lance could wait. "He'll leave a message or call back. I'm with my girlfriend."

His phone pinged a voicemail notification. His hand itched to check it. He hadn't lied to Sadie when he said he would be there for the court date. For the grand reopening. He wanted to be here for those things. And if this call was finally letting him know he'd been cleared to return? He'd set the date for next month.

"Girlfriend?" Sadie walked toward the table, two plates in hand, and placed one before him.

"We're not too old for that term, are we?" He caught her hand and pulled her down so he could brush his lips across hers.

"I don't think we are."

He kissed her again, quick and fast before she returned to the cupboard for two glasses and filled with them water.

His mouth was suddenly dry. Before he'd started working at the hardware store, he'd waited for Lance's call. Convinced the next would be the one to deliver the news that he could return to Costa Rica.

Now? Now the thought of returning—the thought of leaving Sadie—soured his stomach.

Sadie set a glass of water in front of him, and he gulped it down.

"I didn't realize you were so thirsty. You should have said something." She refilled the glass and sat next him, settling her hand on his. "You can call him back or listen to the voicemail. I can step out for a moment."

"No. I'd rather eat with you. That call will be there later." He flipped his hand over and intertwined their hands. He needed the extra contact, the security of her gripping his hand.

David blessed their food and dug in. Sadie hadn't been wrong. Heating the food up on the stove made it...crisper? Fresher? Whatever, it was delicious.

After dinner, David started to stand up, but Sadie's hand shot out and pressed his shoulder. "What do you think you're doing?"

"The dishes. You cooked. I clean. A pretty good deal, right? That's what we do at your place."

"Normally I enjoy that philosophy, but tonight I will clean up. Then I'll get you some more painkillers before I leave. Don't come in tomorrow. Rest up and stay off that foot." Sadie washed the dishes, put them away, and scrubbed the counter.

David kept the place clean, comfortable. But with Sadie here, the place could really be a home.

Home.

David's phone lit up with another call from Lance. Sadie noticed. "I'm going to go get your painkiller. I think I left it in my purse in the car. You answer that call. I'll be back."

David grabbed the phone and swiped to answer. Something was up for Lance to call again. "Hey, Lance. What's up?"

"Glad I got ya this time, David." Lance's perky voice meant something was up. "I have news, and I wanted to talk to you about a new position. Have a few?"

A new position? The front door slammed. It would take Sadie a second to bring his meds back in. "Just a few."

"I'll jump right in then. Marco says the principal at Escuela Bíblica de San José wants to retire. Are you interested? It would get you back to Costa Rica."

Principal? David had never considered that before. He'd been happy in the physical education department. "But what about—"

"I know we said you weren't ready before, but Nate has been really impressed with all you are doing. He seemed confident in your abilities. So, what do you think?"

He could go back. Make sure the teens in Costa Rica had a consistent influence. They wouldn't think he'd abandoned them. But if he took the position, he'd have to leave Sadie.

He'd just called her his girlfriend. Told her he didn't want to leave.

"David? You still there?" Lance probably pulled the phone away to make sure the call was still connected.

"Still here. I had never considered principal before."

"Here's the thing. Wesley just found out his mother-in-law has stage four cancer. He and Jill want to come home as soon as possible to be with her in the end. Why don't you fly down to Costa Rica this weekend. I'll get you a ticket, and you can visit with Wesley in person. Maybe being there will help you make the decision."

"This weekend?" That was really fast. Sadie's face flashed in his mind. He'd already told her he wasn't going back. Weeks ago, the desire to return consumed him, but now? Did he even want to go back? Maybe this was God's way of pointing him in a new direction. Shouldn't he go back and see if this is what God wanted? He still had supporters to consider. Maybe Lance was right, and being on-site, talking to Wesley, visiting all his old hangouts would make the final decision easier.

Or give him peace if he walked away.

He wiggled his ankle. If he wrapped it good, it should be fine. "Okay. Let's do it."

David hung up the phone, with Lance promising to send the flight information later that night.

Just then, the front door slammed, and David looked up to see Sadie breeze into the kitchen, a large smile on her face as she filled his water glass and handed it to him with his pain pill. "Here you go. Drink up. Want me to help you walk down the hall?"

"Totally unnecessary. See?" David stood. Pain shot up his leg, and he sucked in a lungful of air.

"I see a stubborn man." Sadie quickly wrapped one arm around his waist and dropped his arm around her shoulder. Her spicy scent broke through the pain, her soft frame pressed up against him.

Right. He'd wanted to say goodnight and perhaps leave her with a lingering kiss. Not use her as a crutch to maneuver the hallway.

But she nudged him forward. "Come on. I'll help you and then bring the ice pack for you."

Maybe he should have taken the doctor up on those crutches, but he didn't want the hassle of returning them. And he didn't want to buy them and have them around. He could totally tough this out. Besides, it would make traveling easier if he didn't have crutches.

"Thank you." He said the words as he sank onto the bed. He should tell her about the trip. He started to say something, but the pain medication must have been kicking in, because his words jumbled together.

A chuckle escaped Sadie, and she bent down and brushed her soft lips across his cheek. "Any time, David."

She stood up and backed away. His hand itched to reach out to her, to touch her, to hold her, but it wouldn't move.

"I'll bring you a glass of water and the ice pack. Be right back." Sadie slipped out of the room.

The next thing David knew, his phone was ringing. His heavy eyelids blinked open. Sunlight shone through the window. His mouth was dry, a disgusting aftertaste lingering. His phone went quiet, and he rolled to his side. On his nightstand was a glass of water and his phone.

Sadie.

She'd told him she'd be right back, but he must have fallen asleep before she returned. His hand scrubbed his face and landed on his chest. The throw from the couch. Tres protested as David moved, snuggled against him. Cinco stretched and jumped off the bed. Mamá Gata slept at the foot of the bed, but not close enough for David to reach without sitting up.

He grabbed the phone and saw a message from Lance with his flight information.

He hadn't mentioned it to Sadie last night. But in the light of day, he couldn't picture leaving her. Didn't want to picture life without her. He'd already done that. There was no reason to cause her concern with a change in the status quo if there wasn't going to be one. He'd travel down and back without anyone noticing he was gone, and no one would be the wiser.

But what if God did want him to return?

He'd have to leave behind connections he'd made in Heritage. With the teens playing soccer, with Lottie, even with his family. The hardest person to leave behind, though, would be Sadie.

Last time he'd sprung Costa Rica on her, it had ended in disaster. He had no desire to recreate that fight.

It would better to wait and see.

thirteen

"DID YOU KNOW THAT GEORGE H. W. BUSH outlawed broccoli in the White House while he was president?" Lottie stared at the offending vegetable as she looked over the produce Sadie had placed in the grocery cart.

"Yes, and when you're president of the US, you can make the same rule, but growing up, his mother made him eat broccoli—just like your mom." It shouldn't be so hard to convince a growing child to eat some healthy vegetables.

"What if I agree to eat..."—Lottie looked around and picked up a long, skinny cucumber—"this instead. You could put the broccoli back then."

After a full day of school, Lottie shouldn't be so argumentative. It was almost like she'd been saving up her stubbornness for this moment. When she got older, Sadie would encourage her to consider the debate team. "Add the cucumber to the cart, and we'll keep the broccoli. It's packed full of those vitamins and minerals your aunt Doris says you are lacking."

"M-o-o-m." Lottie fisted her hands and placed them on her hips. "Aunt Doris doesn't know everything."

With this much sass now, the teenage years would be a blast. But Sadie couldn't disagree, Doris didn't know everything. But she did want to take Lottie away. And that was enough that Sadie wanted to include a few more veggies, in case anyone asked Lottie if she made her eat her greens.

Irrational? Probably.

Sadie hadn't told Lottie about her aunt and uncle contesting the adoption. With the hearing next week, Sadie needed to tell her so she wasn't surprised. It wasn't an easy topic to broach, though. The girl had lost enough, she didn't need to worry about losing Sadie, because that wouldn't happen. Sadie would fight tooth and nail to be part of Lottie's life.

Lottie threw the cucumber into the cart, and it bounced. "Careful, Lottie. We don't want to smash any veggies."

"Cucumbers aren't even vegetables. They're a fruit." The nine-year-old crossed her arms and grumbled.

Inhaling and exhaling on a four count, Sadie pinched the bridge of her nose and rolled her shoulders. Maybe she should have asked her dad to cover the store at some point during the day so she could have shopped without Lottie. Instead, he was closing, and Sadie was with a nine-year-old stuck in an after-school-funk in the middle of the grocery store.

Sadie deserved a gold star. Or a cup of coffee. Or chocolate. At the very least, a quiet bubble bath. Because shopping was hard enough, but with a little girl's picky palate, it was even harder to meal plan and shop. Next time she'd sneak out before school got out, rather than wait for Lottie to get off the bus.

A bunch of bananas was the next thing to go into the cart next to the..."Lottie, please don't take things out of the cart."

"I won't eat that broccoli. There's no point in buying it." Lottie stomped her foot with her hands on her hips.

Sadie counted to ten. Again. Did she really want to die on this mountaintop?

"Fine. I won't get the broccoli, but you cannot take anything else out of the cart. Besides, I want to take David dinner tonight, and he actually eats his vegetables." He must be in more pain than he let on, because when Sadie suggested that he take the weekend off, he quickly agreed.

Last night, after he'd called her his girlfriend—well, as juvenile as the term sounded, it sent a thrill down to her toes, and she wanted to surprise him with dinner today. They hadn't made any promises, but the intent had been clear. Little dreams about what the future might look had bloomed and played in her mind like movie reels.

Sadie pushed ahead and placed an onion—the one on top of the display—in the cart. A little bigger than she wanted, but she could chop it and freeze anything she didn't use.

Next, she selected a bag of apples and placed them in the cart, but the onion had gone missing. "Lottie."

She turned to see her daughter holding the onion in her hand.

"Don't put that back." Onions were one of the few vegetables Lottie had no idea she ate. Sadie hid them in meat and sauces.

"Onions are gross."

"But when you cook them up—"

"They are always gross." Lottie crossed her arms and placed the onion back on top of the pyramid of veggies on the stand.

Forget shopping in person next time. Sadie would plan ahead for curbside pickup.

Next was the dairy department lining the back wall. Perfect distraction. "Do you want to go pick out some yogurt? I'll be right behind you."

Win-win. She could pack some veggies in her cart while distracting Lottie and keeping her in her line of sight. Sadie grabbed the offending onion and placed it back in the cart. She picked a second one for good measure. She'd chop it and freeze it, so she wouldn't have to have this debate next time she shopped.

Piling in a few more veggies, Sadie parked the cart next to Lottie.

A girl who looked about middle school age with freckles across her nose held a yogurt smoothie, looking at the label. Lottie bounced up to her. "Hi, Trinity."

The two girls chatted, and Mrs. Mathews waved as she approached Sadie. They'd spoken a few days ago when Sadie called about their line of credit. It wasn't the store's biggest loan, but the significant amount would help toward the bottom line she owed the bank. At this point, every penny mattered. Mrs. Mathews had assured Sadie they'd bring the payment by soon.

"Oh, honey, my husband stopped in the store last night." Mrs. Mathews pushed her cart forward. She didn't look much older than Sadie felt, but her hair had started to streak with gray, and she held a wisdom in her gaze that not many people Sadie's age could claim. Calm and confident, the woman oozed a sincerity Sadie hoped to emulate. "Your dad was there."

"I had to step out for a few. I'm sorry I missed him."

Mrs. Mathews nodded and placed a gallon of milk in her cart. "Your dad said you'd taken David to the ER after he'd had an accident playing soccer. The teens around town adore him. Even Trinity has mentioned how much she's enjoyed getting to know him. He's made such an impact by simply taking time to play games with them, talk to them at their level. How is he feeling today?"

Pride filled her for all the good David contributed around town. The man really had started to make a difference. If he could see what he was doing for the area, maybe he would be content to stick around. "It's just a sprain, but I encouraged him to take a few days off."

"So glad to hear he's going to be okay. Anyway, it was so generous of your dad to waive our tab. You have no idea what that means for us. Thank you both so much."

Her dad had waived the Mathews family's credit? Her ears clogged. Had the air been sucked from the store? This couldn't be happening.

Mrs. Mathews said a few more things, but Sadie would have had an easier time talking to the wall. Her dad had dismissed their bill?

Her dad had dismissed. Their. Bill.

A good-sized line of credit. She had two weeks left to scrimp together enough money for the bank. What was her dad doing?

Had he waived anyone else's? Was he trying to sabotage her?

No. Obviously he wouldn't. The store mattered to him. But how did he expect them to raise the money for the bank if he dismissed people's loans?

Sadie's hands shook. She'd done the math, over and over. She didn't have any wiggle room. And without this family's payment, she would be short.

Her dad had said he'd sell things to make up the money. He'd better be ready to follow through with that promise, because Sadie didn't have any extra.

Lottie finished picking out the yogurt. "Let's pick out a frozen pizza for dinner."

Sadie agreed. Because why not? She hadn't told David she'd bring dinner. They hadn't made any plans to see each other. It seemed silly, but she missed him. Missed seeing him at the store. Missed his teasing, his touches, his conversation. But it had only been one day. Still, David would know how she should respond to her dad, and he'd encourage her to stand up for what she believed in.

She could do that without David's encouragement, so she pulled her phone out and texted her dad.

Sadie

Mrs. Mathews said you forgave
their line of credit? Why didn't
you tell me?

Dad
I didn't want to worry you. But trust me, they need that money more than we do.

Sadie
I don't think you understand how much the store needs that money. Just how much is on the line.

Dad
It will come together.

Sadie
How? Cause I've run the numbers. What are you willing to sell to keep the store?

Dots appeared and disappeared.

Sadie
You said you trusted me to run the store. Did you change your mind?

Sadie shoved her phone in her purse. His response didn't matter. If he kept refusing money, the store was doomed. It didn't matter who ran it.

Sadie slowly pushed her cart, following Lottie. The girl picked up a box of Zebra Cakes and tossed it in the cart. Normally Sadie would put it back or tell her to stop.

But that box of Zebra Cakes probably wouldn't be around come morning. Little Debbie comfort for the win.

In the freezer aisle, Lottie opened a door and pulled out a pepperoni pizza and placed it in the cart.

"Mom. What are those?" She pointed at the onions like they were dead fish before picking one up.

Sadie let her breath out. "Please, Lottie. Let's not do this."

"Are you buying them because you're planning for me to leave?" Tears filled Lottie's eyes, and her bottom lip quivered.

"What are you talking about? I would never plan for you to leave me." Sadie tried to hug Lottie, but she stepped back, so Sadie dropped her arms.

"I saw the papers. Aunt Doris wants me to live with her." Lottie's shoulders sagged, and her arms hung down to her side as a single tear spilled over and ran down her cheek. "Do you want that, too?"

"No. Never. I want you to live with me." Sadie squatted down in front of Lottie and waited for her to meet her eyes, then she held out her hand. Lottie's smaller hand gripped Sadie's like she was afraid to let go. "You are my daughter—no matter what the court says, and I will fight for you with everything I have."

"I don't want to live with Aunt Doris and Uncle Patrick. I want to live with you."

"I want you to live with me, too." Sadie tugged Lottie closer, and she wrapped her arms around her. "I should have told you. I just didn't want to worry you."

Little arms wrapped around Sadie, squeezing tight, and Lottie released a small hiccup. Her dad's words from her text floated back to her. He hadn't wanted to worry her. Isn't that what she'd done to Lottie? Sadie had kept information from Lottie because she hadn't wanted to upset her. Good parenting was a lot more than getting them to eat their vegetables. It required a balance of honesty, love, and hard work. Sadie wanted to carry the weight of the world for Lottie, but she wouldn't always be able to do that. At some point she had to prepare Lottie for what the girl would face.

Maybe Sadie needed to spend more time focusing on that and less time worrying about the number of vegetables in their diet.

As if eating a cold sandwich on stale bread wasn't punishment enough, a huge glob of grape jelly rolled down the front of David's shirt.

Of course it did. It was like everything was out to punish him for refusing dinner with Sadie. He hadn't seen her since the Emergency Room visit. Yesterday he'd stayed home resting, considering the upcoming trip to Costa Rica. And now, he'd told her he couldn't make dinner and that he'd see her Monday when he returned. It seemed silly that he missed her. He'd gone ten years trying not to think about her, but now, just a few days had passed, and he missed her smile, her kindness, her kisses.

He could be sitting in her warm and cozy apartment enjoying a home-cooked meal. Instead, he sat in the quiet of his grandparents' kitchen. Not even the kittens were with him, opting for some time outside instead.

He needed to leave for his red-eye flight to Costa Rica in a few hours, and it had been easier to skip dinner and ignore the guilt of not telling Sadie about the job offer. She had so much stuff going on in her life, and with the adoption hearing on Tuesday, he didn't want her to worry about him, too. Not to mention the more time passed, the more certain he was that this job wasn't for him. But he owed it to Lance and his supporters to give it a look.

Pulling off his shirt, David stepped into the laundry room and added some stain remover to the grape-colored spot then laid it over the opening of the washing machine.

A knock rattled the screen door.

"Come in!"

The door creaked open then banged closed. "David?"

Sadie? David stepped out of the laundry room into the living room. She stood inside the door, a plate in hand. A maroon long-sleeve shirt tucked into her jeans hugged her curves. Her gaze dropped to his bare chest as she pulled her lips in and rubbed them before looking back up.

She held out the plate wrapped in tinfoil. "I thought I'd bring over dinner tonight, since you couldn't join us. Plus, I hadn't seen you since I brought you home. And I didn't want you to have to cook on your sore ankle again."

Her cheeks flamed red as her eyes dropped down to his chest again. Never before had he been more thankful for his simple workout routine. He still had a ways to go for a six-pack, but at least he wasn't a slouch. "Thank you for that. It smells amazing." And it did. So much more appealing than his stale PB&J. "Let me go grab a clean shirt, and I'll be right back. Want to set that in the kitchen?"

David stepped into his room and pulled out a freshly laundered shirt he hadn't put away yet. He slipped it over his head as he hurried back to where he'd left Sadie standing by the front door.

The sun shone through the window, highlighting her with soft evening light, her back to him. Outside, Lottie danced around the yard in her black ballet leotard. David crossed the room and wrapped his arms around Sadie's waist and pulled her close. She relaxed into him, and let her head fall to one side. He didn't need any more invitation and dropped a lingering kiss on her neck. A guy could get used to this.

"It's a bit chilly out there, but Lottie wanted to run through her ballet moves. They are performing at the town festival next weekend. But you should eat while the food's still hot." Sadie stepped to the side, knocking over his suitcase.

His suitcase...

Sadie stared at it. David reached for it, but she picked it up before he could, setting it upright. Her eyebrows lowered, and that small V appeared. "Is someone here?"

Danger, danger. The warning flashed in his mind. He had to fix this. He stepped closer to Sadie, hoping to hold her, reassure himself that he hadn't made a fatal mistake, but the expression on her face had him stopping before he could pull her close.

"You're leaving?" Her voice scratched.

"Only for a few days. That's why I couldn't come into the store this weekend. I'll be back on—"

"Where are you going?" Sadie stepped back, the space between them growing.

David fisted his hands, jamming them into his pockets. "Costa Rica."

Sadie's eyebrows lifted. "You're going to Costa Rica."

It wasn't a question, but Sadie studied his face, looking for something. He nodded.

"And you didn't think to mention this?" Sadie crossed her arms over her chest.

"I was going to...The thing is—it's not what you think."

"Not what I think? Is it another job?" When he didn't answer, she turned away and gripped the sides of her head "Oh, goodness. Anna was right. This is just like before."

"No, it's not. I don't even think I'm going to take the job."

"But you might." Sadie sank into the couch, still holding her head.

"I would say I'm ninety percent sure I'll say no." David stepped closer to her, but she sat up straight and held out her hand to stop him. His heart raced. He didn't want to fight.

"But that leaves ten percent. Ten percent that you didn't think I had a right to know when you kissed me after I brought you home from the ER."

"Sadie." David stepped closer and held out his hand.

She looked at it, and then studied his face before slipping her hand into his. He pulled her up and into his arms, running his hands up to her shoulders and down to her wrists. To steady her? Comfort her? To comfort himself? He didn't know, but he needed the contact. Needed to feel her close to him. "I didn't know then. Lance called after that, and the school's principal wants to come home. They asked me if I'd take his place. My hesitation resulted in Lance encouraging me to at least go talk to Wesley."

Sadie let out a breath. "When were you going to tell me?"

"When there was something to tell. I didn't want to upset you, and I haven't decided anything—"

"Upset me?" Sadie broke out of his embrace, her face flushed, and she walked past him to the front window, keeping her back to him. "So what? You were going to make a decision on your own again, and then what...send me a postcard?"

"It's not like that. I just..." The walls between them were too much. David stepped closer and turned her toward him. He wanted to pull her into his embrace, assure her he wouldn't leave. That this time he had no intention of letting go. Except her posture was so rigid. He settled for rubbing his hands up and down her arms. "I just felt like I needed to see it. I don't know yet—"

"Yet? But you will make a decision. A decision that will affect my future—Lottie's future—and you didn't even have the decency to have a conversation with me. Just a few days ago, you called me your girlfriend. What do you think that means?"

When he didn't answer, she shook her head. "I get it, we aren't engaged. But we are too old to just be having fun like a bunch of high schoolers. Either we are in a relationship headed toward something permanent, or we are nothing. I don't have space for the in-between. Not with Lottie's heart on the line as well as my own."

"I get that."

"Do you? Because I want a partner, David. Someone who is going to share life with me—all of it. The ups, the downs. The good, the bad. The decisions."

"I want that, too."

"No, you don't, or you wouldn't have done this." She opened the front door and called for Lottie.

Didn't she get that this decision was bigger than them? He owed it to his supporters.

The door slammed behind her, and he followed her out. He didn't want her to leave angry. "What are you doing?"

"Lottie!" Sadie turned back to him. "It's called leaving. You should recognize it—it's your specialty."

David hurried to block her path. "Don't go. Not like this. Let's talk."

"I've heard all I want to hear." Sadie hurried to her car and opened the door. "Lottie, let's go!"

No response. No little girl's laughter. No footsteps skipping or dancing. Lottie was nowhere to be seen. Lottie didn't seem like the type to ignore Sadie. Or to be quiet.

David scanned the yard. Shadows were lengthening as the chill of the evening hours settled across the field. But there was no sign of Lottie.

Sadie put her hands on her hips. "Lottie? Come on, sweetheart. Time to go home."

Silence.

He lifted his hand to his forehead and looked to the west, the sun on the horizon, but there was no sign of the little girl.

"Maybe she's in the barn." David jogged down the stairs and behind the house to the barn, a slight limp in his step. But the barn was too still, too quiet. There was no way Lottie was inside. Still, he called for her.

Sadie came behind him, their voices blending as they called for Lottie. The shadows lengthened as the sun sank even lower, and a bird cooed.

Only the buzzing of a few bugs met them. David squeezed Sadie's hand, pulling her attention to him as she scanned the space between the house and the barn. "I'll go look in the fairy house. Check inside, maybe she slipped in the house."

They'd find Lottie. But even as he assured Sadie, he spotted the corner of something dark blue in the bush. He hurried over and pulled it out. His passport. His passport that had been on the dining room table when the argument started.

"Sadie." His strong tone stopped her as she put her hand on

the doorknob. He held up the passport, she paled and sank to the steps.

No doubt she had drawn the same conclusion. Lottie had heard them, she'd run off, and it was getting dark. It was autumn, but the night lows this fall were already at a dangerous level, especially for a nine-year-old with no coat. His gaze flicked to the edge of the woods then back to Sadie.

Lord, help us. She could be anywhere.

fourteen

S HE'D ALWAYS BELIEVED THAT NIGHTMARES couldn't come to life—she'd been wrong. Sadie pressed her hand to her chest as she struggled to breathe. She had to find Lottie.

"Lottie!" Sadie's voice scratched on her throat as she called for her daughter again. She checked her watch. It had been thirty minutes. Thirty minutes of calling. Thirty minutes of searching David's house, and thirty minutes of David searching outside.

Thirty minutes of nothing.

Sadie wrapped her arms around her chest and stood on the front porch, looking out over the property. The shadows had grown longer as the sun sank into the horizon, the chill of the night making a shiver run down her spine. And Lottie was out there somewhere in only her black ballet leotard and tights.

What kind of irresponsible mother let her daughter leave home without a jacket at this time of year? Easy—one who didn't deserve custody. Maybe Doris was right, and she didn't deserve to raise Lottie. One who was fighting for custody should never ever do something so...careless. So stupid.

David had a long tube tucked under his arm, and his warm hands gripped her arms. "We need to call for help."

She had no doubt he was trying to sound calm, but his words confirmed that this was bad.

Sadie pulled her phone from her pocket just as it began to ring, and her father's face flashed on the screen. Maybe they'd heard from her. "Do you have her?"

"Who?"

"Lottie's missing. The light's almost gone. I thought—"

"Where are you?" Panic laced her dad's voice.

"I'm at David's—his grandparents' farmhouse."

"Where have you looked?"

"Everywhere. And, Dad, she's not wearing a coat."

"We're on our way, and I'll bring people. There are a lot here standing around that will help."

"What?" But he was already gone.

Sadie hung up and walked toward the house with more purpose. People were coming, she had to get organized. "Dad is bringing help. We need a plan in place when they arrive."

David lifted the tube and slid out some papers then unfurled them across the hood of her car. "I found the plans for the property a while back. I figured they'd be helpful. We can divide the property up into zones. I added the fairy house I built Vangie there." David pointed to a spot close to the pond. Then he ran his finger over the area of the pond. "I moved the fire pit back from the water, but Lottie wouldn't have gone closer to the pond, would she?"

"No. She hates swimming, hates being in the water. There's no way..." Sadie's voice dropped off. She couldn't say the words.

They would find Lottie. She had to believe that.

Nate's motorcycle was the first to pull in the driveway, then a sedan, followed by a truck. Nate climbed off and hurried over to them.

"Have you devised a plan? Because practically the whole town is coming." He motioned to yet another car turning in. There had to be ten cars now and more were still arriving.

"Word travels fast." Sadie wiped her face.

"Helped that we were all together when you talked to your dad. But Lottie is more important. Now where have you looked so far?"

David gave Nate the rundown as more and more cars pulled into the driveway. There had to be close to thirty people already waiting for instruction, and they were all carrying blankets and flashlights. Nate took charge, zoning off the property and sending people in different directions.

"Nate's got this part under control. I'm going to go check the playhouse again." David squeezed her hand then pulled her close, resting his forehead against hers. It was so easy to lean into him, into his strength. To soak in the warmth he offered. "Why don't you stay close to the house, so you're here when we find Lottie."

Words seemed to clog in her throat.

"We will find her." His warm breath fanned her face, and he pressed a quick kiss on her forehead before jogging off.

"He's right, Sadie." She turned to see Nate still leaning over the map on the hood of her car. "We will find her. God is in control of all of this. He already knows where Lottie is. Do you want to pray with me before I head out?"

Pray? She'd trusted God to bless her plans, but could she really trust Him to take the lead?

Then again, look what trying to be in control had gotten her. A missing daughter, a battle for custody, a loan she couldn't pay, and a broken heart. Right now, praying was the last thing she wanted to do, but she couldn't say that to Nate. Couldn't let him know how her entire life was crumbling around her. Instead, she nodded.

Nate gathered everyone together and said a prayer for Lottie's safety and speedy return. He prayed for peace. If only Sadie could get a sprinkling of that. Then he left to look for Lottie.

"I don't think I have ever seen this many cars in the driveway."

Had to park along the road down the street." Her mom's sweet tone nearly broke her last bit of control.

Sadie sank into her mother's waiting embrace. Calming lavender and rose fragrances filled her senses.

"I take it there's no news."

Sadie straightened and rolled her shoulders back. "Not yet. But I think we should find some blankets to throw in David's dryer so they're warm when we find Lottie."

"That's a good plan. Let's head inside." Her mom passed her a coat that Sadie hadn't even realized her mom had been holding. "I figured if Lottie didn't have a coat, you didn't either."

Sadie slid her arms into her coat and zipped it closed, cutting the wind. Lottie must be freezing. Linking arms with her mom, they went inside and tossed some blankets they found in the hall closet into the dryer.

"Dad never did say why he called. Is everything ok?"

Her mom shook her head as she pushed the front door open, the hinges squeaking, loud and sharp.

A cold gust of wind blew through the front porch and stole Sadie's breath. Please, Lord, keep Lottie safe.

"There was an accident at the store."

"What kind of accident?" How much more could go wrong?

A loud breath escaped from her mom. "We're going to find Lottie, and then we'll handle things at the store. But Mrs. Allen crashed into the front window."

"Is she okay? Was anyone hurt?"

"I believe she is okay, but her car isn't. And the store is going to be closed for a while."

"A while like a few days? Or..."

Her mom wrapped her arm around Sadie's shoulder and pulled her close. "Or. Definitely or."

Sadie wrapped her arms around herself. Words failed her before her heart took off racing. The store? But she couldn't even consider that right now. Her hands shook. She needed something to do. "Maybe I should go look for Lottie, too."

Her mom shook her head. "I know you are itching to move. But we're going to stay here and trust God and the others to find Lottie."

"Mom, I'm not good at trusting."

"I know, sweetheart. But it's often in trusting that we find peace. Let's do more than ask God to bless the plans we've made tonight. Let's ask Him to go before us. To guide each person looking for Lottie. And we'll trust Him to watch over our girl, wherever she is right now."

Sadie tried to block out the fear threatening to consume her as she allowed her mom's comforting hug to surround her. Could she really let go and trust God? With Lottie? With the store? With their future?

Tonight, Sadie had already lost David and potentially the store. If she lost Lottie Tuesday...

What choice did she have but to trust?

She'd never wanted to give up control before, but her life was quickly becoming a dumpster fire that she couldn't contain. If she couldn't figure out how to salvage a part of her plans, she wouldn't have a choice but to trust.

Could she afford to wait and see if she could put out the fire on her own?

Sadie didn't know.

And she wasn't sure if she should find out.

David stood next to the fire pit and listened as he moved his flashlight over the familiar terrain of his grandparents' land. The light lit up the playhouse he'd built, and a paper moved inside, but it was empty. Mamá Gata wove between his legs, purring and swishing her tail.

The moon reflected off the pond, and the water gently rippled in the sharp night breeze. Sadie said Lottie hated the water, but what better place to hide than the location she hated most?

His phone vibrated in his pocket, and he yanked it out, but it was a text from Lance. He didn't even open it, just repocketed it and kept moving his flashlight over the ground. He'd have to tell Lance later that he'd missed his flight, but that didn't matter. Nothing mattered right now but finding Lottie.

David's heart pounded dangerously against his chest, and Mamá Gata rubbed his leg harder. If he didn't want to be found, he'd try and find the least obvious place to hide. Would Lottie think like that?

Mamá Gata meowed as if to encourage David to follow his thoughts.

"Lottie!" David's voice mixed with others who called in the distance. The water rippled again, and he jogged toward the dock. It might be a waste of time, but his gut told him to check it out. Using his flashlight to scan the landscape, he called for Lottie again and again.

Only the sounds of the quiet nighttime responded. That and the distant calls from other searchers. He glanced at his watch. How long did it take for hypothermia to set in? Was it even cold enough for that? The cold night breeze fluttered the trees, and David tucked the blanket he carried closer.

"Lottie?" He tried again.

Had he heard something? He paused, listening. The wind rustled the trees behind him, the others searching for Lottie, calling for her.

But there it was again.

A faint sound. He looked down at Mamá Gata, who stared at the pond. He hadn't been the only one to hear it.

He listened as the breeze rippled over the water, lapping gently against the shore as he crept closer. And then, he heard it again—a muffled cough. David shined his light in the direction of the noise. A shadow moved across the dock as a little girl paced back and forth.

"Lottie?" His heart skipped. Sadie had been so confident the girl wouldn't go near water. David stepped onto the dock, his flashlight landing on Lottie.

Her eyes widened, and she turned away from him and jumped into a boat tied to the end of the dock.

Air whooshed out of David's lungs, and he bent over, his hands on his knees. Lottie was safe. He pulled out his phone and sent Sadie a message. Then he shoved the phone in his pants pocket and cupped his mouth. "Found her! Lottie's over here."

David stepped closer to talk to her. "Hey, Lottie."

She sniffed and used her fist to wipe her face.

She stared at him, her lips tight and her arms crossed.

"Lottie, are you okay?" David's voice scratched across his throat.

She glared at him.

David slowly walked to the edge of the dock. Lottie took a step back in the boat, and it wobbled and strained against the rope keeping it tied to the dock. She lunged for it and untied the boat, holding the rope close to her body.

"I don't want to talk to you." Her teeth chattered as she spoke, and the boat floated backward away from the dock. She let out a startled yelp as she sat down, holding the sides of the boat as it rocked, and the rope fell into the water.

"Okay." David held up his hands. "But I want to talk to you."

She crossed her arms and rubbed at her bare skin. "Fine. I'll talk then. You're leaving. You didn't even say goodbye. I thought you liked us." Lottie sniffed again.

David rubbed his forehead. He'd messed up. "I'm sorry Lottie. I'm only going for the weekend."

"I heard Mom. She said you're going away. Why would you leave? Mom likes you. I can tell. And you like her."

"I do lo—" Love. He did. He loved Sadie. Oh man, what had he done? "I do like your mom."

"So why leave?"

"It's not for good. I'm coming back."

"Yet. You said you're not leaving for good yet. I heard the fight. You look at Mom like she's special. Like Daddy looked at my birth mom in the pictures. Why leave?"

For being nine, Lottie sure picked up on a lot, and she was throwing some tough verbal punches.

The boat rocked again, and heavy shivers had Lottie shaking violently as she looked up at the full moon. With Lottie distracted, David took a few steps closer to the end of the dock.

"Why are you here anyway? Don't you have a flight to catch?" The edge in Lottie's voice surprised David, but she had every right to be upset.

David knelt down, hoping he could get ahold of the rope or the boat, before it floated too much farther away from the dock. "I couldn't leave when I didn't know where you were. It's cold out, and you don't have a coat."

"Why do you care?" She shot him a look, but then her jaw trembled.

"Because I care about you." Lottie looked away from him, but her frown lessened.

"Why don't I help you climb out of the boat? We can go inside and warm up. Your mom is worried." He swiped for the rope but missed. He lay flat on the dock and scooted forward, so only his waist and legs were on wooden planks, and then he stretched, hoping to be able to get a grip on the rope. His fingers barely touched it, but he worked it closer until he could grasp it. "I'm going to pull the boat a little closer, okay, Lottie?"

As David scooted back on the dock, Lottie stood up, like she was ready to leap out.

"Lottie, can you sit down?"

Lottie glanced at the water and shook her head stubbornly. "I want out."

The boat tugged on the rope in David's hand, his balance teetering on the dock, as he strained his muscles to scoot back and keep the rope in hand. But when Lottie took a step toward him, the boat pitched to one side.

"Don't move. Hang tight." David slowed his movements, his abs on fire. "Please sit down, Lottie."

"I c-c-can't." Lottie circled her arms, frantically trying to regain balance.

"Lottie!" She was too far away, and he froze as an ear-piercing scream ripped through the night then cut off as Lottie's head disappeared into the water.

David was taken back to that moment when Remy went over the raft. His hand shook, and his breath whooshed out of his lungs as his vision started to tunnel.

David's heart rammed his rib cage. Oxygen became a commodity he couldn't find, and his throat burned. He might as well be back in that river.

This was not the same as Remy.

He was not in a raft.

"Help!" Lottie's shrill plea pierced David's terror.

Not the same.

He could help Lottie. David jumped into the pond and swam two strokes to the boat. Lottie was under water, and it was cold. He dove beneath the surface, but it was so dark, he couldn't see her. He swiped his arms through the icy pond but didn't make contact.

Lottie broke the surface, splashing, several feet to his right, beyond the rowboat.

"Lottie!" Her name ripped from his throat as he swam toward

her, but she disappeared before he got there. He dove under the water again, frantically searching for her, his hands finding nothing.

Lord, please! David pushed forward underwater, completely blind. He couldn't let Lottie drown. His arms burned as the cold sank in. He surfaced, hoping to hear or see any sign of Lottie. Nothing.

Please, Lord. Please let me find her. He again pushed under, his arms moving in front then to the side, and his fingers touched a hand. He pulled her close and hauled them both to the surface. She coughed and spit as he patted her back.

Footsteps pounded on the dock as people approached.

"I found her! We're over here!" David yelled. A grateful heart, a praise to anyone who could hear. Thank you, Lord. He held the shivering girl close, and he swam back to the edge of the pond. People were gathering close, lights bouncing as more people ran toward the pond. He could hear people calling, "She's found!" "Lottie's here!" "Over here!"

He stood up and walked out of the pond. Nate greeted them with a huge blanket and wrapped it around Lottie and David.

"I'm s-s-s-still mad at you." She buried her face against his chest.

"I'm mad at me too. I never meant to upset you or hurt you. I would never have left without saying goodbye." Except as he said the words, the hypocrisy of the moment slapped him in the face. That's exactly what he had planned on doing—even if it was only for the weekend.

Lottie's muscles started to relax, and her breathing deepened.

"Stay awake, Lottie." David jogged toward the house, his jeans sticking to him, stinging his skin, his legs burning with cold.

Red lights flashed in front of the house as an ambulance sat in the midst of the cars, its back doors open. EMTs ran to him and pulled Lottie from his grasp. He staggered after, refusing any medical treatment. "I'm fine. Check Lottie. She was underwater for a while. I don't know how long."

"Mom!" Lottie's strangled cry whimpered as Sadie pushed through the crowd and hugged her soaked daughter.

An EMT allowed the embrace then guided them toward the ambulance. "I'd like to take her to the hospital just to be sure everything is okay."

Sadie nodded, and David held her hand, needed to feel her warmth, to make sure she was okay, too. But the comfort, the friendship he'd come to expect during the last few weeks was gone. Her expression shuttered, blocking him out.

"Thank you for finding Lottie. Good luck on your trip." She pulled her hand, but David squeezed tighter.

"Let me change, and I'll meet you at the hospital."

Sadie watched as the EMT picked Lottie up and set her in the ambulance, wrapping a new, dry blanket around her. "No. I have it under control."

"Sadie—"

"I'll text you that she's okay." Sadie shook her head and tugged her hand again. David let go. "No. I need to focus on Lottie. On the disaster that is my life."

"I want to be a part of that life."

"No, you don't. At least not fully. And that's not enough."

"Sadie—"

"Don't come."

"Sadie?" David's voice broke, as he let his hand fall to his side. She couldn't just jump in the ambulance and leave him.

She looked back at him. "This isn't your problem, David. It's my problem. There is nothing you can do to fix it. This is my family. My responsibility."

The door closed, and the ambulance pulled forward, its lights flashing. David stood there until the vehicle turned out of his driveway. It drove away, his heart inside.

A warm blanket wrapped around his shoulders and gentle hands tugged it closed. Dawn, Sadie's mom, stood in front of him adjusting the blanket. "I don't know what happened tonight. But go change. You're no good to anyone if you're sick. Meet us at the hospital."

"But she said—"

"I heard her. But that little girl will expect to see you. I'm not sure there is hope for you and Sadie after what she just said, but don't break my granddaughter's heart, too."

She patted his chest and hurried to her car. He spun on his heel and headed to the house. Dawn was right—he needed dry clothes before he went to the hospital—and he had to let Lance know he didn't make his flight.

Did he ask Lance to rebook it? Everything in him screamed no—Sadie was his home. But if she was serious, and there was no room for him in her life, what future did he have here in Heritage?

fifteen

A WARM SHOWER AND FRESH CLOTHES COULD change a lot for a guy—except the words still ringing in David's mind. *This is my problem. My family.* Maybe he should have stayed home, but Sadie's mom had said Lottie would expect him. He couldn't let the little girl down. Not again.

The air whooshed as he walked through the automatic sliding doors into the sterile waiting area at the ER. People sat in clumps around the quiet room. Several of them stared at a TV with the closed captioning turned on. Some decorating program played as a couple looked at their stylish deck overlooking the ocean.

In the far corner, Gary and Dawn Hoover sat together with Nate. The older couple held hands, their heads bowed, as Dawn wiped at her cheeks. David waited until they finished and looked up.

Dawn's smile broke through any of the doubts he'd had about coming. But before he could join them, the doors opened and Sadie stood, searching the room, until her eyes landed on him. Heat crept up his chest as she came closer.

His hands stretched out to touch her, to hug her, to pull her close, but she brushed them aside, her voice sharp. "I told you not to come."

"Sadie, that is not how you talk to the man who saved your daughter tonight." Dawn intervened, her hand holding Sadie's, which looked ready to strike him.

"We wouldn't be here if not for him." Her voice cracked, and David's heart seized. "Lottie heard us fighting and ran."

"You need two people to fight, Sadie." Gary's deep, firm voice brooked no argument, Refusing to let Sadie lay the blame fully at David's feet.

"No, she's right." David backed up and ran his hand down his face. "I—"

Sadie turned toward her mom and dad, effectively cutting him out of the conversation. "I came out because I want to update you, and my phone is dead. The doctors say Lottie is fine and should be released later tonight. She's still cold, so they're warming her up with some heated blankets and hot cocoa, but otherwise, she's fine. Her lungs are clear, and all her responses are good. I'm going to head back now so Lottie's not alone."

Sadie hurried back to the door without looking at David. He stood, watching her until the doors closed. He should go since he wasn't wanted or needed here, and staying...well, it would only upset Sadie.

Gary's hand clamped down on David's shoulder, "Sit down, son. We need to talk."

David's stomach churned, and he tugged his coat a little tighter. Even with two pairs of socks on, his toes were still freezing inside his shoes. He shook his head. "I should go."

"Nonsense. You saved Lottie tonight." Gary sat down next to Dawn and nodded to the chair on the other side of her.

"I can't stay, Gary. I've hurt Sadie, again, and I don't think she'll forgive me." David let out a breath and shoved his hands in his pockets.

Dawn hummed her agreement then looked at Gary. The two seemed to communicate an entire conversation in one look. She leaned over, kissed Gary on the cheek, and stood up. "Nate, I feel like a cup of coffee—will you join me? David, you sit here." Sadie's mom guided him to the seat next to Gary and then motioned for Nate to join her.

Nate nodded at David as he walked away with Dawn.

David rested his elbows rest on his knees. Gary's hand clamped his shoulder again.

"What happened?" Gary's gentle voice prodded.

"Where to begin?" Letting out the air in his lungs, David folded his hands together and opened up, telling Gary about the accident with Remy, being sent home, his position being given to a younger candidate. The opening in Costa Rica, the trip down to talk with Wesley. About how much he enjoyed being in Heritage, working at the hardware store, playing soccer with the teens around town. "When Sadie showed up tonight, she had no idea I was leaving for the weekend. No idea about the opening in Costa Rica."

"Why didn't you tell Sadie about the trip?" No sharp accusation laced Gary's voice, just open curiosity.

"Because...quite honestly, I don't want to go back. Telling her about the job, the trip, made it seem like a real possibility. But telling her that I wanted to stay here—with her—seemed like a betrayal to God. To my supporters."

"Why do you want to go back to Costa Rica?"

It's my calling. The words shot to his tongue, but he couldn't get them out. "The Bible tells us to go to the ends of the earth."

"And being a missionary is the best way to serve God, if that's where God called you. But sometimes 'to the ends of the earth' is just helping your neighbor. God calls us all to different things. My calling has been to my family and the people of Heritage as a shopkeeper. Sometimes I help people out when they need things. Other times it is just an encouraging word as they shop. Some people are called to be preachers, others teachers, others businessmen. No calling is lesser. And sometimes callings change. Middle-aged couples take to the mission field, leaving behind lucrative careers. Sometimes missionaries are called to return home. Both are good decisions—but only when the Lord leads."

It sounded so simple. So easy. But there was no handwriting on the wall. No specific direction. "How do you know when it's time for a change?"

"It's a process. And just because God called you to go to Costa Rica alone ten years ago doesn't mean He's calling you to remain there, single, forever. Do you know why we continued to support you financially even after you and Sadie broke up?" Gary's quiet voice encouraged David to sit up and look at him.

Honestly, he'd wondered. Was surprised when he'd heard the Hoovers had committed to supporting him. But he hadn't wanted to seem ungrateful, so he'd never asked.

"It was clear you two loved each other, but it was also clear you two weren't ready for a serious, committed relationship. So, I thought a few years apart might just help you both grow up. Although I'll admit, I didn't expect it to take ten years for you two to get your acts together."

"What do you mean you didn't think we were ready?"

"There's no doubt Sadie loved you. Still does, but despite your feelings for each other, you two didn't communicate. Didn't share pertinent information with each other. If there's one thing I've learned over the years, it's the importance of communication in any partnership—especially marriage."

"You don't even need words to communicate with your wife anymore." David remembered the look Gary and Dawn had exchanged before she left for coffee.

Gary slapped David's shoulder. "Not always. But I'm not stupid enough to think that's always the case. And it took us over twenty-five years of marriage before that became a reality in small areas. So let me ask you, are you really going to make the same mistake again?"

Letting out all the air he'd just breathed in, David looked away from Gary. It seemed the man had an uncanny ability to see right into David's mind.

An older couple walked into the ER, the man shuffling along, pushing a walker, the woman next to him looking pale, coughing as she walked beside him. He guided her to a chair and made sure she was comfortable before pushing the walker over to the registration counter.

"You could have that, David." Gary's voice cut through his thoughts.

"I think it's too late."

"Maybe you just need to start with step one."

"What is that?"

Gary jingled his keys in his pocket. "Go to Costa Rica. Figure out if you want this position or if you want something else. Ask God to make it clear to you."

"You want me to leave?" That didn't seem like the thing Gary would say after his pep talk about God changing callings.

"I do. Maybe God is changing you for something other than Costa Rica. Something better...not because Costa Rica isn't good, but because God's plan is always best. If you're seeking after God, your passions may change. That's God's doing. Follow Him where He leads you. Maybe it will be back here, maybe it won't."

God's doing? Could his change of heart really be God's working? His phoned buzzed in his pocket, and he pulled it out and glanced at the message from Lance. His director had changed his flight time. If David left now, he could make it in time for the next one.

Gary nodded next to him. "I'll talk to Sadie. She told you to leave anyway. So go, David. You have our blessing. Find what God's leading you to do. Trust Him. Not your supporters, not your preconceived notions, but God. He will lead you."

"Thank you." David walked out of the ER with purpose.

He pulled out his phone and typed a response to Lance's earlier message.

Ready or not, he was returning to Costa Rica.

In the light of day, things didn't look any better. In fact, they looked worse.

The wrecker slowly dragged Mrs. Allen's car out of the hardware store as glass crunched beneath the tire wheels. Once the car was cleared from the building, the wrecker towed it away.

The town square was quiet. It seemed folks had slept in after the excitement of searching for Lottie last night. Sadie stood alone outside the store—well, except for Otis, who had moved to the middle of the playground across the street. His bronze eyes were trained on the disaster that was Hoover's Hardware. At least he'd been safe last night.

Careful to miss any large chunks of glass, Sadie unlocked the door and stepped into the store. Instead of the order she'd created, chaos ruled. The glass counter that sat in front of the main window was shattered, the old-fashioned register bent and broken. The car had stopped before it had taken out the aisles—small blessings—but the shattered glass was everywhere, even embedded in the walls. Thankfully, the car had not affected the structure of the building, and she'd been able to stay in her apartment last night. But her mom was right, there was no way the grand reopening could take place next week. Unless they opened with a boarded-up front window and no front counter.

Not to mention Mrs. Allen's insurance had already called this morning and said they'd only cover a few thousand dollars' worth of damage. Nowhere near the amount they would need. Sadie didn't have extra money laying around to repair the store. Everything she could scrape together would need to go to the bank to cover the loan, and even then, she was still short. There was no money to fix the damages.

Her throat burned and her vision blurred. She'd failed. Four generations and she was the one to ruin the family business. She'd gambled her heart, her business, her savings. Her life. And she'd lost.

Lost it all.

At least Lottie had slept soundly all night. She was healthy and being spoiled at Sadie's parents' house this morning. Her mom had made cinnamon rolls, and Lottie ate two of them.

Silence reigned in the hardware store. David was gone. She wasn't sure why that had surprised her after she'd told him to leave. But when she'd gone back to the waiting room and her father said he'd left for the airport, it had been like a punch to the gut. She missed his presence, his friendship, his help. But he didn't want a partner, he didn't want...

Her.

A hand gripped Sadie's shoulder, and she jumped away with a screech.

"I'm sorry, Sis." An apologetic look crossed Romee's face. "I thought you heard me open the door and my footsteps crunching the glass. I wasn't exactly quiet."

Sadie hugged her sister, letting the strength of her embrace soothe the thoughts, the painful reality that she'd lost it all.

"I'm here, Sadie. We all are. Anna can be here next week, and Toby and Clara can be here tomorrow. We're going to get through this." Romee's voice oozed confidence.

If only Sadie could latch on to that, believe that with her siblings' help things would be better.

"It's not that simple." Sadie let go of Romee and turned back to the mess of her store as she walked farther in, taking in the mess. "We can't fix this."

"Of course we can." Glass crunched as Romee walked toward what used to be the front window. "We'll get this place cleaned up in no time."

"It's so much more than that."

"A little sweeping, some organization—"

Sadie spun around. "That won't —"

"I know you like to do things on your own, but I'm here, Sadie. I can help."

"You don't understand."

Romee shoved her hands on her hips. "I would understand if you'd let me in. If you'd let me help."

If it were that simple. If telling Romee all about her problems, if just speaking them out loud would solve them, she'd shout them from the rooftop. "There's nothing you can do."

"I can help. Look—I'm sorry I almost burned the house down when I was eight. It wasn't your fault, and you need to stop holding it over my head."

"I don't—"

"You do. And seriously, you have to let that go. It wasn't your fault, and I'm a grown woman now. I haven't started a fire in the kitchen in twenty years. Let me help with this." Romee stomped closer, reaching for her shoulder with a strength that surprised Sadie. Her sister had grown up, turned into a successful musician, and a competent and caring woman.

"I'm sorry. I have hung on to that. You're right though, we've both grown up a lot since then. But even so, this has nothing to do with not wanting to ask for help. Even with help, things are gone. The store, my home, possibly even Lottie."

"Lottie is safe. That is over."

"I'm talking about Doris contesting the adoption."

"What? Doris is contesting the adoption? You didn't tell me this?" Romee stepped forward and gripped Sadie's arms, shaking her slightly. "Okay, that's it. We're getting out of here."

Romee linked arms with Sadie and pulled her through the door, into the morning sun. She wiggled her fingers for the keys. Sadie handed them over, and Romee locked the door.

"It doesn't really matter if we close it. The front window is wide open."

"We'll have it boarded up soon, but first we're talking." Romee grabbed Sadie's hand again and continued to drag her around to the back of the store, up the wooden steps, and into her apartment. "Go sit on the couch. I'll make coffee. But we're talking about this. Let's talk about the adoption."

Sadie settled into the sofa so she could see the room and wrapped her favorite throw around herself. Soon, Romee came out with two cups of coffee, handing one to Sadie.

"Doris and Patrick are contesting."

"Wait. Hold that thought." Romee pulled her phone out and pressed a few buttons. A few seconds later, Anna's voice filled the room. "Hang on, I'm connecting Toby."

Sadie sipped her coffee as she listened to her brother join the call.

"Okay. Sadie is here with me. You both heard that Lottie was lost last night. And about the accident at the store. But what you haven't heard—" Romee lifted an eyebrow. "They haven't heard, have they?"

Sadie shook her head. "I haven't told anyone. Well, except David."

"Told us what?" Anna. Direct and to the point.

"Doris and Patrick are contesting the adoption hearing. And now that I can't pay the bank the money the store owes, I won't have a job, a home, or anything. I'm not sure that the case will be open-and-shut."

Silence.

Sadie looked at Romee, who chewed on her bottom lip and glanced at the phone between them.

"I really messed up, you guys. And on top of it all, David and I—" What? Broke up? It was so much more than a simple breakup. "He went back to Costa Rica."

"Idiot. Leopards don't change—"

"That doesn't help, Anna." Toby cut off her sister's tirade. "David isn't a leopard, and I am guessing him leaving wasn't just on him. Just like I am guessing him leaving last time wasn't only on him. Am I right?"

"What do you know?" Romee and Anna practically said in unison.

"Nothing." Toby sat in silence as if waiting for Sadie to fill in the blanks, but she couldn't. Not right now. "Sadie, did you ever tell him you wanted him to stay?"

Romee set her cup on the coffee table. "There has to be a way to fight Doris and Patrick. You know what...I think we need Mom and Dad in on this conversation."

Sadie's stomach sank. "I haven't told them. I will. I promise. Just not...yet."

"Not yet? Stop shutting yourself away. From us. From Mom and Dad. From David." Toby let out a sigh, and Sadie could picture him shaking his head.

"It's more complicated with Mom and Dad. I don't want them to blame themselves." She focused on that because she really didn't want to talk about David. Sadie pulled the blanket up, balancing the coffee so as not to spill it. "I gambled. Put everything into the store. All my savings and it's not enough."

"Why does the store owe money? I thought Dad owned that property." Anna's accounting mind was probably crunching all the numbers.

"He said they went through a rough patch, took out a mortgage to pay for things, and it just sorta went south. They never caught up." Sadie lifted a shoulder. If she'd been prepared, she would have known this before taking over. Instead, she'd asked God what to do, her dad fell, and it just seemed right. She'd thought this was God's path, that He'd opened doors and directed in a specific way. So, she'd leapt—and landed in a puddle on the ground.

"And so, you took over the store, didn't tell anyone it was in trouble, and sank everything from Jeremy into the store." Romee's disgust bled through every word. She turned toward Sadie, squeezing her shoulders. "We're here to help. Hoover's Hardware is our family business."

"That you have no interest in. None of you. You took off to travel with your music, only to land in Grand Rapids. Toby settled down in Florida with Clara, doing what God called him to do. And Anna, she left Heritage the moment she graduated high school, never looking back. I don't even know where you are because you move around so much. Why would I think any of you have an interest in the store?" Or her. They'd all left her, just like David had. After she'd been left alone again with Lottie after Jeremy died, she learned to depend on herself. Sadie's hands shook. "I can handle this on my own. It's my problem."

"Except you're not handling it." Toby sighed. A door closed over the phone, and the sound changed. He must be going somewhere. "I'm coming."

"What? No, Toby. There's no need. Really. Not to mention it would take you hours to get here. You can't leave Clara on a whim." Sadie shifted forward out of Romee's grip and placed her mug on a coaster.

"Then listen, Sadie." Toby's deep voice sounded so much like their dad's that Sadie swallowed down her emotions. "You are not alone. God is with you. He did lead you back to Heritage, and He's never going to leave you. We've seen that promise come to fruition so many times, that even when we feel alone, we can trust something bigger than ourselves. Right now is one of those times. We have to trust Him."

"That's easier said than done." Sadie wanted it to be as simple as Toby made it sound. Wanted to just jump in and agree with him. But sometimes, trusting was harder than it sounded. Romee slung an arm around her shoulder and pulled Sadie close.

"Of course, it is. But God never, ever does things in our life without a purpose. And when things are too big for us to handle, that probably means we are trying to handle them in our own strength. We have to rely on Him and the support of the people He put in our life. I don't like this situation you're facing, especially the possibility of losing Lottie, but listen here. None of us—" Romee tightened her grip on Sadie and gestured toward the phone. "I repeat, none of us will let you face this alone."

Anna cleared her throat, her voice oddly gravelly like she was fighting tears. "You can't get rid of us. No matter where I am, I'm just a plane ride or two away. Mom always said siblings have to stick together. So, you're stuck."

Sadie relaxed into Romee's embrace. Strength came in many forms, but she hadn't leaned into the strength of her family. Maybe ever. As the oldest it was her job to take care of them, and she'd done a pretty good job. To have her siblings gather around her, to offer her love and support—her eyes burned. Maybe, with the help of her family, she could trust God. Trust that this path she'd jumped onto wouldn't take everything she loved from her.

sixteen

THE SUN SHONE THROUGH THE FRONT WINDOW
of David's favorite family-owned restaurant on a corner of a resi-
dential area in San Jose. If he could figure anything out on this trip,
it would be with the help of Maria, the tiny, older owner—more like
David's adopted grandma. She rushed around the counter to hug him
when he walked in, asking a long, fast string of questions. He patted
her back as she fired off at least a hundred questions. Then she let go,
put one hand on each cheek, and pulled his face down to her height.

It had been so long since David had spoken in Spanish, not
having needed it since he'd been sent home six months ago, that it
took a heartbeat to catch up. "How was your time away? Did your
family feed you? Did you fall in love? Are you healed?"

A variety of the same questions mingled as Maria made obser-
vations about his clothes, his hair, and even the weight he may or
may not have gained. She squeezed his arm and shook her head,
clucking.

Wise, older eyes studied him, her brown irises darkening. "How
is Leah? And her baby?"

"Great. Isabella is beautiful and growing quickly."

Maria nodded. "If your family is well, then you've found someone, because your heart is sad in your eyes."

He'd found someone over ten years ago. Completely ruined it then. And now? She'd kicked him out of her life. Again. It didn't help that her life was over two thousand miles away. David shook his head, and Maria's hands tightened on his face.

Pain radiated from his spine to his neck to his toes. After the all-nighter he'd pulled looking for Lottie and then driving to the airport in Grand Rapids, only sleeping a few hours on the plane, his body was feeling every ache and pain. None of it compared to the ache growing in the center of his chest, though.

A breeze blew into the café as someone walked in behind him. He struggled to free himself from Maria's grip, but she tightened the hold on his face, pulling it even closer. Her clean scent mixed with all the spices she used in the kitchen. She let out a loud sigh and practically slapped at his cheek. "I'll make your favorite, and we'll talk."

She let go and spun on her heel with more energy than women a third of her age. Her gray bun bounced at the nape of her neck. "Go sit, David. I'll bring you food. And you will talk with me."

David chuckled. The café had become a regular stop for him not long after he moved to Costa Rica. Maria had sensed his wandering and lonely soul and latched on to him. He'd drawn the line at attending her family meals and celebrations, but he had been there when her husband, Ricardo, had passed four years ago. Maria's son Matteo had insisted David attend the family gathering, coming into the school to invite him.

Sadie would like Maria, her no-nonsense business attitude. Her determination, and her ability to read people. Pain seeped into David's chest, and he rubbed at his sternum—it wasn't a physical pain, but it hurt just as much as if he'd broken a rib.

A heaping pile of meat and veggies on a tabla slid toward him, the sweet and tangy scent making his stomach growl. Casado de res—his favorite meal—served on a banana leaf. When was the last time he'd eaten? Had it been the stale peanut butter and jelly sandwich at home? No, surely, he ate in the airport, but he couldn't remember what.

Maria placed a large bowl of soup in front of the seat across from him then gestured toward the kitchen as a young server brought two glasses of Coke. She slid her hand across the table, and David held it, her leathered skin warm against his. David said a quick prayer over the meal and then quickly dug in.

Maria ate in silence, and it wasn't until David slowed down, almost finished with his meal, that she fired the first question. "What is wrong, David?"

"Nothing." David shoveled another bite of meat and veggies into his mouth.

Maria shook her head. "You cannot lie to me, David. I know you. Tell me how you have broken your spirit."

Broken his spirit?

Moving the food around on his plate, he considered Maria's words. She'd been too good to him over the years to give her a flippant answer. Besides, she'd only pry the truth out of him. "I'm not sure my spirit is broken. But I've hurt someone I care about."

"That is not you, David. You love and serve and give. Why would you hurt someone you love?"

Love. That word dug in. It hurt and pinched, and then settled in feeling rather...right. Like he should have grabbed hold of it when he first recognized it and told Sadie. Run to her with the revelation. He had always loved her. "It was never my intent to hurt her. I was trying to do the exact opposite, but I was stupid and wrong. And exactly what I was trying not to do."

"Then apologize and fix it." Maria took another sip of her soup, looking at him like it was the simplest thing to do.

If only it was. David pushed the plate away, the food turning over in his stomach. He shouldn't have eaten so much. "I don't know if I can."

"And why is that, David? What is holding you back?" Maria pushed her bowl away, too, leaning her elbows on the table. If the table wasn't between them, David had no doubt she'd grab his face again and scold him like an errant child.

"Because I'm here." David gestured around the restaurant. The warm colored walls decorated with local artwork. The lunch rush had cleared out a while ago, and David was the only one there. In fact, Maria would be closing soon.

"Are you supposed to be here?" Maria's voice needled the question he'd asked himself over and over. The visit with Wesley this morning had been insightful. The position incredible. He'd be able to return to Costa Rica, his life here, his work, the people he'd made connections with, like Maria, but he'd leave behind his family. Sadie.

"God called me here." He had. David had no doubt that ten years ago the Lord had asked him to follow the calling to Costa Rica, and David had willingly obeyed.

Maria nodded. "Things change, David. Do you remember when Ricardo died and I floundered? You said to me, 'God is full of surprises. And even in this turn of events, He is leading you, guiding you.' Your words gave me the freedom to close up the store, move away, or take over."

And Maria had stayed. She'd taken up the store, coming into the café day in and day out even without Ricardo. "But you stayed here. Kept this place open, loved on everyone who walked in."

"Because that's my calling—to feed the hungry. At first it was to feed my hungry family, and with four boys, they were always eating. But they grew up, and still I wanted to feed the hungry. How I followed God's calling changed. I'd never spent much time in this kitchen when Ricardo was living. I stayed home, kept our house, and I fed him."

That wasn't right. Maria had always been part of the café. "I always saw you here."

"I came to be with Ricardo. But I didn't cook here. Not until he died. Then my plans changed."

"But the school, the students—"

"God will take care of them." And He had. He'd already brought Chris in, and after seeing Chris in action, on the weekend no less, David knew that he brought an energy, a youthfulness to the position David had filled for ten years. An excitement that David could feel in the air. "What did God call you to do here?"

"To love and to share Him." Which he'd been doing in Heritage. His heart sped up, and he wiped his hands on his pants. Was this what everyone had been telling him? That God's calling could change—not because David was no longer useful, but because God could use him someplace else?

"What is holding you back, David?" Maria reached across the table, pushing his tabla out of the way, and wiggled her fingers, indicating she wanted his hand. He offered it to her, and she pulled it closer.

"What if I've mess it up? What if I've completely derailed God's plan and I can't fix it?"

Maria threw her head back and laughed. "Oh, David. You cannot derail God's plan. You may have added a detour or two, but His purpose never changes. He will keep drawing you to Him. Unlike God, who can surprise us daily, you can never surprise Him. You're going to make mistakes, but God offers forgiveness. His mercy will never end, and He will continue to guide you."

He couldn't derail God's plan.

Those words sank in deep, digging in. The truth resonating within.

He couldn't ruin God's plan. Hadn't ruined God's plan.

If he and Sadie had stayed together, who knew where Lottie would be today. God needed Sadie to be there for that little girl.

And David had needed to be in Costa Rica then. But now? Now might be the time for David and Sadie to finally fix their problems.

"What if I've ruined Sadie's trust in me?"

"Ah, I knew there was a woman in your heart." A wide smile broke across Maria's face as she used her free hand to pat her chest. "You are a good man, like my Ricardo. He had to prove to me, too. It took a while, but he did. I heard him through his actions. We had forty-seven years together. Prove to your Sadie, with your actions, that you can be trusted. Do whatever it takes to prove that you will be the man that will stand by her. And every day, you show her you love her."

David squeezed Maria's leathered hand. He could do that, show up in Sadie's life, let his actions speak louder than his words. It might take years, but if God was calling him to be patient for years, he could do that. He'd wait as long as it took, because Maria was right. He did love Sadie.

He stood, and Maria wrapped him in a hug, her strong arms tightening around him as she patted his back. "You bring her back to meet me."

"I will."

It was a promise he'd be glad to keep.

Instrumental music played over the speakers inside the bank. Two tellers behind the counter were already working with customers on Monday morning, and Eddie Fry sat at his desk behind a glass wall.

Sadie adjusted her purse on her shoulder and ran her hand over her stomach. She had a check for a fraction of what was owed.

Eddie came out and extended a hand to Sadie to shake. "I'm sorry about the accident at the store, but thankful no one was hurt."

It had been the sentiment she'd heard all over town, but it didn't make the failure to meet next week's deadline any better. "I was hoping we could talk for a moment."

"Of course." Eddie motioned toward his office, and Sadie followed him in. She sat in the leather chair across from his desk as his thick brows burrowed together. "What can I do for you?"

"I brought a check to apply toward our balance. I know we still owe more. But I'm hoping that perhaps since I've been able to pay so much, that we could work out an extension. After the accident, the store's not open. If I could just have a little more time, I know I could pay off the balance, eventually."

Sadie pulled the check out of her purse and slid it across to Eddie. He glanced at the amount. She still owed thousands. She held her breath as Eddie studied the check. "I talked to Mr. Mackers about this. Knowing the accident would be a severe setback, he still says he can't extend the loan any longer. I'm so sorry."

The tears stung, but she refused to let them fall. She had known it would be the inevitable outcome, but she'd hoped for a miracle. She'd run the numbers last night one more time. If she could collect all the outstanding credit at the store, she'd only be short a few thousand dollars. Maybe she could ask her siblings to cover that. But without the credit, she couldn't ask them to cover the balance. It was too much. She'd tried. Prayed for a miracle, and it just hadn't happened. "I understand. Thank you."

Sadie stood and offered her hand to Eddie. She wouldn't cry in the bank. It wasn't Eddie's fault she'd failed. He squeezed her hand. "I'm sorry."

She nodded and left the bank, walking toward her parents' house. She had to tell her dad. She paused in front of Hoover's boarded-up window. Romee had been true to her word, helping to clean up and organize the store as best they could. They'd been making a list of all the merchandise ruined in the accident, trying to figure out what was left, and pulled the glass out of the walls.

Sadie had found a company she could order new windows from but hadn't placed the order. There was no reason to. She couldn't pay the bank. There was no money left to replace windows and fix the store.

Walking on, she crossed Richard Street and stepped into her parents' house. Her dad sat in the living room while her mother played the piano. She drew the old familiar hymn "Trust and Obey" to a close as Sadie shut the front door and settled into the couch next to her dad.

"Looks like you've got the weight of the world on your shoulders." Her dad closed his Bible draped over his lap and set it on the table beside his recliner.

"I took the payment to the bank. Eddie says there's no more time. October thirty-first is still the deadline." Sadie's heart picked up speed as her dad let out a breath. "There is one chance. If we could collect the credit due the store, we'd be close enough that we might make the deadline."

Her mom settled on the couch next to Sadie and stretched out her hand. Sadie held it and took a deep breath. "There's—"

"I'm sorry, Sadie. I should never have forgiven the Mathews family's payment. I knew how much we needed the money. However, I trust God to see us through. I still think He will."

Maybe God would see them through. Sadie wished she had the faith her dad did. Even with the blow today, he still sat there, confident that the store would be saved.

"I appreciate that, Dad. We do need every payment. But I think it's time to admit that maybe it's God's timing for the store to close." Sadie let out a shuddered breath. Her mom's hand tightened on hers. "But there's something else I want to tell you."

Her mom placed her free hand on top of their joined hands, her long fingers older and more wrinkled than the hands from Sadie's childhood. These hands belonged to the woman who had guided Sadie, loved her, pushed her, and comforted her growing up—the hands of a mom.

"Doris and Patrick are contesting the adoption. With the situation at the store, my lawyer says the case could go either way tomorrow."

Her mom gasped, and she released Sadie's hands, instead pulling her into a tight hug. Her dad stood and pulled them both up, wrapping his arms around them. Sadie let the warmth of the embrace infuse her with confidence. Her mom's rose-and-lavender scent mingled with her dad's leather and peppermint, creating a cocoon of comfort. Of family.

Her dad's deep voice rumbled through their embrace as he tightened his hold. "You are an excellent mother. The judge will rule in your favor."

Sadie longed for her dad's confidence. "Doris and Patrick say I am irresponsible, and they've built a pretty compelling case. The situation at the hardware store doesn't help. Lottie has written a note to the judge, expressing her wishes. But, Dad, what if..."

"No." Her mom loosened her embrace, her gentle hands moving up to Sadie's shoulders. "Absolutely no what-ifs."

"Your mother's right. God has gotten people out of impossible situations before. Look at Jonah. Three days in the belly of a big fish. I cannot imagine a more impossible situation, and God got him out. God is not going to take Lottie from us."

"You are what is best for that little girl." Her mom's hands moved from Sadie's shoulders to her elbows and back up. "There is no doubt in any of our minds. Jeremy knew it, too. We are going to trust God in this. He will do what's best for Lottie, and letting her stay with you—that is what's best."

"But—"

Sadie's mom gently shook her. "No buts. Have faith."

What choice did she have? She couldn't fix it on her own,

couldn't think her way out, couldn't will anything to change. She could only trust God.

"How long have you known all this, Sadie girl?"

"Not quite two weeks." Sadie settled back down on the couch because her legs trembled.

"No wonder you're exhausted. Let me get you something to eat." Her mom stepped into the kitchen.

Her dad sat back down in his recliner. "Have you been carrying this alone since then?"

A rough cuticle poked her thumb as she ran it over her nail. "David knew."

"He's been good for you this time. I'm sure he'll be there tomorrow to support you."

Her dad's confidence was misplaced.

"No, he won't. He's made his choice, and I'm not it." Her dad grunted and Sadie held up her hand. "Don't. I don't want him there. Ten years ago, maybe I should have fought for us. But not now. I'm different now. The situation is different, and I have to think about Lottie. David made his choice. It's time to let him go. Time to move on."

As much as it hurt, as much as she wished things could be different this time, they weren't. This was one thing her dad had wrong. He may be right about God. The good Lord had gotten people out of pretty tough places in the past. Maybe a miracle could be in her future.

"Ok, Sadie girl. I won't say anything more about David. But I'll trust God to work everything out." A confidence and faith that Sadie longed to have flowed from him. Until then, maybe if she said the words, the faith would appear.

"I wish I had that kind of trust, Dad."

Her dad covered her hand with his own. "Trust is a learned behavior. The more you do it, the easier it becomes."

"But I trusted God to work all this out." Sadie had asked His blessing, followed through every open door. Given everything she had to save the store, given her life to care for Jeremy and now Lottie. It wasn't enough.

She had tried trusting.

It hadn't worked.

Her dad's large hand squeezed hers, and he shook his head. "Trusting God isn't a matter of making plans and then asking Him to bless. Trusting God is asking Him what plans to make then doing the ones He lays out. Trusting God is knowing He's already seen your future, already has it planned out, and even if you go through some ups and downs, it's going to be worth it, because He's already taken care of it all."

No wonder trust brought about peace. If she could trust God to work out all the details, if she didn't have to carry that all by herself, it would help. She hadn't really asked God about the move, about the adoption, about David. She'd asked God's blessing, but his advice? Nope, not that.

Her dad gestured toward his Bible. "Before you walked in, I was reading in Exodus chapter eight, where the flies had invaded Egypt during the infamous plagues."

"I know the story of the ten plagues. Learned them back in Sunday School as a kid."

"I know. But this stuck out as I was reading. The flies? They were everywhere. Ruined tons of stuff."

"And Moses prayed, and the problem was solved." See? She'd paid attention. Had even told Lottie the story.

"Yes, but did you notice that after Moses prayed, all the flies left?"

"All the flies? Really?"

"It says not a single fly remained. God controlled them all. Every tiny little detail surrounding each individual insect. If God can take care of each tiny little bug, He certainly can take care of you.

Of Lottie. Of the store. So, we're going to pray, and we're going to trust, okay?"

Perhaps it was time to pray and ask God's guidance, not just His blessing. Pray that God would remove the 'flies' in Sadie's life. She'd pray that Lottie would be protected. That whatever was best for her would happen, even if that meant losing her to Doris and Patrick.

While Sadie had convinced herself that to succeed, she couldn't depend on anyone, she'd unknowingly self-sabotaged it all, allowing all the pesky flies to eat up her life. Without God, she would never have the peace, the love she so desperately wanted.

Her faith might be a little out of practice, but she knew that God would forgive her pride and help her to trust in something beyond herself.

That elusive peace that had been just out of reach filled her. She turned her hand over and squeezed her dad's.

God would work things out. He would be with her to carry her through whatever came next. And she'd trust Him to take care of the flies, because she couldn't do it herself. She trusted that, not because she didn't have a choice, since she had nothing left to lose, but because she knew God had never left her, and He never would.

seventeen

AVID HAD BEEN HOME A FEW HOURS ON Monday, and Sadie hadn't taken his calls, sending him directly to voicemail. His small truck bounced over the dirt driveway as he pulled up in front of Chet's house. He had barely landed this morning when his phone had buzzed with a voicemail from Chet—he'd finished the clock. Maybe it would be enough for Sadie to talk with him. She might not. She might never give him another chance, but regardless, David would be there for Lottie.

He picked up the Styrofoam container of breakfast he'd brought and hurried up the porch.

David knocked, and after a few minutes, the front door creaked open. Chet grabbed the food and waved David in. "Follow me."

Chet's gruff tone didn't surprise David, as the man's message had been just as short and to the point as he was in person. Chet sat in an armchair near a TV tray and started eating the biscuits and gravy. The room was clean, except for a few cobwebs in the corners, the furniture well cared for. The place could be a model home from the 1960's. A picture of Joseph—Luke and Hannah's youngest son—sat framed on the coffee table.

"Finished that clock up. Figured you wanted to give it back. Shame it's not in the square anymore."

David rocked back on his heels. "Agreed."

Chet motioned at the couch. "Have a seat. You're making me nervous. Jon said you were in Costa Rica."

In the voicemail, Chet had said Jon gave him David's number. "Just got back."

"For good?" Chet picked up a mug, looked inside, sniffed it, then shrugged and drank from it.

David scooted back on the couch and rubbed his hands on his knees. As long as it took to convince Sadie he was all in. "That's the plan."

"Good. So, you're gonna fight for the girl?"

David pulled at his collar. "With everything in me."

"About time, boy." Chet cut another large piece of biscuit and stuck it in his mouth. "Have a plan?"

"Never took you for a romantic."

Chet froze. His glare could freeze boiling water.

David sat up straight. "I mean, I just...didn't...well, I guess I could say..."

A slow grin spread across Chet's face. "Easy there, just teasing. It can go both ways."

Unsure if he really was teasing, David tried to relax on the couch without offending the man any further.

"What are you planning to do to win her back?"

Okay, so maybe Chet did have an interest. "I don't know yet, but I thought maybe I could get this clock to them. I promised Sadie I'd fix it, or find someone to, and I'd like to come through for her."

Chet hummed and chewed. "You need one of those big hoopla things. You know, like the ones in the movies."

Chet watched movies?

"You mean like a..." Picnic? A party?

"A gesture!" Chet slammed the fork down on the TV tray. "You need a grand gesture."

"Like showing up every day? Bringing the clock?"

Chet scratched his chin. "I don't know if that's big enough. Let's go see the clock."

Moving the TV tray aside, Chet stood up and shuffled out of the house. David followed him outside and to the barn.

Inside, Chet stood at the tool bench, the clock sitting upright, telling the correct time. "Stretched me. Had never worked on a clock. Lottie was right, there was a twig inside, between the gears."

David stood a little taller. Lottie was a bright kid, smart, intelligent, observant—like her mom.

"The clock is great, Chet. Thank you." Jon had already warned David not to offer to pay Chet, it would only offend him, so David stuck out his hand. "This might be the big thing you were talking about."

Chet gripped his hand and held tight. "No. You need to think bigger. You know Hannah, she pulled the whole town together to petition for Luke to keep his house."

"Sadie doesn't need me to bring everyone together to petition for her home."

"No. But think big, like Hannah did. Really show her that you love her."

Wow, Chet really was a romantic. "I'll keep that in mind."

"See that you do. Now, let's get this loaded up." Chet picked up the box David had brought it in and set it on the bench. "You load it up."

David thanked Chet again after situating the clock in the truck. Off to a good start. He had fulfilled a promise he'd made. Maria said to show up every day, and so far, he hadn't even been home and he'd managed to succeed in one area. One small step—in the right direction.

The ringing of his phone had him pulling over. His heart rate picked up as he dug his phone out of his pocket. Maybe it was Sadie.

No such luck.

Romee.

His heart rate didn't slow. This couldn't be good. "What's wrong?"

"Well, it depends on how you look at things. But I think you might be able to turn things around, if you're willing to help out." Romee's light and airy voice chimed like bells, sounding just as musical as she was.

"If it means helping Sadie, I'm all in."

"I knew you would come through." He could picture Romee throwing a fist bump from the smug sound of her voice. "I've been talking to Anna and Toby, and we're not there to do this, so we need boots on the ground. You willing?"

"If there was ever a time for a Hail Mary, this is it."

"You know Doris and Patrick are contesting the adoption to-morrow. We'd like to get as many people as possible to write letters to the judge, speaking on Sadie's behalf. Also, maybe while you contact people, you could mention the need for them to pay off their line of credit. I haven't seen the books, and Dad can't remember all the names, and he can't find where she's moved it, but you've seen it."

"I know where she keeps it. It's in her desk."

"Dad didn't see it. But I'll have him meet you at the store. How soon can you be there?"

"Ten minutes?"

"Perfect. If we can get those names, we can ask people to take their payment directly to the bank. Dad got it approved that any-thing deposited into the store's account can be applied directly toward our loan. If you encourage them to do it before the month's end, it might save the store."

They talked over a few more details before David pulled back onto the road. Chet would love this—two gestures at the same time.

And if this didn't work, he'd show up every day until he convinced Sadie that this time, he wanted a partner.

This time he wanted it all.

The plastic seats in the sterile hallway outside the courtroom weren't meant for comfort. Still, Sadie pulled Lottie closer, offering what support she could as her daughter twirled a yellow leaf between her thumb and forefinger. The single leaf had blown across their path outside the courthouse this morning and Lottie had picked it up. "It makes me think Daddy's here, too."

The white marble walls rose behind the seats of the group—Sadie, Lottie, Romee, her parents. Anna's flight had been canceled, and Sadie had insisted that Toby not spend the twelve hundred dollars on a last-minute flight. They all waited for the lawyers to arrive.

Small windows at the top of the wall allowed the sun to shine in, the only indicator that the storm raging in Sadie's heart wasn't ravishing the outside world.

Surrounded by family, she clung to her daughter. Her mom's hand rested on Lottie's knee, while her dad occasionally leaned forward as though he were taking a mental picture. Romee hummed a tune, low and slow.

"Oma? Do you think my letter will be enough for the judge?" Lottie's voice trembled as she snuggled into Sadie.

Sadie's mom patted Lottie's knee. "Lottie girl, God will keep watch over you no matter what. We can always trust Him. But I think you telling the judge your wishes can only help."

Doris and Patrick sat several chairs down from their small

group. Lottie had barely said hello to them, instead sticking close to Sadie and her family.

Which was fine by Sadie. She'd rather keep as much physical contact as possible, especially with the possibility that Lottie would go home with someone else. Sadie hugged Lottie closer, her own body shivering. Regret hung in her stomach, highlighting every mistake she'd made as a guardian—David might top the list, but there were plenty more. She'd heard that he'd returned, but probably not for long before he took off on his next adventure. He'd called her yesterday several times, but she'd sent each call to voicemail and hadn't allowed herself to listen to his messages.

One heartbreak at a time.

Blocking out everything around her, Sadie buried her nose in Lottie's hair, trying to memorize this moment. The feel of Lottie in her arms, the peachy scent of her shampoo, the weight of her daughter pressed against her. Please, Lord. Don't take her away. But either way, I'm trusting her into Your care.

Quick footsteps echoed on the floor, and Sadie turned to see Leah hurrying toward her.

Behind Leah a handful of Heritage folks walked toward them, bringing hope and love to the cold hallway. Leah squatted down in front of Sadie and wrapped her arms around both Sadie and Lottie. Sadie stood as the others approached. She blinked back tears when Caroline stepped forward and wrapped her arms around her.

"This time, we're here for you Sadie. David, too." Leah pointed at David, who stood at the back of the group, his dark eyes trained on her.

Oxygen seemed to seep out of the room. She blinked and looked away. She could not deal with him today.

"He's here for support." Caroline squeezed her shoulders. "Not answers."

Sadie couldn't keep the tears at bay, and a few leaked out, trailing down her cheeks. Sadie wiped at them. Hopefully her mascara wasn't streaking, since it was supposed to be waterproof. "Where are the girls?"

"Mayor Jamison's wife has them at a park." Caroline stepped back, making room for people to talk to Sadie.

Mayor Jamison, his usual friendly expression filled with compassion, stepped up, his hands on his belly.

"Thank you for coming today." Sadie needed a tissue. She wiped at her face again.

The mayor crushed Sadie in a hug. "We never let our own face struggles alone. And you, Sadie, are one of us. You may have moved away for a while, but you're back. And you never stopped being one of us. And now Lottie is, too."

He set Sadie back to arm's length and gave her a curt nod before moving down to greet her parents.

Sadie sat back down, and Romee settled in next to her and placed her hand on Sadie's. "Listen, I've been praying and thinking about everything. God's going to see you through this. It's not easy to trust when we can't see the outcome, but that's the time it's necessary."

She couldn't contain the air that whooshed from her lungs. "What if—"

"No what-ifs right now. I want you to remember this—" Romee squeezed Sadie's hand. "You have a host of people behind you. An entire town, really. You are a fantastic mother to Lottie. You'd have to be blind not to see the love between you two. Trust God to work it all out. With Lottie. With the hardware store. With David. Nothing is over yet."

Sadie blinked, the tears that had started flowing coming quicker. God had brought crazy trials into her life. But if she'd married David and gone to Costa Rica all those years ago, she would have missed out on loving Lottie—something she wouldn't trade for anything in the world. God had brought them together. Two girls needing a place to fit in. Two girls loved by a God who would carry them through life, to bring about good.

Through heartbreak, He'd brought Lottie.

Isn't that how God worked—bringing her through heartache to give her gifts?

And He'd brought David back. She easily found him standing at the back of the crowd. He watched her, and his lips turned up. Her breath caught and her heart tip-tapped a merry beat.

He was here. With her. Even when he didn't need to be. Why wasn't he in Costa Rica?

She needed to apologize, but stubbornness and anger plus the stress of the court case had kept her from answering his calls. Kept her rooted in place. Today was for Lottie. He understood—she could see it in his eyes, and in the way he held himself back.

Romee squeezed Sadie's hand once again. Simon Martin, her lawyer, strolled down the hallway in a brown suit. His thick brown hair in a perfect lawyer combover. His stylish glasses sat on his large nose. His facial hair trimmed neatly. Next to him, the older man Doris and Patrick had hired as their lawyer. He wore an equally nice gray suit. His head bald, a thin gray mustache covering his upper lip.

Simon stopped in front of her. "If you're ready, we can head in."

Lottie clung to Sadie. Her small body trembled.

Sadie patted her back and kissed the top of her head. No matter what happened today, she'd had the opportunity to love Lottie like her own, and she wouldn't trade that for anything.

"I love you, Lottie. Regardless of the outcome, you remember that I love you." She hugged her little girl tightly before they stood and entered the courtroom.

They were the last to enter, and Sadie kept her gaze on Lottie as they made their way to the front of the room, hand in hand. Once seated in wooden chairs behind a matching table, Sadie finally glanced around the room, one like every courtroom she'd seen on TV.

A moment later, the judge walked in, carrying a thick black leather folder under his arm, and everyone stood until he was seated behind his desk. His graying hair curled around his ears, and his wire-rimmed glasses sat low on his nose. He settled in his seat, and everyone followed suit.

"Each custody hearing is unique. I've allowed some last-minute evidence to be brought in. Unusual? Yes. But my prerogative. Considering the future of this young child, I wanted to make sure I had all the information before I made a decision. What matters most in these types of hearings is that the child is placed in the best possible home."

The judge nodded and the bailiff handed each lawyer a manila folder.

"Before you open that, I would like to say a few words. Lottie, your letter was heartfelt, innocent, and quite honestly, lovely."

Lottie sat up a little straighter, a small smile breaking out on her face as she continued to twirl the leaf in her hand.

"I received a call last night, and while it is highly unusual to take a call about an open case, I allowed this one through because I want what's best for Lottie." The judge tapped a folder in front of him. He cleared his throat and paused a moment. "In an unusual and overwhelming show of support, an entire folder of letters has been collected from people who know Ms. Hoover and have seen her interact with Lottie."

The judge gestured toward the envelopes. Simon opened his up and scanned over the first few letters. Sadie couldn't look over his shoulder, her stomach too queasy to focus on reading.

"I took the time to read each and every letter, and Ms. Hoover, let me say, you have made quite the impression on your small town. They have the utmost confidence in your parenting skills and in your affection for Lottie. Also, for your business skills. I say that because of the concern over the financial state of your store. However, taking each of those letters into consideration, the letter Mr. Linden left behind and the way he set up his will, not to mention the letter Lottie wrote for herself—well, it made my decision easy." The judge turned toward Lottie. "Miss Linden, I will honor your request and allow you to stay with Ms. Hoover. Ms. Hoover, your request to adopt Lottie Linden is approved."

Lottie launched into Sadie's arms as cheering and clapping rang through the courtroom.

Tears streamed down Lottie's cheeks. Sadie's, too. Lottie's small body vibrated with energy as she squeezed Sadie tighter. Sadie rested her cheek on Lottie's soft hair, her shoulders finally relaxing.

It was official! Lottie was her daughter.

"Court adjourned." He smacked his gavel, nodded, and left the room.

Sadie closed her eyes. Thank You. An inadequate, but heartfelt response to the One who had carried her through. He had never left, and today He'd turned all of Sadie's hard times into something wonderful.

He'd given her something beautiful out of the heartbreak.

He'd given her Lottie.

Doris and Patrick stood in front of the table when Sadie opened her eyes, Lottie still clinging to her. Doris's lips pursed. "I do hope that we can continue to have a relationship with Lottie. She's all I have left of Jeremy."

Heat bubbled in Sadie's stomach, but understanding cooled her temper. Grief made people do unusual things. Sadie nodded.

A look of relief crossed Doris's face, and she offered her hand to Lottie. Lottie glanced at Sadie before slipping her small hand in Doris's. "I do love you, sweet girl. I only want what's best."

Doris left the courtroom, followed by her husband close behind.

Sadie thanked her lawyer, and he handed her the folder full of letters. "I think you should read those, Sadie. Not only do they show support for you, but they all mention payment of outstanding debt to a certain hardware store."

"What?" Sadie flipped the manila envelope open, but she couldn't read anything, her vision too blurry.

God had worked out the details.

"I'm going to hug Oma." Lottie bounced over, and Sadie's mom knelt down so Lottie's arms went around her neck. Tears flowed freely down Dawn's cheeks.

Mayor Jamison and Sadie's dad joined her by the table, and the mayor gripped her shoulder and squeezed it. "Sadie, I want you to read those letters. When David approached me with the idea of a letter campaign, I knew he had a stroke of genius, even if the compilation was a bit of a Hail Mary in the last quarter of the game."

Sadie's traitorous heart leapt at his name. "David's idea?"

"It's right there." He pointed at the stack of letters.

Right there on top sat a letter typed up with a signature she knew too well.

David's.

"He organized this?"

"With my help. Well, it was my idea and David brought it to life since I wasn't in Heritage." Romee walked up and threw her arm around Sadie's shoulder. "Dad cleared things at the bank for people to make payments to be credited to our loan."

Our loan. The word sank in. She wasn't alone. And when she had nothing left to give, God had stepped in and worked out everything.

Romee shook her phone. "I called Toby and Anna. Between the three of us, we can cover the five thousand dollars that didn't come in. Everything from the insurance settlement will be able to go back into the store. Show her the bank account info, Dad."

Her dad pulled his phone out and tapped the screen a few times. He turned it for Sadie to see the total in the bank.

"People paid their loans?" Tears kept streaming down Sadie's cheeks.

Her dad nodded. "I'm sorry, Sadie. It was never my intent to put the stress of the loans on you."

Sadie hugged him, his strong arms coming around her, holding her tight. "You were right, Dad. God worked it all out. Took care of so many of the flies in my life. Even better than I could have imagined."

He pointed at the letters. "Everything but one area. And He will work that one out too. But I'm still holding out hope for a happily ever after for you and David. Especially after today. Maybe I've watched too many of those mushy movies with your mom. Or maybe I know a good team when I see one." He tapped the side of his nose.

A team. A partner. A support. David had been all that and more. Until he wasn't, choosing again to make decisions as a solo unit.

But he'd stepped up today, helping her in ways she didn't even know she needed.

Plus, he'd shown up for the hearing. Several people still mingled, happiness clear on their faces, but there was no sign of David. His sisters still visited with her mom, but David's familiar shoulders, his confident stance—nowhere to be found.

Giving her space, just as Caroline said. Today wasn't about them, it had been about her daughter. He'd been there. For Lottie, for support, but not for reconciliation. Their time had already passed. There was so much hurt, so much history. The saying 'the third time's the charm' didn't apply here. "It may be too late."

"Now see here. Don't be giving up hope yet." Mayor Jamison pulled his pants up by their belt loops and raised onto his toes. "When you get back from your time at the cabin, we have the fall festival. I imagine good things can still come."

Sadie had completely forgotten she'd reserved Jeremy's cabin for a few days for her and Lottie. There was no way she could go now. She hadn't even packed.

Sadie's dad put his arm around her shoulder and pulled her into a side hug. "Lottie's been so excited about that cabin trip. Your mother and I knew you had a lot on your plate. I will watch over the store and continue to work on repairs if anything comes up."

"I'll need to go home to pack."

"Your mom did. You were a little preoccupied. It wasn't hard. Also, you have reservations for lunch—"

"Mom!" Lottie's excited voice rang through the courtroom. Sadie would never get over that title. "The American Girl Store? That's so awesome! Oma packed Amber!"

Sadie's dad nodded at Romee. "Why don't you go help Lottie move the luggage from your mom's car into Sadie's."

Sadie dug into her purse and pulled out her car key, handing it to Romee.

Dad wrapped her in a hug. "I prayed for this outcome. Now, you go enjoy a few days. And when you get back, you can choose the future you want."

Sadie sank into her dad's embrace, his familiar scent of leather and peppermint comforting. Today she'd been granted her biggest wish, her most earnest prayer—Lottie's adoption.

Could she still ask for more?

"Sometimes, Dad, we don't always get what we want. What I have now is more than enough."

And it would be enough.

More than enough.

Because God had never left her, and no matter what tomorrow brought, He never would. She could trust in that.

Her dad placed his hand on her shoulder. "Oh, honey. God is the God of the impossible. Don't settle yet. He will surprise you with what He can do."

eighteen

T HE ENTIRE TOWN HAD TURNED OUT FOR THE
unofficial start to the Fall Festival on Friday night. After working
out all the details with Mayor Jamison, David had helped to install
the old clock on the town square, right across the street from the hardware store, and they'd unveil it to the town tonight, after Sadie arrived.

Last night Otis had moved right next to the clock, as though he
approved of the addition to the square. It seemed everyone waited,
like Otis, with their eyes glued to the clock.

The front of the store would look fresh and new once the window was replaced. Gary had ordered the replacement and the new
front counter yesterday after the check from Mrs. Allen's insurance
came through. They wouldn't have the grand reopening this weekend like planned, but David had put out new flyers announcing
it would take place in a month's time. Hopefully, the store would
see a boost in holiday sales. Sadie had approved everything while
she'd been gone in the one conversation she'd had with Gary.

David still hadn't talked to Sadie. He hadn't called again since
the hearing, hoping a little space would be good for them. Besides,

Sadie should be able to enjoy Lottie this week. It had taken every-thing in him not to rush forward to Sadie and hug her after the favorable ruling. He doubted there'd been a dry eye in the entire courtroom, and he'd wanted to be there with her. Celebrate the win. But he'd meant what he told Caroline, he'd been there for support that day, not answers.

He could support from a distance.

But he'd sure like some of those answers soon. If only the entire town hadn't turned out to watch him lay it all on the line tonight. Maybe he'd wait and try to catch her later.

Gary walked next to David as they skirted around the edge of the crowd.

"Won't be long now. Sadie messaged a while back when they stopped for gas. She said it was a straight shot home." Gary looked over the crowd of people. David had noticed him rubbing his mus-cles as they'd worked side by side in the hardware store cleaning up yesterday. But he seemed to have good movement and rotation, had healed up just fine. Not that he would ever hear Gary com-plain. "You don't have to stay in the back. She's not going to make a scene in front of people. Plus, you've gone to a lot of work for her this week. She'll want to talk to you."

Doubt settled in David's gut. He had worked hard—first on the letters, then the clock and the cleanup around the store. He'd do it all over again. "I don't want to embarrass her in front of the whole town. And besides, I don't want her to feel like she owes me something. I did it because I care for her."

"No one doubts that, son."

A car drove down Richard Street, but it wasn't Sadie's. David let out a breath and rubbed his chin. His hand held a slight tremble, but nothing like the shaking he'd been fighting. As soon as he'd started moving on the path God had for him, as soon as he'd picked Sadie, the shaking had stopped.

A game of soccer took place across the square, next to the library. Maybe if he joined in, he could burn off some of his nervous energy.

Nate waved and walked up to join them. "I've been looking for you. Left a voicemail on your phone."

There hadn't been time to return the call. Or even listen to the message. "Sorry about that."

"Don't worry. I've heard how busy you've been. I wanted to talk to you, though, after we had our annual budget meeting at church. We've approved a youth pastor position, and I wondered if you might be interested."

Working with teens? Staying in Heritage? It almost sounded too good to be true, but if David had learned anything, it was that God always had a plan in place.

Nate waved at Colby Marc as he walked by, carrying a little girl in his arms. "I don't need an answer today. In fact, take some time to pray about it. We can't start paying someone until January, so there's time to decide."

"I'll definitely pray about it." And talk to Sadie, hopefully, because he wanted her input. Although, ideas were already forming. Dreams coming together. Possibilities exploding.

Sadie's blue Honda drove slowly down Richard Street, and David's heart sped up. She was finally back.

Craning his neck, he watched the car pull behind Hoover's Hardware. Romee and Anna hurried behind the building. Anna had arrived after the hearing, insisting on coming even though her flight had been canceled. Although Anna had been distant this week as they cleaned the store, she had eventually told him that if he could convince Sadie he'd stick around, she'd accept that.

Not exactly an open-armed welcome, but Romee had made up for it with constant encouragement to not give up.

The crowd seemed to close in around the clock, and David stepped back, and back again, not wanting to get carried away with the group. But he also didn't want to be so far outside he was easy to spot.

After an eternity, or what was probably a few minutes, Lottie skipped around the front of the hardware store. He wiped his hands on his jeans and waited.

And waited.

He'd seen Sadie Tuesday at the hearing, but he hadn't spoken to her for a week. Seven days. How he'd gone ten years without talking to her, he would never know, because this week had gone on for an eternity.

Finally, Sadie walked around the side of the building, her sisters on either side of her. He stayed back as she talked to people, touched shoulders, hugged Mrs. Allen, even when her hand slid into her jeans pocket, like she needed a moment to ground herself. When she scanned the crowd, he stepped back farther, staying out of sight. Eventually, the crowd absorbed her.

Mayor Jamison cleared his throat and tapped on a portable microphone, making it screech. The crowd quieted. Sadie stood next to the mayor and the clock with Lottie.

Sadie waved at people, her posture stiff. Probably uncomfortable being the center of attention. Mayor Jamison clapped one hand on his protruding belly and the entire crowd seemed to lean forward.

"When little Miss Lottie started asking questions about an old clock tower on the square, our historical person"—Mayor Jamison walked over and clapped Hannah on the shoulder—"dug up some pictures of this old clock here. We haven't figured out why it was removed, but it has been our goal to have a clock tower on the square since we cleared it. David, where are you?" The heads of the people in front of him started looking around.

"David Williams? Don't be shy, throw your hand up in the air." Heat climbed David's neck. This wasn't part of the program.

"Back here," Jon's familiar voice called out in the crowd, and people started moving as Jon pushed his way to stand next to David. The crowd murmured, but Sadie's expression froze him in place. He couldn't read her emotions this far away, couldn't tell what she was thinking.

"Come on up." Mayor Jamison gestured with his arm. "That's it, everyone make room."

The crowd split in front of him, leaving a clear walkway to Sadie. Jon nudged him forward. "Go win your girl, man."

David glanced back at Jon, who grinned. Leah stood next to him, giving him a thumbs-up. He hadn't even noticed his sister there.

As soon as he cleared the crowd, Mayor Jamison grabbed David's shoulder, spinning him to face the group, forcing him to look away from Sadie. "When David here"—the mayor shook his shoulder slightly—"suggested we place the historic clock on the square and he volunteered to do all the work, the town jumped at the opportunity. Even if it was a little last minute. With David's long hours this week, the clock repaired—thank you, Chet Anderson—our vision for the town square suddenly didn't seem years away."

Lottie bounced up next to David and took hold of his hand, awe showing on her cute face. So similar to Bonnie's but with Sadie's mannerisms. His heart swelled as the little girl tugged on his hand. "You put my clock here?"

He nodded, unable to speak past the lump in his throat.

Mayor Jamison gestured toward Lottie. "Before we officially celebrate the establishment of the town clock, there's something I bet you all didn't know. Our very own fourth grade students entered their historical papers into a competition, and I'd like to announce the winner." Mayor Jamison paused and lowered the microphone. A hush fell on the crowd. "It's probably no surprise that Lottie Linden won with her discovery and research done on the clock." A round of applause erupted.

After the cheering quieted, Mayor Jamison continued. "Now,

I'd like to officially celebrate the establishment of the town clock. And, Lottie, we'd like you to do the honors."

The mayor guided Lottie to stand by the clock, and David stepped back next to Sadie.

"Here you go, Lottie. It's a ribbon cutting of sorts." Mayor Jamison laughed good-naturedly. "We've tied a bow, and you can pull right here to untie it."

Sadie pulled out her phone and turned on her camera. With a huge smile on her face, Lottie picked up the ribbon tail and in one quick movement, yanked. The ribbon fell off and Lottie waved it over her head.

"The town festival can now officially begin." The mayor patted his belly and then posed with Lottie, and the crowd cheered before breaking off into smaller groups. A handful of people walked toward the booths, but most stayed close by, sending glances in Sadie's direction.

David turned to face her, the lump in his throat making it hard to speak. But she studied him carefully. "Hi." Of all the things he could say...but there were so many people, and the noise level had risen so he was almost shouting.

"Sadie." Anna threw her arms around her sister. "This was fantastic. I'm glad I could be here to see this."

David stepped back, giving her some space. Some privacy. He'd be around when she was ready.

He turned to slip away, but a hand slid into his. He'd know that hand anywhere, and he closed his eyes briefly to savor her soft skin pressed against his. When he turned around, Sadie's watchful gaze rested on him. "Can we talk?"

Always. He nodded. He hadn't anticipated being able to steal her away. But the look in her eyes gave him hope. Could Chet be right about the grand gesture? Had tonight been enough to tip the scales in David's favor?

Sadie pulled him around the side of the hardware store, away from prying eyes. Closer to the end of the store, she leaned against the brick wall, her hand still tucked inside his.

"Why, David? Why do all this?" She gestured her free hand in a circle. "The letters, the money for the store, the clock?"

David ran his fingers down her cheek, her neck, tracing her shoulder and letting his fingers trail down her arm. Her breath caught, and her skin flushed. "You know why."

"Tell me, please." Something in Sadie's voice cut him to the core. Did she really not know?

"I did it for you." He linked their other hands together, hers trembling in his grip.

"All of it?"

"I'd do anything for you."

"Why? Costa Rica—"

"I'm not going back. God can change dreams and directions. He's changed mine, although it took me a while to hear that. I'm not giving up my calling, I'm still following God, it's just He has a different future in store for me. One that, I hope, includes you."

Sadie's eyes widened and her entire body went still. Had she stopped breathing? David dropped her hands and placed his on her shoulders. Finally, she inhaled, and he stepped a little closer. "I know my actions last week didn't show you that I'm all in, and I'm sorry about that. I should never have agreed to visit Costa Rica, or consider a job opportunity and not have talked to you. I have learned that I need to communicate better. I'm hoping that if you give me another chance, I can prove to you I'm all in. For you. For Lottie. For whatever tomorrow brings. I'm here." David cupped her cheek and rested his forehead against hers. "For us."

Sadie's hands came up and touched his elbows. Who knew that could be so intimate? His skin sparked, and nerves danced up his arms.

They stood there, foreheads touching, his hands on her shoulders, and he breathed her in. That spicy scent he'd come to love.

"David?" Sadie's breath puffed on his face. But her tone held an edge. He straightened, creating some space.

Sadie's brows were pulled together. "What's changed?"

"Nothing." David dropped his hands and stepped back. "Everything."

"I don't understand."

"I've messed up plenty. And I probably will again, but I'm here now. I'm going to show you every day that I can show up, that I can be depended on, and that I love you. I love you, Sadie Hoover. I always have. I promise I'm going to make sure you know it. Every day if you'll let me."

Sadie didn't say anything. Her hand trembled as she brushed at her cheeks. Great. He'd made her cry. More than anything, he wanted to close the distance between them, pull her into a hug, and hold her. But he'd just told her he loved her, and she hadn't responded. Not a peep, only tears.

Not exactly the reaction he'd pictured. He'd wanted her to jump into his arms, returning the sentiment. Preferably with some kisses. Weren't kisses supposed to follow declarations of love?

But he'd determined to be here for the long haul. To show up and give Sadie what she needed. Maybe time and space were the keys for now.

Letting out a breath, he forced his feet backward. "I'll see you around, Sadie."

Chet had been wrong. The grand gesture hadn't been enough. Hopefully, Maria's advice would be better. He'd continue to show up, day after day, and maybe Sadie would understand his intentions.

He wanted forever, and he would wait as long as it took.

The rough brick of the building bit into Sadie's back.

David had really just declared his love.

He. Loved. Her.

She wiped at her cheeks. A few stray happy tears had leaked out. She should say something. Anything. But she watched David walk away, his shoulders drooped. She'd just let him go.

Had she dreamed this conversation? It wouldn't be the first time she'd dreamed of a full reconciliation with David.

She tapped her head on the brick wall and her hair snagged and tugged on the building. Nope—not dreaming. It was the last fly that had buzzed around her the past few days—her love for David. God had worked out all the details, and she let David go and walk away.

"What are you doing?" Romee's voice held a sharp edge as she hurried toward Sadie, Anna on one side and Lottie skipping along on her other.

"Holding up the building?" Sadie crossed one foot over the other.

Anna scoffed and pushed Sadie's shoulder. "We can see that. But why did David leave? You're supposed to be making out. Smoochy, smoochy. The happy ending and all that jazz."

"I like happy endings." Lottie wrapped her arms around Sadie's waist. "And I like Mr. Williams."

"Me too." Sadie let out a breathy sigh. "But..."

"Girl, there are no buts. Didn't he just tell you he loved you?" Romee crossed her arms over her chest and tapped her foot.

"Were you eavesdropping?" Sisters. Unbelievable.

"You betcha. Mom too. And you didn't say anything. Just let that man walk away from you. What were you thinking?"

Honestly? She hadn't been. She'd been so shocked by his admission, she didn't know how to respond. Didn't know what to say. She'd dreamed up his confession of love so many times, and they all paled in comparison to the real thing. And she'd frozen on the spot.

"Mom?" Lottie looked up at Sadie as she squeezed Sadie's waist even tighter. "He loves us."

Anna let out a small breathy laugh. "Both of you. I didn't think leopards could change their spots, but David is in a category all his own. You'd be stupid not to strike that while it's hot."

The street was empty, and there was no sign of David. "I...I don't even know where he went."

Romee stepped to one side, motioning toward their parents' house. "Mom stopped him and dragged him home. Anna and I made sure the fire was roaring, and we may or may not have laid out a blanket in front of it. Some hot cocoa and cookies are there. Candles. We had hoped you wouldn't need us to intervene, but we had a backup plan in place just in case." Romee dug in her pocket and pulled out a peppermint and handed it to Sadie. "You'll need this. Now, hurry."

Lottie's arms dropped, and she put her hands on Sadie's back, pushing her toward the house. "Go, Mom!"

A chuckle escaped, and Sadie popped the mint in her mouth. "Thanks. Wish me luck."

"Go get him, girl!" Romee's voice held a hint of laughter as Sadie jogged across the street toward her parents' house.

Her mom stood out front. "He's inside. But I'd hurry if I were you. He didn't want to stay. Said you needed some time."

Sadie stopped at the top of the steps and turned back to her mom. "I've had ten years. How much more time do I need?"

Inside, the lights in the entryway were off, but a warm glow came from the family room. Leaving her jacket on the coat rack, Sadie slid her shoes off and left them next to David's.

A hand on her stomach, she took a deep breath. If she'd known that David would profess his love today, that she'd get a third chance at this relationship, she wouldn't have used dry shampoo for the third day in a row. At least Romee had handed her the peppermint.

In the family room, the fire crackled, and candles filled the space. A fuzzy blanket sat on the floor with some pillows, the promised hot cocoa in a thermos, two mugs, and a plate of cookies.

David stood in front of the fire, leaning his arm on the mantel. His shoulders sagged, and his eyes were closed, almost like he was praying.

A few heartbeats passed, but he didn't move. "David?"

His head shot up, and he took her in. His arm dropped to his side, and he straightened his shoulders. "I'm sorry. I told your mom you needed time—"

"I don't need more time." Sadie stepped into the room, closing the distance between them. "I'm sorry I didn't say anything. I..." She let out a breath. "Honestly, you couldn't have surprised me more if you tried."

"I meant every word."

"I know." Sadie gestured toward the fuzzy blanket and pillows her sisters had laid out. She had to hand it to them, they had created the perfect setting. "Want some cocoa?"

Sadie settled on the blanket with David next to her. She filled a mug and handed it to him. When his fingers brushed hers, heat crept up her arm.

"Is that the mug I bought you at Cedar Point?"

Sure enough. Romee must not have thrown it out. Probably used it on purpose today. "Yeah. I've kept it all these years."

A wide smile spread over David's face. "That was a good day. I fell in love with you as you looked through the gift store. It's why I bought the mug, because that was the moment I knew you were it for me."

"We'd only been on a few dates. You knew that early?"

"Yeah. I did. And I was stupid to fight it."

He slid closer, and the oxygen must have been pulled from the room. Sadie's breathing became shallow as David closed the space between them, his eyes tracing her face, her skin heating.

"You have a new dream? A new path?" Her breathy voice didn't hide her nerves. She set her cocoa down. David didn't need hot cocoa spilled all over him. He set his mug next to hers.

"An option. But a future with you—that's my dream."

"David..." Sadie's entire body buzzed with energy, excitement. She extended her hand to him, and he held it, pressing it against his chest, over his heart which pounded beneath her palm.

"Please let me finish." He cupped her face with his other hand. "I want to say I'm sorry again. Before I say anything else, I'm sorry for pushing you away ten years ago. I'm sorry for hurting you when I broke up with you. I'm sorry for not talking with you about Costa Rica. For everything that happened that night Lottie disappeared. I'm not perfect, not by a long shot, but I am willing to apologize and to try again. And again. Sadie, I love you. I love you enough to ask forgiveness. To try again. However many times I mess up."

His words settled over her. Warm, comforting, better than any she'd dreamed of. "I love you, David Williams." She brushed her lips to his in just a whisper of a kiss. The look on his face gave her a thrill, sending a shiver down her spine.

He pulled her closer. "Are you cold?"

"Not even close."

Heat flashed in his gaze, but he leaned back, his thumb gently stroking her cheek. "I want to tell you about an offer from Nate."

Sadie picked up her cocoa and took a sip. "I'm all ears."

"I want you to know that I'm in for the long haul. I want it all—marriage, Lottie, all of it." David took her mug, set it back down, then cupped her cheek again, his hand slowly moving to the back of her neck, gently massaging as he spoke. "Nate said the church is looking for a youth pastor. I haven't accepted anything, I wanted to talk things over with you. Make a decision together, be a team."

A team. Sadie squeezed David's hand. "Say it again."

His head tipped to the side. "I'm sorry."

"No, the last part. Say it again, please."

"Be a team?"

She nodded. "Those are the most romantic words you could say to me, David Williams."

"I want to be a team...with you, Sadie." Confidence laced his words and stole her breath. "I could say it again. Or I could do this." Ever so slowly, he started to close the gap between their lips. His nose brushed against hers. Still, she waited for his kiss, her heart pounding against her ribs. It would be so easy to lean forward, close the space between them, but she held still, loving the feel of his breath on her face, the pressure of his hand as he held her in place. Not that she had any intention of moving.

Finally, finally, his mouth claimed hers. Slowly, tenderly, his kiss promised every moment, every tomorrow, every dream. It held all the excitement of a first kiss and the comfort of forever.

She returned his promises with a few of her own until his lips broke from hers, and he moved to the soft spot behind her ear.

His breath tickled her skin as he moved slowly back toward her mouth, his clean fragrance surrounding her. When his lips finally pressed to hers, he tasted of comfort and home. Friendship and forever. Peace and adventure. Her past and her future. As she returned each of David's promises, excitement settled over her.

David slowed the kiss. Lingering. Savoring. She memorized the moment, the start of their forever. When he pulled away, Sadie sighed, his lips addictive. He leaned down and brushed one more gentle kiss on her waiting mouth.

"I love you, David."

"It will always be you." David wrapped his arms around her, and she relaxed against his chest.

The time had finally come for love, for peace, but only after she'd learned to trust God. When she had reached a point where she'd lost it all, God had stepped in, working miracle after miracle, giving her Lottie, saving the store, and restoring her relationship with David.

Ten years ago, ten days ago even, she had no hope for a happy ending, and yet God had worked it all out, giving her everything she'd ever dreamed of. She'd experienced heartbreak, again and again, but to have this moment, she'd face it all over again. "I'm so glad you're here with me."

David kissed the top of her head. "I wouldn't want to be anywhere else."

Bonus Epilogue

Join the Sunrise family and you will receive a special gift, available only to Mandy's and our subscribers. This Bonus Epilogue will not be released on any retailer platform—become a Sunrise subscriber to read this bonus epilogue.

Find out what happens next with David and Sadie. Scan the QR code below to subscribe and get your free gift. You acknowledge you are subscribing to both Sunrise Publishing's and Mandy Boerma's newsletters. Unsubscribe from either newsletter at any time.

Keep reading to enjoy the first chapter of Christmas With You by Tari Faris, Home to Heritage Book 3.

READ ON FOR MORE FROM THE

Home to Heritage

SERIES

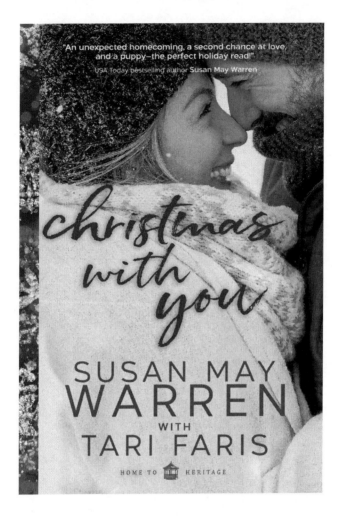

"An unexpected homecoming, a second chance at love, and a puppy—the perfect holiday read!"
USA Today bestselling author **Susan May Warren**

christmas with you

SUSAN MAY WARREN

WITH

TARI FARIS

HOME TO HERITAGE

What do you get when you have an ex-navy SEAL, a Christmas tree farm, and first-time nanny? Find out in the third book of the Home to Heritage series, Christmas with You.

Fallon James has lost everything—her husband, her job, and her home. With nowhere else to turn, she returns to her hometown of Heritage, Michigan, only to find her family's once-thriving Christmas tree farm on the brink of ruin. Determined to save the farm, Fallon throws herself into the struggle, but she can't do it alone.

Enter Cole Scott, Fallon's high school friend and now a single dad working odd jobs to support his two kids. Cole agrees to help Fallon in exchange for her watching his children while he travels for a lucrative security job. As they work side by side, old tensions resurface, but so does an undeniable attraction. However, Fallon harbors a secret that could change everything.

Just as the farm starts to see success, Fallon's former company unleashes a devastating lawsuit, threatening to destroy everything she and Cole have built. With time running out and her dreams slipping away, Fallon must make a choice that could cost her the love and family she's always wanted. Worse, a shocking turn of events forces Cole to confront what truly matters most.

Can Fallon and Cole overcome the secrets, lies, and legal battles that stand between them? Or will they lose the farm, their love, and the future they've risked everything to build?

Filled with heartwarming holiday cheer, pulse-pounding suspense, and the magic of second chances, this unforgettable tale of love, family, and the true meaning of Christmas will keep you turning pages late into the night. Perfect for fans of small-town romance, single dad heroes, and holiday happily-ever-afters, this book is a must-read for anyone who believes in the power of love to overcome even the darkest of times.

one

FALLON JAMES'S ENTIRE LIFE HAD BEEN RE-
duced to a small storage unit back in Detroit and whatever
would fit in the back seat of her new-to-her-but-very-old Chevy
Impala. She eyed the cardboard boxes and bags in her rearview mirror
as she exited US 31 and drove east toward her childhood hometown
of Heritage, Michigan. Soon she would be snuggled up in her pink
comforter under the poster of Justin Bieber and could pretend like
the past three years hadn't happened.

She might not be a fan of the Bieber anymore, but no matter
how many years went by, her parents' home always seemed as if
she had been gone only a few hours. It was both why she had been
excited to leave and why it always felt so wonderful coming home.
This place had always been her safe haven, her constant, and her
parents a steadfast source of strength.

She bypassed the turn that would lead to the heart of the small
town and a hot cup of Donny's amazing coffee. She actually could
use a coffee after the four-hour drive from Detroit, and the warmth
of the diner would sure be nice. They might only be ten days into

November, but the chill of northern Michigan had arrived even if the snow hadn't. But there was no such thing as a quick stop in Heritage. The same people would be there talking about the same old things, and Fallon's return would be noticed by all of them. It would be an hour visit minimum and right now, all Fallon wanted to do was be home—for a peaceful Sunday evening.

The houses of the town slowly gave way to the larger properties and driveways that disappeared into tall pine forests. The phone rang through her car and the face of Sadie Hoover, her childhood friend, popped up on the screen. Fallon tapped to accept. "Are you ready for the big day?"

"Not even close." Sadie released a deep sigh as if she'd just flopped on her bed. "Was your wedding this stressful?"

There was that all-too familiar ache in Fallon's chest.

"I'm sorry." Sadie's voice dropped lower. "I shouldn't have—"

"It's fine." Fallon was tired of the apologies.

I'm sorry you lost your husband.

I'm sorry Robert kept so much from you.

And the big doozy she'd gotten last week. I'm sorry but you are no longer welcome here.

She shook her mind away from the memory and back to her friend. "Weddings are probably less stressful if you don't try and plan them in four weeks."

"Eight weeks." Sadie's voice carried a touch of attitude. "I only have seven left."

"Because eight weeks is so much longer. Are you sure you are ready for this?"

"When you know, you know. And face it, David and I have been waiting ten years for this. We weren't waiting for another year."

"Not a year but maybe a few months. And it isn't the ten years that you have been in love that has me concerned. It is the nine years and eight months that you weren't speaking." She was happy for her friend. But marriage had been the hardest thing she'd ever

ies at JJ's of all things. But I don't know more than that." Sadie's voice muffled a moment before she was back. "Hold on a second, David needs something."

Fallon released a wry laugh. A hot, successful Cole Scott, to whom she'd lost the valedictorian spot by a tenth of a GPA point, might be intimidating. But she could handle an old, fat, and—with any luck—balding Cole Scott who stocked shelves and bagged canned goods at the local grocery store. So much for Mr. Most Likely to Succeed. Maybe some people did peak in high school.

At least she'd been the lead designer for Winterbourne Industries for eight years—eight long years that should have earned her some loyalty.

Fallon flipped on her blinker and began to slow as she neared her parents' property. The twenty-foot white pines lining both sides of the road were like a channel leading her home. She opened the vent and let the woodsy scent fill the car. It smelled like safety, comfort, and a happy childhood all rolled into one. Her constant. A constant that was just over forty degrees. She shut the vent and slowed as she neared the drive.

Why was there an obnoxious yellow sign swinging from a wooden post in the ground that was rudely planted right in front of the James Tree Farm welcome sign? Taylor Realty? No. No. No. It had to be a mistake.

Fallon turned in the drive and stopped just off the road. A small part of her mind told her the obvious truth—the sign wasn't a mistake. But the rest of her thoughts raced through even more far-fetched scenarios like a local teen prank. Anything other than the one that simply couldn't be true.

Her parents were selling the Christmas tree farm. The thought pressed in on her like a crushing weight.

Her childhood home. This place was all she had left.

"Fallon, are you still there?" Sadie's voice came through the speaker again.

done, and she just hoped Sadie knew what she was getting into. Fallon released a sigh—then again, David wasn't the heir to Winterbourne Enterprises who refused to grow up and had never cut the apron strings. "Sorry, I'm happy for you. It's just—"

"Fast? I know. But we are ready, trust me. Besides, we want to start the new year as Mr. and Mrs. Williams. When are you getting to town?"

"I'm here. Well, sort of. I just passed Dearing Road."

"I thought you weren't coming until next weekend."

Right. But that was when she still had a job, a house, her Tesla, and a bank account. "Plans changed. I'm here through the wedding. Figured it would be good to be home with my parents for the holidays."

And who knew how long after that?

"Yay, then you can go cake testing with us tomorrow." The lightness in Sadie's tone lifted something in Fallon. At least the whole world hadn't turned against her. "But if you are going to be here for the next few weeks, I should probably warn you..."

"Warn me? That's ominous. I've already seen the glow-up in the middle of town. Isn't that about as much change that Heritage can handle for a decade or two?"

"It's just..."

"Say it."

"Cole's back."

Fallon's breathing slowed.

So many emotions swirled through her with the name that she couldn't even land on one. "Cole Scott?"

"Do you know another Cole?"

"What is he doing back?" And why hadn't her mom mentioned it? She gave a hard blink and kept her focus on the road. "Last I heard he was living out in California, married to the wicked witch of Heritage High."

"Tiffany's not with him. I'm not sure why. He's bagging grocer-

in the gravel was the only sound on the farm as she approached the house.

Her hand paused on the new white railing. If her dad had fixed this, why hadn't he bothered with the rest of the place? Maybe that was in the plan.

She offered two quick knocks and reached for the knob. After all, this was home and her parents were probably stretched out in their recliners as they watched their evening round of Jeopardy!

She pushed through the door and stepped into the mudroom, securing the door behind her. Her father's tan Carhartt coat hung on his usual peg, her mom's fall hat up on the shelf, and the same green-and-brown carpet that she'd stained with mud as a kid were all there to welcome her.

But instead of the voices of game show contestants, "Dance to the Music" blared from the stereo at a volume level she would have never been allowed in her teen years. She hung her coat on a hook then stepped out of the mudroom into the wide family room.

She paused by the back of the brown couch straight from the nineties. It was same couch, facing the same two gray recliners, all sitting a few feet from the same dining room table she'd sat at to do her homework. She even recognized her mother's prized collection of Hummel figurines on the wooden shelf her father had made.

What she didn't recognize was the little girl with blonde curls, who was maybe seven, spinning in circles or the teenage boy with dark hair lounging on one of those gray overstuffed recliners with his nose in his phone. The little girl bumped into the five-tiered shelf full of figurines. Fallon winced as they rattled, but none fell.

"Careful!" the teenage boy yelled at the girl, his gaze never leaving his phone.

If it weren't for the row of her school photos on the far wall showing Fallon's annual progression from kindergarten to graduation—including those special middle school years—Fallon would

"Are my parents really selling the tree farm?"

"Oh, Fallon. You didn't know?"

"Why didn't they tell me?" She put the car back in gear and wound down the long dirt drive.

"The sign just appeared last week. Maybe they planned on telling you when you got here. I can't believe there will be no more tree farm. It's been a staple in the community for my entire life."

"Since my grandfather opened it back in the sixties." Fallon navigated around a large rut in the dirt path. "In its heyday people would drive up to four hours to get their Christmas trees here." The car jerked as it hit another pothole. "Why would they close it?"

"I know you weren't here, but the past few years it's been different."

"Different how?" Fallon eyed the broken fence as she made her way toward the house.

"It's not like when we were kids and it had a live nativity, cookies with Mrs. Santa, sleigh rides, and remember when we could get photos with Santa himself? Last I heard it was more of a stop by and cut down your own tree and leave money in a box."

Fallon parked in front of the white two-story farmhouse with a wraparound porch and took in the place with critical eyes. The arch over the entrance of the tree lot had fallen over. The windows of the Sugar Shack were so dirty she doubted any light was getting in. And the wooden letters that hung by the old barn just spelled Jam s T ee Fa m. Maybe it had seen better days, but her dad loved this place. It wouldn't take much for him to fix it up. "They still should have told me."

"You're right. But hear them out. I'm sure this is hard on them too. I've got to go. Sorry, but it's going to be okay. We can talk more tomorrow. I'll text you the time of the cake testing."

Fallon ended the call and climbed out. As she pulled her coat from the back seat, a chill ran down her neck. Her boots crunching

owned her house, her car, and all her accounts, they also owned her rights to the entire series. None of it was hers anymore.

She couldn't have imagined how different her world would become when she took her brush to paper that day to create her mom a Christmas gift. Those fat cherubs quickly became a series that was bought up by Winterbourne Enterprises. And just like that she'd become an overnight success in the world of wall-art and ornaments. The next Thomas Kinkade, that's what they had called her. What would they call her now?

"Maybe she'll paint you something else." Her mom's hand landed on her arm. Her mom understood the legal ramifications, but what she didn't know was that Fallon hadn't been able to paint anything even halfway decent since Robert's death. The inspired part of her seemed to have died with him.

"That's Zane." Her mom motioned to the boy in the recliner. "Zane, say hi to my daughter, Fallon."

Zane offered a grunt with a slight nod. His dark mop was in need of a haircut but the long gangly arms and legs plus the attitude probably meant he was in junior high.

She focused back on her mom. "So why are they here?"

"They've been here for the weekend. Their dad was supposed to pick them up this afternoon but he was delayed."

Delayed. Great. Some deadbeat dad had somehow convinced her mom to watch his kids. No doubt playing into the fact she didn't have her own grandkids. Not that that had been Fallon's choice.

Wasn't that just wonderful.

"Where's Dad?" Fallon took the tie from her wrist, pulled her long blonde hair up in a loose bun, and then bent over and started picking up strewn clothes and toys.

"He's in bed. Threw out his back again last week trying to move some boxes in the Sugar Shack."

have believed her parents had already sold the house, furniture and all.

She opened her mouth to ask the kids who they were, but stopped as her mother walked through the swinging door that led to the kitchen. She wore an apron that was dusted in flour and her hair pulled up into a messy gray bun, most of which had escaped. Her face was a little flushed. Maybe the doctor needed to up her blood pressure medication yet again.

Her mom paused by the dining room table and leaned down to pick up a pink backpack that lay open on the floor, then grabbed a child's stray sock. "Your dad just texted. He should be here soon. Let's get you ready."

Fallon blinked from her mom to the children then back to her mom. "My dad or their dad?"

Her mom stood up with a jerk. "Fallon! You startled me. I didn't hear you arrive."

"I wonder why." Fallon stepped over to the stereo and turned down the music, earning her a mid-twirl "aww" from the girl, then wrapped her mom in a hug. Did she feel more frail than the last time she was here? "Who are these kids? And why are they here?"

The little girl stopped dancing and waved with a big smile that stretched from ear to ear, revealing two front teeth that were only half-grown in. "I'm Susie. Are you the daughter who painted that?"

Susie pointed to the wall, but Fallon didn't have to look to know what she was talking about. It was the first of her Tiny Angel series with two fat cherubs looking up in awe at the star of Bethlehem. The abstract watercolor technique had given the quaint scene an unearthly quality. As if looking into a dream.

"That's me." She didn't clarify that she was the only child so she had to be "the daughter."

"Can you paint me one?"

Legally? Nope. Because the Winterbourne family not only

when you were young? It's what kids do. We'll just clean it up." With that, her mom pushed back open the kitchen door. "Susie, put away the dolls, please."

Fallon followed her mom back out as Susie wandered over to the pile of dolls and dresses and started dropping them in their box. Fallon did a double take. Those were her dolls. Dolls that she'd been meticulously careful with. Dolls that now had messy hair and mismatched clothes and were being tossed in a box. They were dolls she'd saved for her future daughter.

The familiar pain squeezed her chest.

She was about to give her mother a few words about the value of those dolls when the doorbell rang. Susie jumped up and ran over to the door. "I bet that's my daddy. I have so much to tell him."

Her daddy? Fallon had a few things she wanted to tell him too. Like he would no longer be taking advantage of her mother's kindness. Couldn't he see that she was in no shape to do this? All so he could go have a weekend away kid free.

Susie flung open the door, and Fallon took a step forward and froze.

Cole Scott?

What? Cole Scott was a dad. Of a little girl. And a teenage boy. And oh, she should have seen the resemblance in the kid's surly expression and arrogance. It was so obvious now that she was looking. He had Cole's chestnut brown hair and those cold blue eyes. And Susie was the spitting image of Tiffany at that age. Back when she'd been Fallon's best friend.

Any hope that Cole had gone fat was dispelled by the way the tactical gear molded to his upper body, highlighting an impressive set of shoulders. Drat. He bent down to pick up his daughter with a smile that highlighted that familiar set of dimples. But his boy-next-door baby face that she'd last seen those dimples on had been replaced with a strong jaw covered with a full day's scruff.

Fallon dropped the bundle into an open duffel and stood upright. "You didn't think to tell me?"

"He's fine. This isn't our first rodeo with his bad back. Just needs a little rest."

"So you've been playing nursemaid and watching some guy's kids. No wonder you look exhausted. Maybe I should check on Dad."

Her mom dismissed the idea with a wave. "He's asleep. Those pain meds knocked him out."

"Then at least sit down. Let me do this."

"I'm fine." But she still sank into a chair with a sigh and checked the time. "I'm not as young as I used to be, that's for sure. But I agreed to this before your dad hurt himself."

"Let me guess, you didn't mention to their father that Dad had gotten hurt either." When her mom didn't respond, Fallon sat on the edge of the recliner and rubbed her forehead against the building headache. First the house, then her dad's back, and now these kids. What else hadn't her mother told her? "Is this about money? How much is he paying you?"

She blinked at Fallon a moment then reached for another sock. "Nothing. I offered for free."

"Free?" She stood and motioned for her mom to follow then walked into the kitchen. She could calm down easier away from the mess and the noise. Or maybe not. The remains of a cookie-making endeavor were everywhere. There was even batter on the cupboard.

She turned to her mom. "You are too nice. You are giving the guy free childcare and he can't even show up on time. He's taking advantage of your kindness. You should've called me to come help."

Her mother grabbed a rag from the sink and wiped a splatter off the cupboard. "I have it under control."

"Are you sure? Because this"—Fallon motioned to the mess surrounding them—"doesn't look like it's under control."

"Relax, Fallon. Do you think you didn't get the house this messy

you don't know because you didn't ask. You never think through things. You do what you want regardless of how it affects others. Then again, why should this surprise me. Same ole Cole."

His face reddened slightly as his jaw twitched. He opened his mouth but the door opened and he instantly transformed his expression into something soft and sweet as he took in his kids. "You guys ready?"

"Yup." Susie slipped her hand in his, but Zane just grunted and walked toward an old blue Chevy Blazer that was idling behind her Impala.

Cole glanced back at her but seemed to change his mind about what he was going to say. He just nodded. "I'll make other arrangements next time."

The door opened again and his dark stare instantly turned soft once more as her mother walked out. "Thank you again, Mrs. James."

"I told you, call me Deb. You aren't seventeen anymore."

"Bye, Deb." Susie waved with her free hand as she hopped down the first step.

Cole tapped her gently on the head. "Mrs. James to you."

Susie giggled and waved at Mrs. James again, then turned to Fallon. "Thanks for letting me play with your dolls. Sorry I got that hair tie stuck in the one doll's hair."

Fallon flinched at the words but just smiled.

Cole walked off the porch as her mom offered a wave. "Bye. Come again soon."

Her mom slipped her arm into Fallon's. "He's like fine wine, he has really improved with age."

She looked at her mom, who was sending her a pointed look. "No, Mom."

"No?"

"No. I had my chance at love with Robert. Besides, the last person I'd want in my life is Cole Scott. Trust me."

And when his daughter yanked off the black beanie, underneath revealed a full head of thick dark hair with just a hint of wave to it.

Shoot. He wasn't just not fat. He was handsome too.

Could nothing go her way?

His gaze met hers, his piercing blue eyes creasing at the corners as he seemed to shift from surprise to confusion to recognition all within a matter of seconds. "Well, if it isn't Feisty Fallon James."

Her lips pressed together a moment as she drew a calming breath. "Well if it isn't Can't Keep—"

"Why don't you two continue this reunion outside while I get the kids ready." Her mom rushed forward and grabbed Susie's hand.

Cole lifted his brows but Fallon just grabbed her coat and marched past him out the door and waited to see if he'd follow. But by the sound of footsteps on the porch behind her, he had.

Fallon spun toward him but the move put him just inches away. She took a hasty step back, and for some reason it bugged her when he did the same. "Why are your kids here?"

Cole crossed his arms over his chest, annoyance settling into his gaze. "Nice to see you too, Fallon."

"She's busy enough with taking care of my injured dad. She doesn't need to take care of your irresponsible life." Okay, that didn't make sense now that she was face-to-face with him. One look at what he was wearing and anyone could guess that he'd been working. But she'd already been rehearsing the speech before she had that bit of information. "Why can't Tiffany watch the kids?"

"Tiffany's gone."

"Well, maybe you two need to figure out your work schedule better."

Something dark passed over his features. "I am sorry I'm late. It was out of my control. But I didn't even know your dad wasn't well. What's wrong with him?"

She didn't buy the concerned look. "He threw out his back. And

TARI FARIS

"I think if you knew everything about Cole, he might surprise you."

"Surprise me? Like when we were best friends and then—surprise, he chose my nemesis over me?"

"That was a long time ago. You really should let it go. Cole's grown up and so have you."

Maybe she had grown up, but somehow, she'd landed exactly back where she started. "Cole is a part of my past. Not my future."

"You can't keep a mom from praying." Her mother patted her arm, let go, and then moved toward the door.

Fallon watched the Blazer back down the driveway, kicking up late season dust.

She wanted to argue, but what did it matter? She'd long stopped believing in the power of prayer. Her mom could pray all she wanted. If God had wanted to answer prayers, He'd have kept the man she loved alive.

She turned away from the cloud of dust but her mom stood at the door. "Now, want to tell me why that car is packed to the ceiling? And where is your Tesla?"

"The Tesla wasn't in my name either." Fallon cast a quick glance at the 2004 Impala. "I was hoping to move in here until I can get back on my feet."

A touch of weariness pulled at her mother's eyes. "There's nothing I would love more, but we are—"

"Moving. I saw the sign. When?" Please say January.

"Someone is coming to look at the place tomorrow."

"Tomorrow?" Her voice hit an all-time high.

"It's all happening much faster than we planned." Her mom motioned her back in the house, the weight of the world on her shoulders. "But they want to break ground by spring and need to start working on permits."

"Break ground?"

293

"It's some developers. But they are offering decent money, so maybe it's better this way."

Better? For who?

Her mom kissed her cheek then turned toward the hallway. What was happening? This place was supposed to be her constant, her anchor. She stared into the tree line. Soon it would be gone. Not just owned by someone else but gone. Bulldozed. All replaced by cookie-cutter houses.

She really had nothing left.

You do what you want regardless of how it affects others. Fallon's words from the night before still rang through Cole's head as he slathered peanut butter on a piece of white bread. Do what he wanted? Because making sandwiches and hurrying his kids out the door to the bus, all the while trying not to be late for his pathetic job at JJ's Foodmart where a kid half his age took perverse pleasure in bossing him around, that was what he really wanted. Forget being one of the top technical surveillance specialists in the SEALs just a year ago, he'd thrown all that away because he wanted to make sandwiches.

Cole grabbed the jelly from the fridge and added it to both sandwiches, then finished them off by cutting one into triangles, leaving the other whole. He slipped them each into a Ziploc bag then added one to Susie's pink My Little Pony lunchbox and the other to the brown paper sack for Zane. Because evidently a lunchbox at age thirteen was embarrassing.

He had no doubt he'd had just as much attitude once upon a time, but sometimes it was hard to imagine.

Cole walked to the bottom of the stairs of the small two-story rental house and looked up. "Bus will be here in fifteen minutes. And breakfast is getting cold. I made waffles."

He pulled up his work scheduling app on the phone and grimaced. He stared at his watch and then back at his schedule. No. How could he be opening this morning? Cameron must have adjusted the schedule this weekend while he was gone. He should have double-checked last night, but he'd been so exhausted. As soon as he got the kids down, he'd just showered and climbed into bed. Not that he'd been able to sleep with Fallon's words running through his head on a loop. She had no idea what his life was like.

Irresponsible? What about her? She'd tossed their friendship away like it had meant nothing when he'd needed her the most. Maybe he had been irresponsible for a moment, but he'd been taking responsibility for that moment ever since.

He pulled the Christmas lists that the kids had presented him last night from his pocket and unfolded them. Their top items were so out of his budget that it was laughable. Zane had starred, circled, then highlighted the latest Xbox that was supposed to drop this week. And Susie had drawn all sorts of pink and red hearts around the word "puppy." Like he had the money to feed one more mouth. Or the time to clean up after the other end.

He'd figure it out. Not the puppy, but something just as good. Maybe he could pick up double shifts stocking shelves at JJ's.

He'd already canceled his NFL+ this fall so he could afford new coats for the kids. But that was him, being irresponsible. He dropped the lists back on the table.

Okay, so maybe it wasn't just her words, but also Fallon herself that had occupied his mind. He hadn't seen her in what, thirteen—maybe fourteen—years? Time had been good to her. Before recognition had settled in, he'd taken full notice of her curves and intense green eyes and quickly wondered how long he had to wait until he started dating again. That was until she opened her mouth.

Still as sharp and quick to judge as she'd always been.

Susie was the first down the stairs but Zane was only a few steps behind. His hair was not combed, but the kid didn't seem to care.

He wore a black hoodie and a scowl on his face. He stood in the entry to the kitchen and stared at the waffles stacked up on the table. "You made waffles?"

"Yup. Me and Mr. Eggo." Cole pointed to the box next to the toaster.

A slight smile twitched at Zane's mouth as he sat and pulled a few to his plate. Then he seemed to notice what his face was doing and the scowl returned. It wasn't much of a reaction, but Cole would take it.

"I love waffles." Susie pulled one onto her plate then got to her knees and reached for the syrup. She had convinced Cole to do two braids in her hair this morning. He'd learned that skill last month via YouTube. He still wasn't great at it, but it had gotten to the point the casual observer could at least tell it was supposed to be a braid. But it was clear as she poured way too much syrup over the single waffle on her plate that one side was definitely higher than the other.

She smiled up at him, her blue eyes bright. "We're like one of those TV families."

"Yeah, just like it." There was a fair amount of sarcasm in Zane's tone but he smiled at his sister.

The sweet exchange was both a gift and a punch to the gut. The kids were close because they weren't like a TV family. They had spent much of their lives depending on each other rather than a parent. But he was determined to do right by them no matter the cost.

His phone rang on the counter and he snatched it up. Walker. His old teammate had started working in the private sector in security a few years back and now designed security systems for the rich, famous, and sometimes sketchy power brokers of the world. Walker had gotten him the gig this past weekend. It had felt good to get back in the field, but it was a one-off thing. He couldn't justify that much time away from the kids, but he'd agreed to consult for Walker when he could. It paid a lot better than JJ's.

Cole walked over to where he'd left his laptop and opened it as he accepted the call. "Cole."

"Did you get the file?"

Hello to you too. Cole didn't expect anything different. Walker had served with him for over ten years and when he had a task at hand, the guy had always been straight to business.

Which felt right, since he spent most of his life compartmentalizing. Work. Family. Cover job.

"I looked it over briefly." Cole opened the file and scanned through it. It had appeared in his inbox at five this morning, but he'd only had a few minutes of downtime to look at it. "I think your problem is in the southwest quadrant. I'm marking three spots I see as potential weak points. Probably big gaps in camera coverage." He sent the file back. "I can't be sure without getting eyes on it, but you definitely want to double-check those."

"This would be a lot easier if you'd just come work for me instead of just consulting on the side. I got more accomplished this weekend with you on-site than what we could have accomplished in a month of back and forth. Not to mention good pay and seeing the world."

"I've seen the world." He glanced back at where his kids were finishing up. He wet a cloth in the sink and carried it over to Susie. "I have to be here."

Susie took it and wiped at her face and hands as Zane stood, carried both plates to the sink, and then disappeared back up the stairs.

"Doing what? Bagging groceries and being a part-time rent-a-cop?" The disdain dripped from Walker's tone. He should have never told his friend about his current jobs. "Those are jobs for a high school kid, not one of the top surveillance guys in the country."

Maybe his jobs weren't every former Navy SEAL's dream, but he needed to keep his kids in Heritage for now. They had both been through enough and he wanted to offer them some stability even if it meant stocking bananas.

But Walker wasn't done. "I have the perfect job for you this weekend. Fly out on Friday, back by Sunday."

"I have kids. You forget that part?" He glanced back at Susie but she'd left to get her school backpack. He claimed the rag from the table, walked back to the steps again, and covered the phone. "Five minutes before the bus gets here!"

"Find a babysitter. With the kind of money I'm talking about, hire two."

"Do you have kids? Didn't think so. Finding a babysitter isn't that easy. I can't just leave them with anyone, especially overnight." Even though he'd been back for almost six months, he hadn't connected with anyone yet. He hadn't had the time with working two jobs.

He'd just been thankful that Deb had taken him under her wing. He wasn't sure if it had been because of her friendship with his former mother-in-law or because of his long-ago friendship with her daughter. Either way, he'd been thankful. That was until Fallon ended that connection with her little tirade last night.

His gaze lingered on the Christmas lists still lying face up on the counter, but shook away the idea. If his ex-in-laws weren't in Florida, it would be a no-brainer. But they were, and besides, it was his job and his alone to protect and provide for the kids. He'd learned long ago not to depend on anyone else. "You know I'd have your back if I could, but I just don't think—"

"Don't say no. I can give you twenty-four hours to figure out your complications. But you're the best—maybe the only man for this job. I'll be waiting to hear from you." Walker ended the call.

Cole pocketed his phone. "Two minutes!" Though he itched

to get back to that type of work, he didn't see changing his mind. Because his kids weren't complications.

They were his life.

Zane hurried down the stairs, his backpack on one shoulder. Cole did a subtle sniff test as Zane walked by and came up with only a heavy dose of Axe body spray and morning breath. So either he'd showered recently or just slathered on enough deodorant to cover it up.

Cole pointed back up the stairs. "Go brush your hair and brush your teeth. It smells like something died in your mouth."

Zane offered a hefty eye roll but did as he was instructed just as Susie ran down the stairs with one shoe on. "I can't find my other shoe."

"Then wear the brown ones I just bought you. They're by the door."

"Today's gym day!" Her hands flew into the air. "I have to wear my tennis shoes. Maybe I left it at Mrs. James's house yesterday."

"Didn't you wear them home from their house yesterday?" He wouldn't classify himself as the world's best parent, but he would have noticed if she didn't have any shoes on. Wouldn't he?

"I wore my boots." She slapped her head. "I got mud on one shoe, so I left it in their mudroom to dry. We have to go get it. It's kickball day."

Cole checked his watch and ran his fingers roughly through his hair. He needed to head to JJ's as soon as they were on the bus if he was going to be on time for work. But his kids came first. He needed them to see that. "I'll figure it out."

Cole hurried up the steps to change. He grabbed a pair of jeans that were mostly clean and his work shirt from the closet. At least he'd showered last night, but his hair didn't look that much better than Zane's had a few minutes ago. He hung his head over the sink and splashed some water on it. He brushed his teeth, grabbed his sweatshirt, and hurried back down just as the front door shut behind Zane, who hurried off the porch toward the bus. So much for "have a good day."

Susie sat on the couch, her feet swinging back and forth. Her one foot wore the pink glittery tennis shoe, the other empty. "Zane went to the bus."

"We'll run to the James's before I take you to school. Grab your backpack and put your boots on for now."

They hurried out the door toward the Blazer but Susie paused on the sidewalk. "Otis moved across the street. Can I go see him?"

"What? Not right now. We don't have time."

"But Jane at school said she's going to figure out how he moves and I don't want her to figure out before I do." Susie's eyes rounded in despair.

Cole scooped her up and set her in the back seat of his Blazer. "Well, since generations of kids have been trying to solve that mystery with no luck, I think you can wait until after school."

She nodded, but the moment her eyes began to tear up, Cole was undone. "I'll tell you what. After school you and I will go together and try to look for clues. But right now we have to go. Now buckle up."

She offered a watery smile and did as he said. Cole circled the Blazer, hopped in, and hurried toward the James's farm. With any luck, Fallon would still be asleep or have gone back to wherever she had driven in from last night. She didn't know him anymore and he didn't like the fact she acted like she did.

But that small hope he wouldn't see her died ten minutes later as the bane of his sleepless night opened the door of the James's home. She was not as put together as she'd been last night. She wore a thick gray robe with turquoise polka dots. Her hair testified to a rough night's sleep of her own, and her face was scrubbed free of makeup. Was it bad that he preferred this Fallon?

She pulled the thick robe tighter around her middle. "What do you want?"

Right, because again, she was sure she knew him.

"Good morning to you too." Cole motioned to Susie who still sat in the car, waving through the window. "She left her tennis shoe here. She said she left it in the mudroom. Can I get it? Or do you need to lecture me on being irresponsible again?"

Fallon stepped back, allowing him entrance, then pointed at a small shoe in the corner of the mudroom by the door. "That one, I'm assuming."

He bent down and grabbed it but paused in the doorway. "I know you said my kids were too much for your mom. But I have this opportunity this weekend—"

"No."

"Can I talk to her?"

"She's still in bed. I told you, you wore her out."

He winced. He hadn't meant to be too much, but he needed this job and he didn't have other options. Maybe Deb could at least give him another suggestion. "If you'd just hear me out. It is a job where I could—"

"What about the word no do you not understand? Besides, shouldn't the great Tiffany be returning soon?"

"She lives in Vegas."

"Oh." That seemed to blow away some of that attitude. She cleared her throat and crossed her arms. "Well, did you know my mom has high blood pressure and the doctor told her to take it easy?"

"I didn't know that." Cole pressed his lips together to keep from saying anything else. He offered a curt nod and turned away. "Me and my irresponsible self have to get this girl to school."

"See, we finally agree on something."

"See you around, Fallon." Cole hurried out the door, letting it shut behind him, but not before he heard the mumbled word "Typical."

If he hurried, he might be able to make it to his shift on time.

Cole navigated to the elementary school just as kids were climbing off the bus. At least Susie wouldn't be late. He got out and led her across the parking lot and headed her to the kids in her class who were starting to line up.

Her teacher, Mrs. Miller, stepped toward them and his heart sank. The woman was kind as could be, but she had been his second-grade teacher as well and Cole had not always been the model student that year.

"Good morning, Susie. What did you bring for special snack today?"

Susie's eyes rounded, and she looked up at him. Oops. She seemed to be holding her breath as her eyes filled with tears.

"Don't worry. Your dad can drop it off."

Drop it off? He didn't have time for that. Then Mrs. Miller shot him the look, the one-eyebrow up frown, and yup he was back in second grade. He'd faced terrorists and drug lords, but one stern look from a five-foot gray-haired woman had him nodding. "I'll figure it out."

Her face morphed into a wide smile. "It just needs to be here by eleven."

Eleven? Which meant the first thing he'd have to do after arriving to work late was ask for a long break. He'd be lucky if they didn't fire him, and then where would he be? He needed this money, even if it was only minimum wage.

This single parenting thing was tougher than a lot of the ops he'd run. If Fallon thought he was irresponsible, maybe she should give it a try.

P.S. Goodbye

What if a woman who's all about the goals and plans falls in love with man who no longer believes his life has a purpose?

A novice life coach needs to cement her reputation with one great success story. When a wounded ex-Army officer walks in looking for a job, she decides to work with him—a win-win for them both.

If Caroline Williams had her way, she'd help everyone in town find their purpose in life—unfortunately, no one seems to want her help. But she refuses to give up, and her new status as a certified life coach should provide her with some badly needed credibility. All she needs is her first client. When Grant Quinn walks in looking for a job, Caroline knows he needs more than that—he needs a new plan for his life. But when Grant refuses to be honest about his dreams and his struggles, Caroline's business might come crashing down before it starts.

Wounded former Special Forces operator Grant Quinn understood the cost when he enlisted and served his country with pride. The scars on his face are reminders of what he lost, but he is moving on—now if he could just convince his family that he's fine. When Caroline steps back into his life and offers to help find him a job in exchange for being her Guinea pig in her new life coaching business, he agrees. After all, what better way to show his family he's okay than with a new, stable job? But when the anxiety he's been running from ruins his one interview, his plans come crashing down. Can he trust Caroline enough to be honest about everything?

Get your free copy today!

Want more Heritage now?

Come see what has one Goodreads reviewer saying "I love this small town of Heritage, MI . . . where gossip blooms like wildflowers but also where love, acceptance, and mercy flow like a wild river."
(MJSH, Goodreads)

Six books, nine couples, and one mysterious hippo!

Start where it all began with Tari Faris' FREE prequel novella *P.S. Goodbye*.

Scan for a free download or go to:
www.tarifaris.com/my-free-novella

More from Mandy Boerma

Escape to Hearts Bend for a sweet
story of romance, faith, and
an unexpected happy ending.

All she wants is a fresh start...

Chloe Beason LaRue left Hearts Bend after high school, determined to never look back. She shed her unrequited crush on Sam Hardy, moved to Paris, went to pastry school, found a good job, fell in love, and got married. She was happy in France. Then her husband tragically died. Now, Chloe just wants to move forward...but when her mom's health is in jeopardy, Chloe heads right back to Hearts Bend where she's hired as head baker for Haven's, the premier bakery in town. She has no idea that moving home will push her right into the arms of the man who broke her heart.

He's not looking to fall in love...

Tennessee Titans quarterback Sam Hardy has too many broken memories in Hearts Bend to Return. But when he's sidelined by an injury, he desperately needs to invest in something to safeguard his future. Haven's Bakery is up for sale—and his business partner believes the deal is too good to pass up. He has no idea that the owners have hired the one girl he can't seem to forget...and the last thing he expects is to be her boss.

But it's a recipe for romance...

Back in Hearts Bend for the first time in ten years and thrown together at Haven's Bakery, Chloe and Sam have a second chance at first love. Indeed, the more time Sam spends selling pastries, the more he sees a new future. But when Paris beckons Chloe back, where does her heart belong? Can they find the recipe for leaving regrets behind and start something new?

More Sweet Sunrise Romance

Faith. Forgiveness. A future they never imagined.
It's time for a fresh start for the Fox Family.

Return to Susan May Warren's beloved town of Deep Haven now!
Find out more at sunrisepublishing.com.

Connect With Sunrise

Thank you again for reading *Here with Me*. We hope you enjoyed the story. If you did, would you be willing to do us a favor and leave a review? It doesn't have to be long—just a few words to help other readers know what they're getting. (But no spoilers! We don't want to wreck the fun!) Thank you again for reading!

We'd love to hear from you—not only about this story, but about any characters or stories you'd like to read in the future. Contact us at www.sunrisepublishing.com/contact.

We also have a monthly update that contains sneak peeks, reviews, upcoming releases, and fun stuff for our reader friends. Sign up at www.sunrisepublishing.com or scan our QR code.

Acknowledgments

Writing a book is never a solo project, and there are so many people to thank.

Tari Faris, thank you for working with me and allowing me to bring David and Sadie to life on the page. Without your encouragement, this story would not be here. I've learned a lot through this process and through all our crazy conversations. It's finally done.

To the team at Sunrise Publishing, Susan May Warren, Lindsay Harrel, Rel Mollet and Sarah Erredge—thank you for all the time and effort you poured into getting this novel out there. And to my editors, Barbara Curtis and Kristyn Fortner, thank you for all the little details you caught.

Thank you to my huddle buddies: Tammy, Jennifer, Sara. You ladies make every day great. Your friendship, prayers and encouragement have kept me going. And to my friends, Andrea, Alena, Jeanne, Kariss, Lisa, Michelle and Rachel. Thanks for believing in me.

For the always full cup of coffee that has seen me through this process, I have Angela, Kiefer, Trevor, and Hannah at JoJo's Coffee and Goodness to thank. Keeping my cup full kept me going. And for Steve. I'm so glad you sit beside me.

Obviously, I wouldn't have finished this process without the love and support of my real-life hero. Thank you, Sam, for always letting me follow hair-brained ideas. For supporting me as I wonder what I've gotten myself into and encouraging me to seek

God when I am overwhelmed. Stella and Johanna, thank you for letting mommy follow this dream, talk to imaginary people and for laughing at my stories when I needed a pick me up.

And Mom, Dad and Julie, thank you for being the listening ear. My support, and for telling me I'm doing ok, even when I know I'm not. Thanks for making dinner, picking up kids and groceries and acting as my very own laundry fairy.

I saved the most important for last. I had no idea the lessons I'd learn through this process, and I wouldn't have completed it without the overwhelming graciousness of my God. He is always good.

About the Author

Mandy Boerma lives in the Florida Panhandle with her very own Prince Charming and two of the most amazing girls. She loves writing, drinking coffee, and hanging out at the beach. In her free time, wait—free time, what's that? But she does love spending time with her family, reading while snuggling her cat, and walking her dog.

Mandy loves to hear from readers, and you can connect with her at mandyboerma.com

Made in the USA
Monee, IL
23 October 2024